Flirty Dancing

Also by Jennifer Moffatt

THE FALLING HARD SERIES

A Hard Sell

A Hard Fit

Flirty Dancing

A NOVEL

Jennifer Moffatt

ST. MARTIN'S GRIFFIN
NEW YORK

First published in the United States by St. Martin's Griffin, an imprint of St. Martin's Publishing Group

FLIRTY DANCING. Copyright © 2025 by Jennifer Moffatt. All rights reserved. Printed in the United States of America. For information, address St. Martin's Publishing Group, 120 Broadway, New York, NY 10271.

www.stmartins.com

Design by Meryl Sussman Levavi

The Library of Congress Cataloging-in-Publication Data is available upon request.

ISBN 978-1-250-37928-3 (trade paperback)
ISBN 978-1-250-37929-0 (ebook)

Our books may be purchased in bulk for promotional, educational, or business use. Please contact your local bookseller or the Macmillan Corporate and Premium Sales Department at 1-800-221-7945, extension 5442, or by email at MacmillanSpecialMarkets@macmillan.com.

First Edition: 2025

10 9 8 7 6 5 4 3 2 1

To Hanna, who loved this book before anyone else did, and has believed in me with her whole heart since the day I met her

Flirty Dancing

Nathan Lane Is Watching

"Twenty-seven is too old."

Not *the* most devastating words ever spoken, perhaps, but close.

They echoed through Archer's head again as the subway car rattled around him. *Twenty-seven is too old.* Objectively speaking, it was not old. It was just a beginning, really. Too old to start a family? Of course not. Too old to go to college? No way. Too old to write a novel? Don't be ridiculous, have at it. Too old to quit your job as an accountant and move to New York City with dreams of making it as a Broadway dancer? Well, that answer had to be no too, or else . . . fuck.

Archer's phone lit up with a text from his mom. **Why aren't you returning my calls? Did you get the part?**

No was all Archer could bring himself to type.

Oh, hon. I'm sorry. I hate to say I told you so, but . . .

Twenty-seven is too old.

That still counts as 'I told you so,' Mom, just so you know.

You're a brilliant dancer and you gave it a good try, but maybe it's time to come back home. You belong here, Archer.

Archer slumped into his seat, eyes shutting over the sting of tears. Five months, thirty-six auditions, twelve callbacks . . . and exactly zero roles. But he couldn't do it. He couldn't quit. His very soul would shrivel up and die if he had to move back to Ohio. Maybe he didn't belong in New York, but he sure as *hell* didn't belong there.

I have two more auditions this week, and a callback, he informed his mom. The callback was for the most ridiculous gig ever, but she didn't need to know that. **If I don't get those, then we'll see.**

Okay, hon. Have a good night.

The train shuddered to a stop and Archer joined the flow of people up the stairs out into Hell's Kitchen, duffel bag slung over his shoulder. The evening air had cooled but was still thick with the promise of the stifling summer heat that was not far off.

"Hey, gorgeous," Lynn called from the bathroom when Archer shut the apartment door behind him. "Watch out, Leak Perry is back."

Archer dodged the half-full bucket of water sitting in the middle of the faded linoleum floor. "And I'm sure Fletcher is on his way to fix it right now?"

"Ha!" came Lynn's reply. "Yeah, and he's giving us free rent for the month."

"Right," Archer muttered, not even bothering to look

up at the wet patch on the ceiling. Fletcher had come to investigate the leak twice already, finally, after multiple texts and phone calls, then informed them both times it was fixed. It was not. Archer dropped his bag on the floor and threw himself onto the old couch that was wedged against the wall, only inches from the kitchen on one side and the bathroom door on the other.

"How was your day?" Lynn came out of the bathroom attempting to jam her abundant dark brown hair into a bun, curvy figure wrapped in a killer sequined dress. Despite the damp and closet-sized apartment that was rapidly draining his savings, he adored living with Lynn.

Archer whistled. "Damn. Where you headed?"

"Out," she mumbled through a hairpin before she took it from her mouth and stabbed it into her bun. "As are you."

"Ugh, pass. I'm wallowing." He clutched a magenta throw pillow to his chest and tried to look pathetic. It wasn't hard.

"The fuck you are." She examined him, hands on hips. He didn't even need to tell her he got another no. His silence said it just fine.

"It's Sasha's birthday," she reminded him. Lynn was an actual responsible adult, with a responsible adult job in a law firm in the Garment District, and she even had a responsible adult relationship.

Archer sighed. He wasn't sure Sasha's birthday was occasion enough to be forced off the couch on, this, the day of his thirty-fifth rejection.

"Plus"—Lynn gave him a look that pierced right through him—"you need to get out of your head a bit, my friend. Get drunk. Maybe even get laid."

"I do not," he said, even though they both knew all of those things were absolutely true.

Lynn didn't dignify it with a response. "Let's go. We're

meeting Sasha at The Fiddler in thirty and she hates it when I'm late."

He tossed the pillow aside. "You're only ever late because of me."

Lynn sighed. "I know, boo. I mean she hates it when *you're* late. Now get changed!"

* * *

Ten minutes later, Archer followed Lynn out onto the sidewalk. The bar was only a few blocks away and she had decided a speed walk would be faster than a cab. He had gone with jeans and a fuchsia button-down. It was a great color on him against his golden skin and dark blond hair, which he kept shorter than he would strictly like, not wanting to look anywhere near scruffy at auditions. He had left two buttons undone until Lynn had added a third with a wink. "You gotta sell the goods, Arch."

The bar, dark and well-worn, walls lovingly plastered with queer Broadway paraphernalia, was already packed when they arrived, on time and everything. The music was so loud he couldn't quite make out Sasha's shouted greeting before Lynn cut it off with a kiss.

"Happy birthday!" he yelled at Sasha, adding a peck on her cheek. "How dare you look hotter than me?" She was already glowing with sweat and a bit drunk, short blond hair sticking to her forehead.

"Thanks for letting Lynn drag you out," she yelled back, her eyes a little too wide and lingering on him a little too long. Great, so she knew he was a pathetic loser, too. He threw Lynn some side-eye. She shrugged, handed Archer her handbag, and pulled Sasha back out onto the dance floor.

Archer sat at the table Sasha had pointed to and nodded

at a few of her and Lynn's lawyer friends. That was another thing. He'd been in New York for five months and had zero friends of his own. Thank God Lynn took pity on him.

He ordered the cheapest beer they had from a passing server and eyed the dance floor, wondering if maybe he could relax enough to actually try and hook up tonight. It seemed unlikely because, so far, he'd only managed it once, and the guy—part of the lighting crew on an experimental nudist *Hamlet*—left right after, mumbling something about an early call time, then ghosted him entirely.

Not like he wasn't used to rejection in New York. No doubt the audition tomorrow would result in more of the same. He nursed his beer, talking himself even deeper into a pit of despair, until there came a tap on his shoulder. Archer turned and was startled by the beauty of the man looking at him. He smiled on instinct, even though he was sure this guy had made a mistake.

"Hey," the man said, sliding onto the stool next to Archer. "I'm Lachlan." Lachlan had light brown hair styled into an achingly perfect tousle, thick eyelashes, and, quite frankly, a killer body, from the very quick and discreet glance Archer took.

"Archer." They shook hands, Lachlan holding on a second longer than necessary. "Nice to meet you." He waited for Lachlan to realize his error and make an awkward excuse as he slipped right back off that stool.

"Who you here with, Archer?" he asked instead, eyes narrowing as he smiled.

Archer liked the way his name purred off Lachlan's tongue. "Just my roommate and her girlfriend," he said, nodding at them on the dance floor.

"Hmm." Lachlan leaned forward and Archer caught a

whiff of his cologne—something spicy that sent his stomach swirling. "So, you're all alone, then?" The curl of his lips suggested this was a good thing.

"I guess," Archer replied, then cringed. *God, I'm terrible at flirting. Say something flirty.* "Less alone now."

He must have said the right thing because he got a heated look in return. "And what do you do, Archer?" Lachlan's eyes slid up and down Archer's frame.

"I'm a dancer." Still sounded ridiculous to say out loud, but *accountant* was worse.

His eyebrows jerked up. "Oh, yeah? Broadway?"

That was always the first thing everyone asked. "Not yet."

"Off, then? Anything I might have seen you in?"

And the second thing. "Not unless you caught *Guys and Dolls* at the Beavercreek Community Theatre in Dayton five years ago."

Lachlan bunched his brow. "Uh . . ."

"I mean, I just moved from Ohio and I'm, um, still looking to, you know, break my way in."

Lachlan took him in again, only this time his gaze was analytical. "Aren't you a little old to be 'chasing your dreams'?" He gave a derisive chuckle but read the clench in Archer's jaw. "Don't get me wrong! You're crazy hot, but how old are you? Twenty-six, twenty-seven?"

Archer cleared his throat. "Twenty-seven." For another month anyway.

Lachlan grimaced. "No offense, but, like, you showed up here, have zero connections, and you're almost thirty. What did you think was going to happen?"

The cheap beer gurgled up Archer's throat, fighting with the welling disappointment and leaving no room for words.

"Anyway." Lachlan laughed, although nothing was funny. "Bet you could make a killing if you started stripping."

Archer stretched the corners of his mouth out to nowhere, and then he lurched to his feet without looking at Lachlan. *Twenty-seven is too old.* "I just have to . . ." He dashed through the bar and into a bathroom stall before the tears spilled over.

Twenty-seven is too old. He heard it in his own voice now, instead of his mom's.

He pressed the heels of his hands to his eyes. Is this what his stupid dream had come to? Crying in a bathroom with a picture of Nathan Lane over the toilet, all because a hot guy told him he should be a stripper? "Goddamn it, Archer," he muttered to himself, furiously wiping the tears away. His head *thunked* back against the closed stall door under Mr. Lane's steady gaze, unsure if he was more mad at himself for bolting, crying, or being a total failure in general. He decided it was a three-way tie, then stayed there for a good twenty minutes, figuring Lachlan wouldn't wait around for more than five, but just to be sure.

And he was right. When he made it back to the table, Lachlan was already chatting up a new guy across the bar, younger and hotter. Archer diverted his gaze to Lynn and Sasha's smiles as they bounced around and forced himself to stay for one more beer, three more songs, then he stood.

"I gotta go," he yelled at Lynn over the music.

"Nooo, staaaay!" Lynn was drunk now and leaned on him heavily. "Who was that hottie you were talking to?"

"Just another reminder of my horrific life choices."

"Archer . . ." Lynn threw her arms around him and squeezed. "I love you. I'm so glad you answered my roommate ad."

"Me too." She was, after all, the only good thing he had going in New York. "But I gotta get out of here."

"Okay. Don't wait up."

He kissed her forehead and waved at Sasha. "I won't."

"Liar."

* * *

Each audition had gotten harder over the months, as the desperation grew. The pressure, then the panic, layer upon layer, hunching his shoulders, tightening his muscles, wringing the air from his lungs. The audition the day after Sasha's birthday was a no, as was the one the day after that. His mom sent him a link to available accounting jobs in Dayton.

The night before the callback, a foreboding sense of It All Comes Down To This hung over him, and he barely slept. If he failed again, on a gig this lowbrow . . . surely that would be the final sign that this whole attempt was ridiculous. He'd have to go back to Ohio, tail between his legs, back to the place that had never really wanted him to begin with. Dancing was the only thing that had given him comfort growing up, that had made him feel like he had gifts to offer the world. The only time he really felt like himself. He definitely did not feel like himself drowning in tax forms and spreadsheets. He could not go back.

It was cliché, but it was true. The big city. The freedom to be unapologetically yourself. In some ways he had never been happier, dedicating himself to dancing. But how long could he keep pretending he belonged here? He needed a yes.

The callback was nothing to write home about, that was for sure. He certainly hadn't. He was almost embarrassed to admit he even went to the audition in the first place, but, well, something about desperate times . . . The show was not Off Broadway, or even Off Off Off Off Broadway. It wasn't even a real fucking show. It was a summer cabaret at an LGBTQ+ resort in the Catskills called Shady Queens. But it was a gig, and at this point he had no business turning one down, no matter where it was. In fact, it was his only hope.

He might have slept a little, finally, slipping in and out of restless dreams, then dragged himself out of bed at eleven, equal parts dread and exhaustion. Lynn had long since left for work, but she propped a note next to his granola. YOU'RE GONNA KILL IT, ARCH. He stared at it while he crunched, holding his bowl at the counter.

The audition was in an old warehouse two trains away at the ass end of Brooklyn, the building so run-down he almost didn't go in for the first round. The only thing that actually got him in the door was the fact that the director of the show was Stewart Harpham-Lale, a figure well-known in the musical theater crowd who had never quite found mainstream success. Apparently, retirement bored him, and he was now filling his hours at Shady Queens. Worst case, Archer figured he could learn a thing or two from Stewart.

He approached a woman sitting at a folding table inside the rusty doors. "Hi, I'm Archer Read, here for the callback?" His voice was small in the vast space.

She barely glanced at him as she checked a clipboard and gave him a sticker with a number ten. "You can go ahead and warm up," she said, nodding at the floor.

He slipped his sweats off and did some stretches at a shaky barre. There were about twenty other people in the room who clearly couldn't land anything better either. And yet . . . each one of them was incredible. That made him feel worse. Talented and *still* not happening.

They started with Latin ballroom. He was paired up with a tiny slip of a blond girl for a samba, which worked in his favor because he was able to whirl her around with ease. Next, they danced hip-hop to Missy Elliott, which he felt good about, pushing through the tiredness and hitting it as hard as he could. Last was lyrical, his favorite, thanks to his ballet training.

As he stood in that moment of stillness before the final run, between the last breath and the first note, the thought came to him. *This could be it.* Inhale. *This could be my last one.* Exhale. The tightening in his chest loosened.

He danced. The beat of the music thrummed in his blood, the stretch of each finger and toe reached to the ends of the earth, every breath was fuel in the fire. He flew around the floor like gravity was merely a suggestion, with a lightness that he hadn't felt in a long time. When he stopped and stood in the silence at the end, his eyes were wet.

He stood, heaving in formation with the other dancers, while the panel sat staring, impassive.

"If you could all give us a few minutes," the one who seemed to be in charge said, before they turned their chairs and huddled for about ninety seconds. They turned back again. A silence grew, stretched, grabbed Archer's chest and squeezed. "Numbers three, four, ten, and fourteen, you can stay. The others, thank you."

Archer stared at his number ten. He blinked, confused. Surely not. He watched as the rest turned and left, leaving him, two other men, and the tiny blond slip on the floor.

"Congratulations," the boss said, now allowing a smile. "We would love to offer you a spot at the Shady Queens cabaret this summer."

I did it.

He sucked in a shaking breath. *I fucking did it.* He didn't care how small it was, or that it was a two-hour bus ride away. He did it.

Archer called his parents on the way home. "Don't get too excited," he started, once his mom put him on speaker, "it's totally not a big deal, but I got a small job."

"Honey, that's great! What's the show?"

"Well, it's a cabaret . . . for the summer . . . in the Catskills."

There was a pause. "The Catskills?"

"I know it sounds crazy, but Stewart Harpham-Lale directs the show, he's kind of a big deal, and tons of theater people go to the resort and it might actually help me network and stuff, you know. Someone might even see me in the show and remember me." He was babbling but couldn't stop. "I feel like it'll be good for me, then I can come back to the city and give it one last try, after that. Just a few more months."

He could feel his parents having a silent conversation with their eyes. "That sounds fun, Archer," his mom said.

"So I'm actually gonna bus up there tomorrow and I'll be there for about four months, until the end of August," he continued, blazing through the noticeable drop in their enthusiasm. He forced a laugh. "It'll be just like camp."

"Mm-hmm," his mom said absentmindedly. There was rustling in the background. "What about your apartment?"

"Oh, uh . . ." His mind whirred. "I don't know, I'm sure Lynn will—"

"You should get something in writing, so she doesn't try to scam you."

"What? Lynn would never . . ." He trailed off. What was the point?

"Have fun, Arch," his dad said after a beat of silence. "Let us know when you get there."

* * *

Lynn was much more excited for him—more than she should have been, really.

"That's amazing news!" she cried, jumping onto the couch, bag of roasted chickpeas flying. "Babe, I'm so proud of you!"

Sasha retrieved the bag from the floor and gave Archer a much more reserved look. "Congratulations." She tugged at Lynn's shorts. "Sit down, sweetie."

"It's not that amazing," Archer said, trying to suppress the smile that wanted to unfold across his face.

Lynn flopped back onto the cushion. "It is. It's a great gig. You'll have so much fun."

"I guess so."

"When do you leave?"

"Tomorrow morning."

"Then you know what this means . . ."

He watched her grinning when it clicked. He grinned back. "You're right. This is the moment we've been waiting for."

Sasha looked back and forth between them. "What?"

Archer hustled to the fridge and dug around in the back until he found what he was looking for. He held it up for Lynn with two hands, like Rafiki presenting Simba on Pride Rock.

Lynn cackled while Sasha looked perplexed. "A bottle of gross, cheap champagne?" She squinted at the label. "Jesus, how much did you pay for that? Five bucks?"

"Two ninety-nine," Archer said proudly. "From the first liquor store I saw when I set foot in Manhattan."

Lynn jumped up and took the bottle from him, cradling it lovingly. "He's been saving it to celebrate his first job. Go grab some glasses . . . Ew, Archer, why is it sticky?"

It was the worst champagne he'd ever had, and the best.

2

Shady Queens

It was depressing how Archer's entire New York life fit into a suitcase and a duffel bag. Just his dance gear, clothes, and toiletries, really, plus a few books he'd been meaning to get to, including his old, battered copy of *The Hobbit* that he reread every summer. He left his little collection of succulents on the only windowsill in the apartment, which got a pathetic trickle of sunlight around noon. He hadn't managed to kill them yet and pleaded with Lynn to keep them alive.

"I promise," Lynn said solemnly. "I'll take care of little Danny Zuko and Belle and . . . What was the other one's name again?"

"Spot Conlon."

"Yes, of course, also Spot Conlon."

That morning, he was up early and caught a bus from the Port Authority with time to spare and only a slight cheap-champagne headache. The two men he remembered from the callback were waiting, too. Both were solidly built, with thick shoulders and dark brown hair. One sat on the

other's lap in the crowded terminal and ran his fingers up
and down the other's neck while they scrolled through
their phones. The lap-sitter leaned in for a kiss, then they
smiled at each other before going back to their phones.

Archer's heart clenched. It had been a long time since
anyone had looked at him like that. When his bus pulled
in, he joined the line behind them.

"Oh, hey," the slightly taller of the two said when he
saw Archer. "You were at the callback, right?"

"Yup. Archer."

"Ben. This is my boyfriend, Beau." He had a trace of a
French accent.

"That's great that you both got in," Archer said, shaking
their hands.

"There were some tense moments." Beau laughed. "But
we're kind of a package deal. And I told him if he got in
and I didn't, I'd break up with him." Beau had the same accent, and Archer tried to commit to memory that Ben was
the taller one.

Ben rolled his eyes. "He's joking."

"Kind of." Beau pecked Ben on the nose.

Archer took a seat across the aisle from the two of them,
and they leaned toward him to continue their conversation.

"So how much do you guys know about this show?
Have you ever seen it?" Archer asked.

"Nah, never seen it, but we know a man who works in
maintenance at the resort," replied Beau. "The guests don't
arrive until Sunday when the season opens, so we have
five days left for rehearsal."

"Left?"

"Yes, the rest of the cast is already there. We were last-
minute fill-ins. We'll have to play catch-up."

"Where are you from?" Ben asked. Or was it Beau?

"Ohio. Been in New York for five months."

"Only five months?"

"Yeah. I, uh . . . I was an accountant." Archer flushed.

"Chasing the dream, eh?" Beau (or Ben) asked kindly.

Archer chuckled, running a hand through his hair. "I suppose so." He changed the subject. "Where are you two from?"

Ben and Beau were ballroom dancers from Quebec who decided to audition for the show on a bit of a whim, thinking it would be a fun summer job. Normally, they taught ballroom in Montreal. Archer remembered the way they moved as one at the audition during the samba and wasn't surprised they had been chosen together. They chatted easily the rest of the way, and Archer was glad he would arrive already knowing these two.

The buildings gave way to trees as the bus rolled north. To Archer, when he was growing up, New York meant skyscrapers and sidewalks, and, for some reason, he had never considered the rest of the state. Leafy green trees covered gently sloping hills, with the odd flash of a placid lake or frothy waterfall visible through the foliage.

He had stalked Shady Queens' Instagram, so he had some idea what it would look like, but the place was much more charming in person. There was a large main building waiting for them at the bottom of the maple-shaded gravel drive. It was a three-story white Victorian shingle with rainbow trim, and there were three bright and new-looking pride flags hanging from poles across the front. A WELCOME STAFF sign was tied to the front railing. Other smaller white buildings and cabins spilled down the hill toward the lake, which sparkled in the afternoon sun.

Archer trudged up the creaking steps, suitcase in hand, and pushed open the front door. A woman stood behind the reception desk in a flowery yellow and orange dress with gray hair twisted into a messy knot.

"Hi, I'm Archer Read," he said, showing her the paperwork they'd given him after the audition.

She didn't look at it but smiled at him instead. "Department?"

"Uh . . . dancing?"

"We call you *Entertainment*, dear." She pecked at the keyboard.

"Oh."

He stepped aside to let Beau and Ben introduce themselves.

"Nice to meet you all. I'm Macy Cunningham, but everyone calls me Mrs. C. Any of you been here before?"

They shook their heads as she handed them each a welcome package. "Dinner is in the staff dining hall from four until seven sharp, every night." She looked at her watch. "But I believe rehearsal is still going on. Perhaps the three of you should hustle over there first." She pulled a map out and began marking it with firm Xs like she'd done it a thousand times, which she probably had. "We are here, your bunks are here. You can drop off your bags, get changed, and head here." She Xed another building down by the lake. "This is the theater. There's a door for the talent in the back." She handed the map to Archer and passed them each a room key. "Heads up, Stewart doesn't like to be interrupted, but better that than missing altogether, hmm? Well, don't stand there blinking at me, off you go!"

* * *

The three of them were assigned the same four-person room in one of the staff dorms, their beds waiting empty and neat. The bed on the end was rumpled and covered in clothes. They dropped their bags, threw on their rehearsal gear, and ventured in the direction of the theater, map in hand.

The building was old but lovingly refurbished. A wrap-around veranda with cozy bench seating looked like the perfect spot for a drink before or after the show. They could hear "Ladies' Night" blaring before they even opened the back door. It was dark inside, but lights from the stage reached them through the side-masking draperies and down a short flight of stairs. Archer realized he was holding his breath as they climbed the stairs and approached the stage. The air thrummed and the pounding of feet on the boards shivered down his spine. He exhaled as he took in the movement.

The troupe danced like a well-oiled machine, like the most seasoned of Broadway performers, tight, deep in the pocket, not a step missed, not a finger out of line. And young, so young. Most of them looked to be early twenties, at best. Except for one face at the front—a face that sent Archer's jaw plummeting to the floor. A handsome face—gorgeous, really—that had been featured on his bedroom wall from the ages of fourteen through eighteen. Black hair, heavy, serious brow, a stick-straight nose, full lips, square jaw. Mateo Dixon, Broadway star, all-around breathtakingly talented and devastatingly hot. Archer was distantly aware his mouth was hanging open, but his body was not responding to signals from his brain.

Archer's parents took him to New York City for his fourteenth birthday, and he had fallen in love with Mateo Dixon when he saw him as Danny in *Grease*. Archer had followed Mateo's career, until, five years ago, Mateo had abruptly left a show and disappeared off the face of the earth.

What the fuck was he doing here?

Besides the hustle, that is. Mateo was in a very loose black tank top and black tights, chest rippling and glistening with sweat. Archer's gaze lingered on the perfectly sculpted arms and shoulders. He had only a vague impression of Mateo's partner, a shapely redhead spinning in front of him.

"Dude," Ben or Beau murmured at him. "You're staring."

"That's Mateo Dixon," he stammered in reply, as if that explained everything.

"Who?" said Ben or Beau.

"Oh, I think I've heard of him," Beau or Ben interjected. "He was the lead in *Robin's Egg*, wasn't he, when it took off?"

"Yup." Archer swallowed and nodded, eyes still not leaving Mateo as he lifted his partner and spun her around on his shoulder like it was nothing.

"What's he doing here?" Beau or Ben wondered.

"I don't know . . ." Archer trailed off, realizing he was about to spend the summer dancing with Mateo Dixon. Except no, this was a mistake. Surely, he was just visiting? Choreographing? There was no way he was actually in the show?

Right. Show. Archer tore his eyes off Mateo and tried to take in the choreo. The blond slip from the callback was there already, following along by herself at the back. Now that Archer wasn't a ball of audition nerves, he realized she was a cutie pie with a little button nose and a dusting of freckles over her fair skin. She must have made the trip to Shady Queens right away when they got selected.

But Archer's attention went back to Mateo. His face was stern, eyes dark. He kept his gaze on the back of the theater, with the odd flick over to his partner. He was flawless and . . . distant.

And there was Stewart Harpham-Lale seated in the front row, one hand gripping the cane propped between his legs, the other petting a Yorkshire terrier in his lap. He wore a wrinkled linen suit, rings on each finger, and his mouth curled down in a frown.

When the song ended, the troupe held their final pose. Stewart stood and regarded them for a moment before he approached the stage, wiggling dog under one arm. "We're lucky we have five more days," he said in a rasp as he climbed the stairs. "That was . . . mediocre." Then he turned to the three of them huddled offstage and waved them forward with his cane. "This is the rest of my troupe, is it?"

They shuffled toward Stewart while the other dancers watched.

It was very quiet in the theater when Archer spoke. "Yes, sir. Archer Read. It's an honor—"

"Indeed, likewise," Stewart Harpham-Lale said rapidly, already moving on to Ben and Beau as they introduced themselves.

Archer's gaze slipped back to Mateo. His stomach jolted when he discovered Mateo was watching back. Archer offered a small smile. Mateo's face remained blank as he looked away, wiping his forehead with the hem of his shirt.

"Well. We're polishing up our *Club Retro* show right now, or we're trying, God help us. Why don't you three watch a full run-through and see what you can pick up, then the others can break it down for you after. From the top!" Stewart spoke with very few pauses. He stood at the front of the stage this time as they did another run. Archer's brain hummed trying to take it all in.

Stewart frowned again when they were done. "Passable. Mateo, you'll see to these three? Eight o'clock sharp tomorrow morning, do *not* be late. Dominik, *yes*, I'm looking at you. Come, Judy." His dog yipped. He turned and swept off stage right, the back door clattering shut behind them in the silence.

"Alright." Mateo looked at them like it was the last thing in the world he wanted to do. "I'm Mateo, this is Dominik, Gage, Iris, River, Seta, Caleb . . ." Mateo rattled through the names of the other twelve, making sixteen dancers in total. All Archer could remember was Dominik, because he had a purple mohawk and made a horrified gasp when Stewart Harpham-Lale called him out, and Caleb, because he was beautiful and smirking right at Archer. "You can learn names tomorrow. They're going to go eat while I run you through *Retro*."

The crowd shuffled out, a few saying hi and offering handshakes and backslaps on their way. They laughed and joked with each other like they'd been dancing together for years, although Archer supposed that some of them had.

"Hi, I'm Archer." He took a step toward Mateo, hand out, insides churning, and suddenly, he was living his teenage fantasy. He'd imagined walking up to Mateo a thousand times, introducing himself, Mateo smiling, taking his hand. *It's so nice to meet you, Archer,* dream Mateo would say. *Tell me, are you a fellow dancer?* Then sometimes he would even lean in for a kiss—

Actual, very sweaty Mateo looked at Archer's outstretched hand a second too long before shaking it without enthusiasm. "Mateo."

"Yes, I know, I—I'm a huge fan."

Mateo raised a skeptical eyebrow at him. "A fan?"

"I saw you in *Grease.*" Archer was about to start babbling, but he couldn't help it. "My parents took me for my fourteenth birthday, and I've been a fan ever since. I never got to see *Robin's Egg* live but I—"

"That was a long time ago." Mateo cut him off as his gaze swept over Archer.

This was not going as expected. "You were brilliant, that's been my favorite show—"

"Look, Archer." Mateo's voice was a heavy bass, a vibration in the center of Archer's chest. "That was another lifetime. Now here we are in the fucking wilderness and you have six entire shows to learn and I'm missing dinner, so I suggest you stop talking and put your ballroom shoes on."

"Okay. Yeah, sure." Archer fumbled with the zipper on his bag. "You're teaching us the choreo?"

"Is that a problem?"

Oh my God, Mateo Dixon is going to watch me dance. "No, sir." *And I called him* sir. *Fuck.* Archer wanted to smack himself in the forehead. But a hint of a smile flickered on the corner of Mateo's mouth for a second—no, probably his imagination.

"Betty's your partner for *Retro*," Mateo said, nodding at the tiny blonde when she appeared from the wings with a water bottle and towel. She smiled at Archer, at least.

"Hi, I'm Archer," he whispered to Betty when Mateo went to fiddle with the audio equipment. "Is your name actually Betty or does he call you that because you've got a blond ponytail?"

She laughed. "It's actually Betty. Nice to meet you, Archer. Or should I say Archie?"

Now it was his turn to chuckle as he bent to lace his ballroom shoes. "When did you get here?"

"Yesterday. I drove—left right after we got the gig. There's so much choreo to learn—"

"If you two are done talking," Mateo interjected, "we start in the wings."

"Right. Sorry." *Come on, Archer. Time to focus.* "I'm ready."

Mateo led them through the blistering choreography for "Disco Inferno" and "Ladies' Night," and Archer did his best to keep up, despite the fact that he was still completely starstruck. *Mateo Dixon is touching my arm. Mateo Dixon's thighs are like tree trunks. Mateo Dixon smells amazing.* Betty was a huge help, having already picked most of it up, and gave him little nudges here and there to keep him on track.

"Thanks," he whispered when her chin bob once again told him which way to go.

"I got you," she whispered back. "Archie and Betty need to stick together."

Archer was starving and dripping with sweat himself when Mateo declared them done at six thirty. "Hurry and grab dinner before the dining hall closes. Be back here ready to go before eight tomorrow morning." Mateo wiped his forehead with his shirt hem again.

"Thanks for . . . Thanks," Archer said, not staring at Mateo's abs.

Mateo took a long pull on his water bottle, throat bobbing, before he looked at Archer again. "You don't need to thank me. Here to do a job, same as you."

Archer nodded, tongue-tied. They said never to meet your heroes. It seemed they were right. Not that he expected Mateo to be his instant best friend, but Mateo seemed to actively dislike him. The disappointment was heavy in his chest as he changed into his flip-flops and gathered his belongings before heading down the stairs.

"Archer."

He startled at Mateo's deep rumble and turned around, hopeful. "Yeah?"

"That's the wrong door. The dining hall is this way."

3

The Cabin

Archer stood next to Betty with his dinner tray heaped high, surveying the crowd and waiting for Beau and Ben. He couldn't pick out any of the dancers in the sea of faces and suddenly he was in high school again, wondering where he should sit. He was eyeing a nearby table that had some room when Betty murmured in his ear.

"That's the housekeeping staff. We don't eat with them."

"We . . . What?" Oh shit, it *was* high school again.

Betty cackled. "Nah, I'm fucking with you. This isn't high school. Of course we do."

Archer sagged with relief and followed her over to the table. "There's so many people here though," he said as he sat. "I feel like I'll barely be able to remember all the dancers."

"Don't worry, I'll help you," Betty said. "Everyone's been really nice so far . . . mostly."

When they came back from dinner to unpack and settle in a bit, Caleb was stretched out on the fourth bed scrolling his phone. He was strikingly beautiful—Black with deep eyes, thick lashes, and full lips that seemed to be permanently curled into a suggestive grin.

"Welcome," he said, getting up with a grand gesture, as if they were in the guest suite at the Ritz. "I'm Caleb. The most important roommate rule this summer is if you're hooking up or jerking off or something, sock on the doorknob. If you forget, it's your fault if someone walks in." Caleb's gaze ran up and down Archer's body. "Archer, was it?"

"Er, yes," Archer stammered. Caleb's frank pause at his bulge heated his cheeks.

Caleb's gaze flicked back up, the grin curling farther. "You single, Archer?"

He shifted. "Why?"

"Just wondering how often you might need a sock on the doorknob."

"I'm single but . . . not really here to hook up?"

Caleb smirked. "Heard that before."

To his relief, Archer's phone buzzed in his pocket, which reminded him he hadn't checked in with his parents when he arrived. "Excuse me, I need to . . ." He waved his phone in the air, then eased back into the hallway, sure Caleb's eyes were on his ass.

He was expecting a message from his mom but instead it was Lynn. **Hey! Did you arrive okay???**

He leaned against the wall, happy to hear from her. **Yes! Sorry, bit of a whirlwind. Listen, MATEO DIXON IS HERE. IN THE SHOW. (Do not ask who that is, just Google.)**

While he was waiting for Lynn's reply, he fired off a quick message to his mom. **Arrived okay. Busy day. Will call you tomorrow.**

Then Lynn replied. **HOLY SHIT, ARCHER. HE'S HOT. WHAT IS HE DOING THERE?**

I don't know . . . dancing, I guess?? But I
was IN LOVE with him as a teenager. It's
very weird.

You were??? THIS IS AMAZING. Is
he nice?

So far, I think he hates me.

No way. How could anyone hate
you?

Lol, I'll ask him. How are you?

Good! But I need to talk to you about
something when you have time.
Maybe tomorrow? We're heading out
now.

Everything okay? Did you kill my plants
already? Tell me Spot is alright.

Lol, no! Everything's great, including
Spot. Just need your advice about
something.

Okay. Have fun. I miss you.

Miss you too. Kick some ass, okay?

Xoxo

He slid his phone back into his pocket and went back
into the room.

Caleb was stretched out on his bed again watching Beau
and Ben unpack. "How long have you two been together?"
he asked them.

"Three years," they said at the same time, then smiled at each other.

Caleb whistled. "Three years, shit. No little breakups in there at all? Three years solid?"

Both men stiffened. One of them (Ben?) offered a forced smile. "There was a brief, er, *pause* a year or so ago, but"—he pressed his lips together—"only a pause."

"We don't count it as a breakup," the other said firmly. He stopped what he was doing and went to kiss his boyfriend on the shoulder before resuming his unpacking.

"Hmm." Caleb's eyes twinkled as he gave Archer a knowing look. Archer tried to keep his face noncommittal. "Yeah, sounds like it doesn't count."

They continued to settle in while Caleb gossiped about the rest of the dancers. "River is nonbinary and is definitely trying to get with Gage, who is bi. I already tried to fuck Gage last summer, but he wasn't interested. Seems like he's into River, anyway. Speaking of fucking—"

"How many summers have you been here?" Archer interrupted, not at all interested in who Gage was or was not fucking.

"This is my fourth. Gage, Grace, Seta, and a couple of the others are on their second. Dominik and Harley have done three. They work here for the summer semester then go back to college."

Does anyone dance on Broadway? Archer wanted to ask, but it felt like an idiotic question.

Mercifully, Betty rapped on their doorframe before the hookup report could continue. "Hey guys, you ready to go?"

Caleb swung his feet to the ground and stood. "Hell yeah. I'll meet you there, though. Gotta go see a guy about a thing." He winked and strolled out. Archer had an immediate sense of relief without Caleb's presence in the room. The man was intense.

"Go where?" Archer asked, eyeing his bed. It had been an awfully long day.

Betty laughed. "You're not actually thinking about going to bed right now, are you?"

"No?"

"Archer! Holy shit! The entire point of coming to work at Shady Queens for the summer is the partying! You two are up for it, right?" she asked Ben and Beau.

They looked at each other. "Sure," they said together.

"Archie, darling, it's time to get our drink on."

* * *

Betty led them down a path that curled around the west side of the lake. The setting sun had turned the trees around the lake black, while the sky was soft and purple. Music and shrieking laughter reached them before the light flickering through the maples. "Is this not a guest cabin down here?" he asked, dodging under some low-hanging leaves.

"Nope. It's sort of the employee lounge, and a few of the more senior staff have private rooms upstairs. Everyone calls it 'the cabin.' I think Mateo stays here," Betty replied.

One more curve of the path, then a large, faded cabin was visible, hunkered down only a few feet back from the shore. A weathered dock jutted into the lake, where a handful of silhouetted bodies hurled themselves into the darkening water, hooting and hollering, spurred on by cheers from the rest. The porch of the cabin seethed with bodies, flashes of color and skin.

Ben and Beau went to check out the dock while Betty took Archer by the hand and pulled him up the steps to the house, smiling and nodding as she went. Inside was one big, low-ceilinged room with a kitchen in the corner and the rest of it old, beaten-up couches and tables, plus a foosball table in another corner. There was a hall in the back where Archer could make out a set of stairs.

"Well, stop standing there like you carried a watermelon. Grab a beer," Betty said, nodding at the fridge.

"I didn't bring anything with me."

"It's fine, there's a beer fund you can contribute to. Go ahead."

Archer took one of the cheapest cans by habit, added a twenty to the jar on top of the fridge, and popped the top, taking a nervous sip as he looked around.

He recognized a few of the other dancers and some of the housekeeping staff from dinner. He definitely wasn't looking specifically for Mateo, but he got a thrill when he saw him lounging on a couch by the back hall, and, damn, did he look sexy. His hair was wet and falling onto his forehead in pieces. His pale blue patterned button-down was only half done up and was paired with tight faded jeans. He held a bottle of something Archer didn't recognize in one hand and the other was stabbing the air as he made a point to the person he was talking to.

"I know, right? I can't believe he's here," Betty whispered in his ear.

"Who? What?" Archer said, scratching the back of his neck.

"Please. You haven't stopped staring at him since you arrived."

A protest formed on his lips but it seemed pointless. "So what's he doing here?"

"I don't really know. Have you heard the full story about him, though?"

Archer shook his head. Betty grabbed a drink for herself and pulled him back outside. "Come on." They went and leaned on the railing, watching the splashing and pushing and cannonballing off the dock.

"Okay, so, you know how after *Grease* he got the lead in *Robin's Egg*, right?"

That musical had taken Broadway by storm six years ago. The main character was a trans woman and Mateo had played the Latino love interest. "Of course, yeah."

"They say the fame went to his head, he started strutting around like he was king of Broadway, drinking and partying too much, treating the rest of the cast like shit, apparently said some really awful things to his costar, and he got fired and then he . . . disappeared."

"Wow." All Archer had heard was the statement Mateo had released at the time that he was stepping down from the role for personal health reasons, which admittedly was usually code for drug or alcohol problems. His brain spun as he filed away the new information, heart hurting a little at the idea that his teenage crush was maybe not a very good person. "How long has he been here?"

"No idea. It was a surprise for me yesterday, too."

Archer took a thoughtful sip of beer and stared out at the lake. There was no moon, and the night was dark, save for the glimmer of the resort's lights on the water. Someone turned on a lantern on the dock. "I kind of had a massive crush on him when I was a teenager."

"For real?"

"Yeah, I had a picture of him on my wall and everything." Archer chuckled at the memory. "I even used to practice writing my name *Archer Dixon* and imagined going to prom with him."

Betty laughed and took a drink. "Well, good luck talking

to him. Aside from choreo, he hasn't said two words to me. Seems kind of . . . grumpy."

At least it's not just me. "How did you end up at Shady Queens?" Archer asked. "A fun summer job for you, too?"

"Sort of? I just graduated from NYU with a BFA. My uncle knows Stewart a little and he thought this would be a good experience for me before I dive into the audition circuit."

Archer was relieved that someone else was here for more than just a good time. "Maybe I'll see you out there pounding the pavement."

"That would be fun." They clinked bottles, then sipped in silence, lost in their own thoughts, until their drinks were empty. "I'll get you another one," Archer said and headed back inside with their empties.

He dug into the fridge for two more beers, then turned and almost ran straight into a huge solid mass of . . . Mateo Dixon. Archer swallowed as their eyes met. "Hi."

"Hi." Mateo pushed his hair back off his forehead, biceps flexing.

They stared at each other, Archer worrying that he'd eventually have a heart attack this summer if his heart started pounding this hard every time Mateo spoke to him.

The silence stretched on. Mateo's lips were so full . . . Why was he still staring?

"Are you going to move?" Mateo said, pointing at the fridge.

"Right." Archer scooted out of the way, cheeks flaming. *Idiot.* "Sorry."

Mateo reached in and took out a bottle of an expensive-looking craft beer.

Archer desperately searched for something to say, but, coming up empty, reached over to tap their drinks together. "Cheers."

"Cheers," Mateo mumbled in reply, looking annoyed. He popped the cap off and took a slow drink, throat rippling. Wiping the back of his hand across his mouth, he regarded Archer with heavy brows. "Look, I'm here to work, alright? I don't really . . . socialize."

"Why are you at the party, then?" The question burst out of Archer's mouth before he could think about it. *Shut up, Archer.* He smiled, trying to soften it.

"My room is upstairs," Mateo replied shortly, jerking his chin up at the ceiling. "Not much point in sitting up there trying to read or sleep with music blaring down here."

"Yeah, okay. Makes sense." Archer bobbed his head. *God, as if he cares what you think.* "And," he continued too quickly, "you don't need much sleep anyway." *Oh, Christ. Shut up, Archer.*

"I—what?" Mateo's eyebrows pinched together.

"Uh." Archer scratched out a laugh, tugging at his shirt. "I remember reading that about you once. In an interview or something."

Mateo's brow softened. "Oh."

"Like I said, I'm a fan." He shrugged and took a sip of his beer, cheeks flaming.

Mateo studied him for a second, then clenched his jaw. He huffed a humorless snort. "You're going to have to get over that pretty quick." He turned to leave, then tossed over his shoulder, "We have a lot of work to do."

Archer blew out a breath. *Way to go, Archer. Mateo Dixon hates you.*

* * *

The night got blurry after that—two beers became four, then beer pong broke out, then shots. Archer was intro-duced to every person at least twice by an increasingly gregarious Betty, even when she didn't know their names, and Beau and Ben ended up shirtless and doing a rather explicit rumba in the middle of the cabin, much to the delight of the crowd. Archer didn't see Mateo again after their brief conversation.

When Archer's alarm went off at seven the next morning, he cracked open an eye with great difficulty. He spent most of his life running a few minutes late for everything, and getting up early was not his thing, but he'd be damned if he was going to be late to his very first day of rehearsal.

Caleb was already gone, and it was a relief not to have to face him a little hungover first thing in the morning. A few sips of Gatorade helped settle Archer's stomach, then it took him a good couple minutes to shake Ben and Beau awake and out of bed. He pulled on shorts and a tank top and grabbed his duffel. They stopped by the dining hall for eggs and sausage, then made their way to the theater with a few minutes to spare.

The troupe was milling around, downing coffee and Gatorade in equal measure. There was no sign of Stewart Harpham-Lale yet. Archer studied the wheeled white-board that was up against the wall stage right that showed the weekly performance schedule and daily rehearsal plan. There would be two shows every night in the theater, at six and nine o'clock. There was *Club Retro*, *Latin Flame*, a hip-hop night called *Urban Beat*, *Around the World*, *Broadway Boulevard*, and a contemporary show called *From the Heart*. Every Sunday was a drag show, and the dancers had the night off.

They would be working on *Latin Flame* today, according to the sense he could make of the scrawled writing. There was the Argentine tango, paso doble, samba, and cha-cha, and his partner was . . . Mateo?

"Uh . . ." He turned to Betty when she appeared at his elbow. "This can't be right?"

"It sure is," she said when she saw where he was pointing. "Every show has some same-sex couples."

"But I—" His heart hammered its protest against his rib cage. He was going to be dancing with Mateo Dixon? Like, with him? In his arms?

Betty smirked. "Wow. You must be feeling a lot of feelings right now."

He glared at her. "I've just . . . never danced ballroom with a man before. I mean, who even leads?"

"Mm-hmm."

"That's all."

"Your face is sure bright red about it."

Archer's jaw flapped.

Betty patted his cheek. "You're adorable, Archie. This is going to be really fun for me."

Tango

Archer and Betty warmed up with the rest as eight o'clock passed, then 8:05 and 8:10. He was on the floor stretching and wondering where Stewart was when he saw Mateo look at the clock and sigh.

"Alright," Mateo said to the group, hands on hips. "Let's run through the tango duets first, no music. Beau, you're with Seta. Ben, Caleb. Archer"—their eyes locked—"with me."

Archer stood and gulped as the rest of the dancers paired off and began to work through their intro sequences.

"Have you danced the Argentine tango before?" Mateo asked, rolling his shoulders.

He had taken a few Latin ballroom classes over the last few months, but he was no expert. "Some."

"Great. So like that, only now you do it backward."

"I do?" Archer frowned. "Wait, why do you get to lead?"

Mateo looked taken aback. "I'm taller."

Archer squinted at the top of Mateo's head. "I don't think you are. I think we're the same height."

"Well, my shoulders are wider."

"What does that have to do with anything?"

"Uh . . ." Mateo's brow furrowed.

A smile played at the corner of Archer's mouth. "Alright, teach me the choreo for now, and we can measure width later."

Mateo huffed and crossed to the center of the floor. "We start in opposite wings and walk to meet in the middle on the second eight-count and then—" Mateo took Archer in his arms in a close hold and fucking *smoldered* at him.

Archer dropped his eyes while he filled his lungs with Mateo's scent. The reality of what it would mean to dance in this man's arms hit him hard. "Got it," he rasped.

"We start with a walk in promenade. Make sure you hold your frame . . ." He began to lead. Archer tried to let himself be moved by Mateo's hands and arms. "Slow, slow, quick, quick . . ."

He thought he was settling in well when Mateo stopped. "Archer, you're leading."

"What?"

"You're leading."

Archer blinked. "How can I be leading? I don't know the steps."

"And yet . . . you are."

Archer exhaled. "Sorry."

Mateo took hold of him again. "From the top. Slow, slow . . ."

It wasn't long before Mateo stopped again. "Relax your shoulders," he told Archer.

Shit, I suck at this. "I thought I was supposed to be erect in the tango."

The faintest hint of a smile fluttered over Mateo's mouth. "Your posture is erect, yes, but your shoulders also need to be relaxed and over your hips." When he said the word *hips*, he took Archer's hips in both hands and pulled them forward so they were under his shoulders. And right up against Mateo's hips.

Archer stifled a whimper. "Got it." He knew he was too tense—he could feel the rigidness in his body, like he was trying to maintain a boundary between himself and Mateo. A professional I-didn't-spend-most-of-my-teenage-years-in-love-with-you wall.

"Then same-foot lunge . . ." Mateo continued.

Forty-five minutes later, Archer—sweating and trying to be erect, yet not—noticed Stewart shuffling in from backstage, dog under one arm, cane in the other. "Good morning, my darlings!" he announced. "You'll have to forgive my tardiness this morning. One of us . . ." He paused and lifted the dog up to press a kiss to its shiny fur. ". . . was having a bit of a lie-in this morning, weren't you, Judy? Well, enough faffing about, from the top!" He settled into his usual front-row seat.

"He's late 'cause of his dog?" Archer murmured under his breath.

Mateo shot him a sardonic look. "He told me that he takes an entire week off every year for Judy's birthday."

The opening tango number began with a series of partner duets, Mateo and Archer first. The pairs split up into the left and right wings while Francisco, their tech guy, fiddled with some knobs. Then the music began.

Archer started his walk in time with the music, matching Mateo's pace, until they met in the middle in their hold. *Slow, slow, quick, quick . . .* Archer blew out a breath at the halfway point of their duet. *Okay, this is—*

"Stop!" Stewart shrieked.

Archer and Mateo dropped out of their hold as the music cut off.

"Stop, stop, STOP!" Stewart stomped up the stairs in his leather sandals, Judy still tucked under one arm. He reached the top and thrust an accusing finger toward Archer. "*You.*"

"Me?" Archer squeaked, as if there was any doubt as to whom Stewart was pointing at. Mateo shuffled back a few inches. *Oh God, am I getting fired? Do I suck that bad?*

Stewart marched toward him, although it was really more of a waddle. "This is the tango, boy. The *tango.*" He waved pinched fingers at Archer. "It is *hot.* It is *spicy.* It is *sex on the dance floor.* I need to believe you want to *devour* your partner."

Archer licked his dry lips and flicked his gaze over to Mateo, who looked only amused.

"Well?" Stewart barked.

"Um." Archer blinked at him.

"'Um,' he says. So help me, Judy, he says 'um.' Mateo, get over here. Let me see your hold."

Archer's cheeks flushed as Mateo took hold of him, their noses only an inch apart. He stared at Mateo's chest.

"Now, see, you can't even look at him. Look into his eyes! See that he wants you!"

Archer was only seconds away from melting into a puddle and seeping through the cracks in the floorboards, never to be seen again. He lifted his chin to find Mateo's dark stare boring into him.

"Yes! Yes. Feel his desire. Yearn for him. Smell him!"

"Smell—?"

"It's pheromones, boy! We've got to believe he is driving you insane on a *chemical level.* Breathe him in."

Archer inhaled. Fuck, he did smell good. Forest and sunshine. Mateo's nostrils flared too. Archer figured he smelled like sweat.

"Can you feel how he wants you?" Stewart asked, voice a low, urgent simmer.

He could, in fact, feel every inch of Mateo's body, even though most of it wasn't actually touching him, but it was only a breath away, radiating heat and muscle and power. Mateo's gaze dipped to his lips and back up, eyes flashing with desire.

"Yes," Archer whispered.

Stewart leaned in. "Say it."

Their eyes were locked. "He wants me."

Stewart's voice dropped to a hush. "Then fucking dance like it." He whirled, his sweater flapping like a cape. "And that goes for all of you! Again!"

"He's right, you know," Mateo murmured as Stewart clomped back down the stairs. "The audience has to believe the chemistry. These dances, they have to be sexy." Mateo was still holding Archer, but now he was looking at him like he was just some dumb kid who couldn't do his job.

Archer stepped back out of his arms. "Got it," he snapped, face hot. He turned and marched to his place on stage right. *Alright . . . You want sexy? I'll give you fucking sexy.*

When the music started, Archer began his walk. He attached his gaze to Mateo's, imagining it was the face on his bedroom wall. He rolled his hips. He dragged his tongue along his lower lip. He didn't look away. This time when Mateo took him in their hold, Archer tilted his head a smidge, parted his lips, looked at Mateo through lowered lashes. He had imagined this moment many times before. All that was left to do was kiss.

The duet began. Each pause, he pressed his chest to Mateo's. He pushed his foot hard against Mateo's leg for each caress. When they stopped in hold, he let out a faint moan. Mateo's eyes widened when he felt the vibration in his chest.

"How was that?" Archer whispered into Mateo's ear when they hit their finishing pose. He tried not to grin when Mateo shivered.

"Good," Mateo rasped. He let go of Archer like he was a hot poker. He cleared his throat and tried again. "Good. That was good. Better. Uh." He looked around. "Can we take five?" He bolted for his water bottle.

Archer found Stewart watching him.

The bastard winked.

* * *

"How was the *tango*?" Betty said in a deeply meaningful way, bumping Archer's hip with hers on their way out the theater door.

He suppressed a grin. "Fine."

"'Fine,'" she repeated. "Yeah, if by 'fine' you mean 'the eye-sex was great, thanks.'"

Archer tried to pretend he didn't know what she was talking about for a hot second, then the grin won. "Okay, more than fine."

Betty cackled. "Holy shit, it was *fire*. God, how did you manage to do all that without ripping your clothes off and yelling 'take me now'?"

Archer chuckled and made a show of examining his nails. "I mean . . . only doing my job."

She laughed again. "You're dedicated to your craft, Archie. Just try to leave some sexual chemistry for the rest of us, hmm?"

* * *

The blistering water cascaded down Archer's aching shoulders and back. He wasn't used to being in a ballroom hold for half the day. In Mateo's arms though. He grinned at the shower tile. He'd be looking forward to *Latin* night each week, that was for sure.

When he decided he had been in there long enough, he reached out for his towel, but his hand only met the bare wall. He frowned and stuck his head out from behind the curtain. It took a second to process the empty stall. His clothes and towel were gone from the hook. "Are you fucking kidding me?" he asked the wall.

Archer groaned and stepped out of the shower, shaking water drops from his hair. "Hello?" he called to the rest of the bathroom. No answer. Of course. Fortunately, the prankster had left his toiletry bag, and he had a washcloth in the shower. He eyed the barely adequate white square. "Fuck."

He packed up his toiletries and, holding the bag behind him and the washcloth over his junk, tiptoed past the sinks and over to the door. He poked his head out and looked up and down the hallway. No one. With a deep breath, he bolted for his room, rounded the corner, and screeched to a halt when he found Mateo Dixon standing outside his door.

"Uh . . ." The shock on Mateo's face would have been fucking hilarious if Archer wasn't about to incinerate on the spot and blow away in a billion pieces of ash. "Where are your clothes?" he stammered.

"I don't know," Archer replied, gripping the washcloth.

Mateo looked confused. "Did someone take them?" Mateo's eyes began to drift down Archer's chest and got somewhere around the *v* of his hips before wrenching back up to Archer's face.

I'm naked, Archer's brain screamed. "I guess, since I got out of the shower and they were not there." He laughed. It bordered on hysterical. "Did you take them?"

"What? No? Why would I take your clothes?"

So, so naked. Archer closed his eyes. "I was joking. Uh, do you mind?"

"Sorry." Mateo lurched away from the door. "You probably want to . . ."

"Uh, yup." Archer shuffled forward, staring at the doorknob. Using the hand with the washcloth was out of the question . . . but if he used the toiletry bag hand, his naked ass would be facing Mateo. He swallowed a whimper and turned to face him. "Could you . . . ?"

"Oh, shit, yeah." Mateo jumped forward and swung the door open for him. Thank God no one had locked it. The key was in the depths of his toiletry bag.

"Thanks," Archer murmured as he dashed through the door, not able to slam it behind him because, again . . . hands. Instead, he fell onto his bed and wiggled the covers around him. His clothes and towel were sitting folded neatly on his pillow. Ben and Beau were curled up together on a bed watching something on a tablet, although they were both now staring at his entrance, wide-eyed.

"Who put my clothes there?" he mumbled into his pillow, too embarrassed to be mad.

"Caleb," one of the B-Boys replied.

Archer sat up. "You didn't think it was weird Caleb had my clothes?"

They shrugged and went back to their show. "He said you asked him to drop them off or something," one of them muttered.

Archer grabbed his clothes and realized Mateo was standing in the doorway still, looking very uncertain—a look Archer had not seen on him before. He pulled his boxer briefs and shorts under the blanket and awkwardly clambered into them before letting go of the blanket and wrestling his T-shirt on.

"Thanks guys," he snapped at the B-Boys as he stood and smoothed his hair back. "Did you need something?" he asked Mateo with more irritation in his voice than was fair.

"Uh, no," Mateo said. "No, not really, I was walking by and I was just going to ask—or say—good job today."

Right at that moment Caleb strolled in. "Hey, Matty," he said casually to Mateo. "How are things?"

Archer bit his lip, not wanting to lose his shit in front of Mateo.

"Fine, Caleb. I, uh—I've got to go. I'll see you guys tomorrow morning."

"What the fuck, Caleb?" Archer snapped as soon as Mateo's form retreated from the room.

Caleb fell back onto his bed. "Oh, just a bit of harmless fun, Archer. Relax. Welcome to the troupe."

"Fun? Mateo Dixon basically saw me naked!"

Caleb laughed. "No one is going to be mad about seeing you naked, not even Mateo."

"That's bullshit and you know it. This is my job. I'm here to work."

He rolled his eyes. "You don't need to take this quite so seriously, Archer."

The words piled up in Archer's mouth. Maybe this wasn't serious for Caleb or Ben and Beau or anyone. Maybe they were only here for fun. He was here because no one else wanted him, and he had to do it well.

"Just . . ." Archer ran his hands through his hair. "Leave my stuff alone, okay?"

"Fine." Caleb sniffed.

Archer spread his comforter out in the icy silence, which was interrupted by his phone buzzing. Lynn was calling him. He ducked into the hall, ignoring Caleb's sulk on the way.

"Archer! I miss you!" Lynn cried as soon as he answered.

"I miss you too." He walked down the hall and out the door onto the creaky porch. It was already dark, but the night was warm. Crickets chirped in the greenery.

"How's it going? Have you kissed Mateo yet?"

Archer laughed ruefully. "No, but he just saw me practically naked."

"Ooh, do tell!"

"Unfortunately, not like that!" He told her the story.

"Okay, dick move by Caleb," Lynn weighed in, "but . . . like, your body is objectively amazing. I bet Mateo enjoyed the experience."

Archer flushed. "Maybe. So what did you want to talk to me about?"

"Hmm, okay, I'll allow you to change the subject, only because this is important. As you know, Sasha and I have been together for six months now—"

"Mm-hmm . . ."

"—and I'm thinking about asking her to marry me."

"What! Lynn, that's amazing!"

"Is it? You don't think it's too soon? We haven't even lived together yet . . . although we basically have been since you left."

Archer considered what he had observed the past five months, and they seemed like a perfect pair, but he didn't want to influence such an important decision. "Only you can know what feels right."

"It feels right, it does."

"Then that's great." His heart swelled with happiness for his friend.

"Great!"

"So, how are you going to ask her?"

"I was hoping you would help with that! Something cute and creative. You're so good at stuff like this."

"Hmm, let me think about it. Do you have a ring yet?"

"Nope. I have nothing, Archer. That's why I need you."

He laughed. "Okay, you look at rings, we'll both think about the proposal, then we'll talk again soon."

"Thanks, boo."

"You're welcome."

They chatted a bit longer about Shady Queens and Lynn's work, then they hung up. Archer smiled at the forest around him. A breeze tickled his cheeks, and he could maybe hear the distant shriek of someone jumping into the lake. A thought wriggled through his brain—what would Lynn do with her apartment once she and Sasha were engaged?

Speaking of intrusive thoughts, he figured while he was out there he might as well make another call, though it wouldn't be as fun. "Hi, Mom."

"Oh, he finally calls us! One sec." His mom put the call on speaker. "Your dad is here too."

He sighed. "Hi, Dad. And you can call too, you know."

"You never answer."

"Yes, I do."

"So, how is it at . . . What's it called? Shady Pines?"

"Shady Queens."

"Queens? Why would it be called Shady Queens?"

"It's an LGBTQ+ resort, Dad."

"So?"

"Like . . . drag queens?"

"You're not a drag queen . . . are you?"

"No, Dad. They perform on Sundays. A different one comes in each week."

"Are they paying you well?"

"It's decent, plus I get room and board."

"How much are you making, though?"

Their barrage of questions continued until Archer's defenses were weakened and he told them he had rehearsal and hung up. He leaned against the railing, head drooping. Why did his parents make him feel like such a loser? He slapped at a mosquito and headed back to his room. The others were gone. He looked at his bed.

Five minutes later, he had brushed his teeth and was burrowing under his covers when a text came in from Betty. **You coming?**

Ummmmm . . .

You're already in bed, aren't you?

Little bit.

Sad.

The saddest.

Caleb says hi.

What? No, he doesn't.

Fine, he didn't exactly say hi, but he asked me where you were.

Gross.

He's hot.

Yeah, but . . . **And psychotic.**

Well, one out of two ain't bad.

You go for it, then!

Maybe.

Archer laughed. **Good luck.**

It wasn't until he woke up in the middle of the night and stared at the ceiling for a while listening to Caleb snoring that it occurred to him that Mateo must have asked someone which room was his.

5

Blurry

Thursday was a blur. They ran through *Retro* again and also had to learn the hip-hop show. Mateo was all business, barking orders and nagging at him about his turnout. "It's not ballet, Archer. You need to settle into your knees."

"I am," Archer muttered through gritted teeth, not quite loud enough for Mateo to hear. He wanted sexy, smoldering tango Mateo back, or the uncertain, fumbling Mateo who came to find him in his room, not the drill sergeant ragging on him about his knees.

They were taking a water break when Caleb approached. "Mateo's extra pissy today, hey?"

"Mmm," Archer replied, pulling his heel back for a quad stretch.

Caleb chewed his lip for a moment, looking uncustomarily sheepish. "Listen, I'm sorry about taking your clothes and stuff yesterday."

Archer dropped his foot. "Thanks. I appreciate it, Caleb."

"It was supposed to be funny."

"Yeah. It wasn't."

Caleb shrugged. "Your body is scorching hot though."

Archer took a drink of water, considering. "Are you hitting on me while apologizing?"

"Maybe." Caleb's normal mischievous grin crept back. "Is it working?"

Archer chuckled and shook his head. "No."

"Damn it. Better try something else." Caleb winked at him and sauntered away. Archer watched him go. Awfully cute, though. And, he had to admit, the attention was flattering, considering he had been rejected by everyone and everything the last five months.

"If you're done daydreaming, Archer"—the drill sergeant was back—"we're taking it from the top."

* * *

Archer had another long, hot shower—this time his thighs ached—taking quick peeks past the shower curtain at the slightest sound in case Caleb decided it would actually be fucking hilarious to steal his clothes again. When he got out of the shower, he saw that Lynn had sent him a picture of the most beautiful engagement ring—gold with a pink teardrop diamond—and the caption **I found it, Arch!!!**

GORGEOUS, he texted back. **Omg, she's going to love it. Good job, you.**

Any brilliant proposal ideas? she replied.

Archer sagged. No, in fact. He hadn't even thought about it since they talked the day before. What a terrible friend. **Well,** he typed, brain whirring. **You guys met in the library, right? What if you went back there and hid the ring behind a book on marriage law or something?**

YES! she replied. **Love it! It's quiet, not super public, cause she would hate a spectacle, cozy and romantic . . . Okay. I think I'm gonna do it.**

When?? Archer asked, with some relief that he thought of something at the last second that didn't suck.

We're planning on a date Saturday. Maybe then?

So excited for you, babe. You've got this xx

* * *

Caleb sat next to Archer at dinner and peppered him with questions about his background. It would have felt a little interrogatory, if not for the fact that their thighs kept brushing together.

"So mostly ballet?" Caleb asked, dabbing a piece of lettuce into the side dressing.

"Yup." Archer had second thoughts about the fry in his hand, but he ate it anyway. "My parents took me to see *The Nutcracker* when I was four, and I've done ballet ever since, then jazz, contemporary, and acro as I got older."

"Cool, cool." Caleb nodded and set down his fork, half his salad uneaten. "Same for me, but I did tap, too, and some ballroom. My parents have a studio so I kind of did it all."

"What was your favorite?" Archer asked, sneaking one more fry.

"Um." Caleb blinked at him for a second. "My mom said I was best at tap."

"Yeah, but . . ." Archer studied Caleb for a moment, once again appreciating his beauty. "That's not what I asked."

"Oh. I, uh . . . I love ballet. I like that it's so rigid and controlled, so many rules, but then from that, something fluid and beautiful emerges—something close to perfection." He shrugged, then snuck a fry off Archer's plate and winked. Their thighs touched again.

"You heading to the cabin tonight?" Archer asked.

"Yup." An easy grin stretched across Caleb's face. "You?"

* * *

The party was extra that night. Extra loud, extra drunk, extra naked. The music blared, swimmers hurled themselves into the water bathing suit–free, and someone had brought a keg. Perhaps it was that they only had three nights left before the guests arrived, or perhaps it was that they were all getting to know each other better, but whatever it was, the cabin vibrated with a near-manic hum of lust and urgency.

Caleb hadn't left his side since dinner, and Archer was still enjoying the attention. And the guy, while maybe a little too self-assured, was funny and extremely charming and displayed occasional glimpses of unexpected layers. They were lounging on the couch, swapping audition horror stories, slightly buzzed and nearly yelling over the music and ruckus from the group playing beer pong.

"Can you sing?" Caleb asked, leaning so close his breath brushed Archer's cheek.

"Yeah." Archer shrugged. "I did some musical theater stuff in Dayton."

"I went to an audition once that didn't say anything about it in the ad, then I got there and they wanted me to *sing!*" Caleb laughed. "I can't fucking sing! But I was too embarrassed to bail at that point, standing up there in a line, so I panicked, and I'm like, what musical do I know all the words to? And I go with *The Book of Mormon.*"

Archer was delighted. "Which song did you pick?"

"'I Believe.'"

"No!" Archer cackled.

Caleb cracked up. "I know, worst choice ever! And then I ended up forgetting all the fucking words anyway."

Archer tipped his head back and laughed, feeling wonderfully loose and warm up against Caleb's side.

Caleb nodded at his empty bottle once their laughter had faded. "You want another?"

"Sure, thanks." Archer watched Caleb's tight ass make its way over to the fridge. He caught Betty's eye across the room where she was chatting with a bunch of the other dancers. She gave him an eyebrow waggle with a pointed glance at Caleb.

Archer grimaced and shook his head.

Sure, she smirked back at him.

Archer turned his head to ignore her, pointedly.

"What do you think?" Caleb asked when he got back, extending his bottle toward the beer pong table. "Think we can take those assholes from maintenance?"

Archer studied the fluid, muscled lines of Caleb's body. "Hell yeah, we can."

They could not. But they drank and laughed even more, fingers brushing, shoulders bumping, as they got their asses handed to them by the sturdy, well-practiced maintenance crew.

Mateo was there early on, hovering around the edges, glowering at his beer. Archer tried to ignore him, but his gaze continued to find that thick, brooding frame. Then, when Archer was leaning against Caleb, laughing at a catastrophically bad beer pong shot, he looked up and saw Mateo watching them.

Mateo's face was blank, unreadable. They held eyes for a moment as Archer's laugh faded. Something flicked over Mateo's face, then he turned away. Archer watched his back disappear down the hallway toward the stairs.

"Okay, my turn," Caleb said, nudging Archer aside with a hip, words slightly slurred. "I've got this."

Archer shook himself and clapped Caleb on the shoulder. "Here we go. We need this shot."

The night got louder and fuzzier after that. They did some shots with Betty and Dominik, then ended up back on the couch, Caleb edging closer and straightening the collar on Archer's shirt. They might have danced for a while, bodies liquid, sweat beading on Archer's hairline, Caleb's hands on his waist, then back to the couch again.

"Archer!" It was Betty, he was able to determine, once the blond head floating over him came into focus. "Dude, it's three A.M. You good?"

"So good." Archer knew he was hammered, and his wide, blurry smile was fooling no one. Caleb's hand was on his thigh. He blinked at Betty. "What're you still doing here?"

"Get to bed, you guys." She patted his shoulder. "Rehearsal is in five hours. And please, for the love of God, drink *so* much water." She fluttered her fingers at them, shaking her head, then she was gone. Archer realized it was much quieter now, not many people left. One couple was slow dancing—if he squinted, it looked like Gage and River—and someone was passed out on the couch across from them.

"Fuck, man," Archer mumbled. "We should go." He stood and hauled Caleb to his feet. Caleb leaned on him, laughing as he sagged, and they managed to stumble outside and down the stairs to begin making their way up the dark, uneven path.

There was a bleary moment when Caleb paused, took Archer's hand, and tilted his lips toward his, but Archer swayed and stumbled on.

That was the last thing he remembered.

* * *

"Archer! What the fuck? Wake up!" Ben's voice called to him from far away. No, wait, that was Beau. "Archer!" A pissed-off Beau. "Get up, man! Rehearsal starts in five!"

"Wha?" Archer pried his eyes open. The light in the room clawed at his eyeballs. "Fuck." He closed them again.

"Seriously, get your ass out of bed."

A rueful chuckle from Ben. "We tried. See you there, Archer!" The door closed, a sound that bounced off the inside of his head in a clatter.

"I'm coming," Archer mumbled, sitting up and trying to hold his throbbing brain in place. He swung one leg out of bed, then another. His stomach roiled. "Oh God," he muttered. "What did I do?"

The night came back to him all at once. The drinking. The laughing. The flirting. Caleb. His head jerked over to Caleb's bed, a move he instantly regretted. His bed was empty.

Then Archer realized he was naked. His boxers were crumpled under the covers. And so was another pair that he didn't recognize. "Oh *God*." Did he and Caleb sleep together? Or only . . . sleep together? And where was Caleb?

Archer rested his forehead in his hands, mind and stomach spinning. "Okay," he breathed, hoping the burst of oxygen would help. "Get it together, Archer." Rehearsal was now officially starting and he was still in bed. Not great. So he got up and stumbled to the bathroom, puked in the toilet, scrubbed his face with cold water, and studied himself in the mirror.

He looked *exactly* like he had been partying all night. He pulled on tights and a tank top for rehearsal, threw sweats on top, tried to drink some more water, and jogged over to the theater, despite his pounding head. Only ten minutes late. Could be worse. Except it was only day three. Fuck.

He resolved to not be late the rest of the summer, knowing he was likely fighting a losing battle against his nature.

They were already into choreo for the *Around the World* show. Looked like some country and western line dancing. Caleb was in place, fresh as a spring day. Archer approached the stage, gnawing on a lip.

Stewart stood from his usual front-row seat. "Well, well. Archer has decided to join us."

His stomach quivered. The last thing he needed to do was give Stewart a reason to dislike him. "Sorry, Stewart. I, uh, slept in."

Someone in the ranks snorted.

"Do not apologize to me, Archer." Stewart waved his hand at the other dancers. "Apologize to your colleagues whom you have let down."

Archer faced his troupe. Most of them looked amused, including Caleb. Mateo's face was a storm cloud. "Sorry, guys."

Dominik grinned at him. "It's fine, bro. We've all been there. Well . . ." His eyes shifted. "Most of us."

Stewart sniffed. "Indeed. This reminds me of the morning after Matthew Broderick's bachelor party. Quick warm-up, Archer, then fall in."

He didn't get a chance to talk to Caleb until the first break. He sat next to him on the floor for a stretch. "Why didn't you wake me up?"

Caleb smirked and pulled his cowboy boots off to rub his feet. "I tried. You were out cold, princess."

"Were we, uh . . . Did we . . ." He leaned closer to Caleb and lowered his voice. "Did you sleep in my bed?"

Caleb grinned. "You don't remember?"

Archer's cheeks flushed. "No."

"Yeah, we both passed out in your bed. Nothing happened, though."

Archer breathed a sigh of relief. "Okay, good."

"Ouch."

"No, it's not that, it's—"

"Relax. I'm messing with you. Trust me, if we fucked, you'd remember."

Heavy feet stopped next to them. Archer looked up to see Mateo's frown. "Hey, Mateo, I'm really sorry—"

Mateo shook his head. "I was right about you."

Archer furrowed his brow. "Right about what?"

"You're just here to party."

"What?" Archer's stomach dropped. "I'm not—"

"Look." Mateo's face was twisted with distaste. "All I'm asking is that you do your job like a fucking professional, and part of that is showing up on time."

"I'm sorry, I—"

"Save it, Archer. I don't give a shit about your apology."

Archer's jaw wobbled as Mateo turned to leave. Yeah, he messed up, but Mateo didn't have to be such a—

"Look who's talking," Caleb mumbled.

Mateo stopped and marched back. "Excuse me?"

Caleb sighed and rolled his eyes. "Nothing."

"Say what you need to say, Caleb." Mateo looked huge, towering over them where they sat, hands on his hips.

Caleb stood. "It's rich, you lecturing us about being professional."

Mateo's eyes darkened.

Jaw clenched, Caleb stared back.

Mateo opened his mouth, then closed it again. Then he whirled and stormed off, barking at the troupe to get in formation.

"What a dick," Caleb muttered.

Archer gave him a weak smile of agreement, but his heart sank.

* * *

"What did you mean about Mateo being unprofessional?" he asked Caleb later at dinner.

"You've heard the stories, haven't you? He got fired from the role of a lifetime for being 'unprofessional.'"

The other conversations around them quieted, heads turning in their direction.

"Like how?" Archer asked.

"Same old. He started drinking and partying, missing rehearsals, making demands of everyone to treat him like a fucking god. And I guess he was an asshole to Abby. Refused to even talk to her backstage."

Abby Hodge was perhaps the most famous trans actor in America these days, certainly the most famous to ever make it big on Broadway. She had even been nominated for an Oscar this past year. And Mateo was . . . here. With Archer, who couldn't get a job to save his life. Ouch.

"So, why is he working here?"

Dominik shrugged. "No one knows. He hasn't exactly been making friends."

There was murmured agreement around the table.

"This is his first season?" Archer asked.

Dominik nodded, purple mohawk bobbing. "Yeah. We were all shocked as hell when Stewart introduced him the first day. One thing's for sure though," he added, popping open a can of sparkling water. "That man can *dance*."

The conversation drifted onto other topics, but Archer's thoughts stayed on Mateo. How does one go from being the toast of Broadway to toiling in a tiny cabaret show upstate? He finished his stuffed peppers in silence.

"Cabin tonight?" Caleb asked him, feet bumping under the table.

Archer's stomach quivered. "No way, man. No drinking for me."

"Come on, Archer," Dominik interjected. "Cannonball contest!"

"Everyone's doing it." Betty poked him and grinned.

Archer groaned. "Okay, fine. I can beat you all sober, anyway."

Caleb sighed and stood, stretching his arms above his head and revealing a rather impressive six-pack. "You can try." His voice was low as his gaze dropped to Archer's. "But you're going down."

Archer raised an eyebrow at Caleb. Maybe.

6

Moonlight

"Dancers!" Stewart paced along the front of the stage, Judy trotting at his heels. "For those disinclined to observe such things, I would like you to note that it is Saturday." He stopped and stared at them, gripping his cane, eyes wild. "Saturday! Do you know what this means?"

The dancers shifted, eyeing one another.

Betty raised her hand. "It means that . . . tomorrow is Sunday?"

"Yes!" Stewart bellowed. "Yes, Betty, very well done. Tomorrow is Sunday. And what happens on Sunday?"

"The guests arrive?" Betty continued, on a roll.

"The guests. Arrive. *Tomorrow.*" Stewart took a deep breath then threw his head back. "Tomorrow! Tomorrow, people! *Retro* is merely passable. *Latin* is middling. *Urban* is abysmal. *Around the World* and *Broadway?* In utter shambles! I need your blood, your sweat, your very *tears* today, my darlings. Today . . . we dance!" He flung his arms out and froze as if waiting for applause.

"Uh, Stewart?" Mateo pointed behind him. "The costume designers and photographers are here, though."

Stewart turned to verify that they had indeed interrupted his big finish, then sniffed at them. "Oh, yes. Very well. We dance . . . later today."

The seamstresses descended with their racks of costumes, paying special attention to Archer, Beau, Ben, and Betty, who hadn't had a chance to try anything on yet. The photographer and her assistant took over a corner of the stage and began setting up their equipment. Stewart shuffled and sighed his way around the hubbub while Mateo got them organized.

"Let's get everyone into their contemporary costumes first for the headshots," he decided, "then we'll do a few pairs for each show after."

The others seemed unimpressed with all the bustle around them, but Archer was secretly thrilled. This made it feel less like summer camp and more like an actual show. He stood patiently for the seamstress as she measured and pinned and sorted through his clothes. Each dancer would have their own rack backstage, a neat row of all their costumes for the six shows. His favorite had to be the *Latin*—slinky black pants and a loose-fitting dark purple and scarlet top cut down to his waistband. Mateo's costume was black and sparkly, with hints of matching purple and scarlet shimmers. For a second, he pictured the two of them together, tight in their hold.

"You're up, Archer," Mateo called when the seamstress had finished checking Archer's billowy contemporary shirt.

"Okay." He stepped over to the screen, a little nervous. He hadn't had dance photos taken in a long time.

"Stand on the X, please," the photographer said. "Chin down a bit . . . That's it. Now take a breath, and smile."

Archer sucked in a lungful of air and let it out in a *whoosh*. It was hard to relax with Mateo and half the troupe milling around watching. He tried to think about the moment when he got this job and let that smile come out.

"Gorgeous," the photographer said to him. "Just beautiful. Give me another smile. Great. Now how about a serious face . . . Ooh, sexy. Perfect. Do you want some with your shirt off?"

"Um, sure?" The rest of the men had done it, so he figured he should. He whisked off his floaty shirt and tossed it onto a chair, then turned back to the camera. Archer swore he caught Mateo's gaze lingering before he whipped it away.

After the individual photos were taken, Mateo began sorting them into small groups. "We need a few shots for each show. How about Dominik and Daniella in their *Grease* costumes for *Broadway*, Nijah and Iris into belly dancing, and Caleb into capoeira for *Around the World* . . ." He continued giving instructions until only he and Archer remained. "And we can do *Latin*," he finished.

Archer gulped. Guess he wouldn't have to imagine how they'd look clinched together—he was about to find out. Archer slid into his *Latin* costume, then watched as the others took their turns posing.

"I want these really dynamic," the photographer said when Mateo and Archer were up. "Can you give me a few steps?"

Mateo took hold of Archer. "Let's do the eight-count from the first lunge?"

"Sounds good," Archer gasped, breathing him in and trying to keep his pulse from racing.

"Gorgeous," the photographer mumbled, pulling back to study her screen for a second. "Do that again. God, you two can smolder, can't you?"

Their eyes met.

Yup.

By the time the costume racks were sorted away and the photographer was packing up, Stewart was sipping tea in the front row with Judy in his lap, having lost his momentum for inspiring speeches.

"Alright," Mateo said. "Time for *Broadway.*" He and the others helped Archer, Ben, Beau, and Betty break down the choreo, and, God, Archer loved it. They were doing a collection of songs from so many of his favorites—*Grease, Newsies, Hairspray,* and *Beauty and the Beast.*

Watching Mateo dance to the *Grease* song was so exhilarating he was nearly dizzy. Archer would be one of the greasers during "Summer Nights" and watching Mateo as Danny . . . He was transported back to the theater when he was fourteen, falling in love with him. Not that he was in love with him *now*, of course. Just, professionally . . . admiring him.

The day ran long and they were cooling down on the stage, in danger of missing dinner entirely, when Stewart shuffled over to speak to them.

"As you know, normally Sunday is your day of rest, but tomorrow we will use it for a dress rehearsal for *Retro*, and a run-through of *Latin* and *Urban*. Be here by eight o'clock sharp. We must be out by two o'clock to allow setup for the drag show."

Archer let out a low groan. He had been really looking forward to sleeping in tomorrow.

"So excited to see Eva Stiff again!" Dominik piped up.

"Who's Eva Stiff?" Archer murmured to Caleb while

Stewart launched into a story about the early days of drag in New York.

"She's a drag queen from Manhattan. There's a group of them who usually rotate through and come out to do the Sunday shows. Eva is getting pretty big but she started out here so she always comes back for the opening and closing shows."

"Can we watch if we want?"

"We never miss it."

* * *

So? Archer texted Lynn, flopping onto his bed with wet hair and rubbery muscles after dinner and a shower. **Are you engaged??? Are you having celebration sex this very minute??**

It took a minute but her reply popped up: the grimace emoji.

Oh no, what happened?

The library is undergoing renovations! The section where we met was closed and I got flustered. Plus Sasha had a bad day at work and she was kind of in vent mode and it didn't feel very proposal-y.

Aw, that's okay! You can try for another time when the mood is right.

Yeah, I will. Let me know if you have another idea! In other news . . . A picture of their living room came through showing three buckets now instead of one. **Leak Perry brought his friends, Jason Trickley and Tori Spilling.**

Archer groaned and cackled at the same time. **At least you got to come up with more names.**

Lol. A small consolation.

> **You going full lawyer on Fletcher's**
> **ass?**

I'm trying. He's rather impervious.
Unlike our ceiling.

> **If anyone can tear him a new one,**
> **it's you.**

On it. Gotta go, we're grabbing
dinner. Kisses!

> **Backatcha.**

Archer put his phone down and folded his arms under his head. He really missed Lynn. Even though they'd only been living together for five months, it seemed like they'd been friends for years, and it felt shitty not to be there for her when she was ready to make such a big leap.

"Archer!" Caleb burst in, eyes lit up, teeth gleaming white in a broad smile. "Last night! Let's go!"

Archer moaned. "I'm so tired, Caleb."

"Oh, no, no, no." Caleb took his arm and tried to heave him off his bed. "It's the last night before the guests arrive. We all go skinny-dipping and drink our faces off."

Archer let Caleb pull him to a seated position but retrieved his hand from Caleb's grasp. "I'm so confused as to how that's different from what we've been doing all the other nights."

"Come on! We have to tone it down once the guests are here. It's our last chance to go crazy."

Archer sighed and scrubbed his face.

"You can sleep in plenty this summer," Caleb continued when he saw the chink in the armor. "Once the shows are running and Stewart leaves, you can sleep in every morning."

"Wait, Stewart is leaving?"

"Yeah, you know, like in an actual Broadway show. The director gets the show going then takes off to do other things."

"Like . . . drink tea and pet their dog?"

Caleb laughed. "Exactly. He'll show up a couple more times for a check-in, but mostly we'll be on our own. Anyway"—he grabbed Archer's hand again—"it's the *last night*. Let's go, sexy."

Well, then. Caleb's hand was warm. Archer stood. It was the last night, after all.

* * *

It was close to midnight when they were stretched out on the dock with a few of the other dancers, legs dangling over the side, panting after the exertion and skin tingling from the cool water. Archer studied Caleb, his features aglow and more beautiful than ever in the lantern light. The water beaded on his smooth skin, running down the groove between his abs until it collected in the fuzzy pineapple-yellow beach towel that was slung low around his hip bones. And below those hip bones . . . Archer had a peek as they threw themselves off the dock into the dark water, and that part of Caleb was, well . . . it was rather beautiful, too.

As if he knew what he was thinking, Caleb whipped his head around and threw him a devilish grin. "Aren't you glad you came along?"

"Yeah." Archer brushed a hand over the goose bumps on Caleb's arm. "You were right."

"I usually am, Archer." Caleb's eyes dropped down to Archer's hand for a second, then back up. "Last one inside does a shot!" he announced. In one fluid motion, Caleb was on his feet, chucking his towel in Archer's face and running down the dock back to the cabin, whooping as he went. The rest of the crew followed, shrieking and laughing.

Archer shook his head, chuckling. Cute ass, too.

* * *

Idea! Archer texted Lynn the next morning. **Why don't you take her to that pop-up bar in Tribeca? The one that's in the alley, which sounds creepy, but it's all strung with a million fairy lights. I saw some pics on Insta and it's gorgeous. You could get the bartender to garnish her drink with the ring.**

Ooh! That sounds beautiful, she replied. **I'll suggest that for our next date. I think we're going out tomorrow night. Thanks, Arch! How are things going with you? Mateo in love with you yet?**

> **Lol. Mateo is all business. He barely talks to me. But . . . remember Caleb? The one who stole all my clothes? Turns out . . . he's kinda cute.**

Oh yeah? Like fuckable cute?

Archer considered for a moment. **Maybe? I don't think it'll be anything serious, but . . .**

Get it, girl. Keep me posted. And GOOD LUCK TOMORROW! BREAK A LEG!

> **Thanks, babe. You too.**

* * *

Sunday rehearsal went smoothly. Archer was confident with *Retro*, which they would perform tomorrow on their opening night. *Latin* was always fun—even though Mateo barely looked at him when they weren't dancing—and hip-hop felt good, too. There was more to learn later in the week, but he was ready enough.

Archer was pulling his sweats on after rehearsal when Mateo approached.

"Archer, can I talk to you for a second?"

He sucked in a breath and waited for Mateo to give him shit about his turnout again. "Yeah, what's up?"

"I was just wondering if you wanted some extra rehearsal? I don't mind meeting with you a few times to go over the choreo this week. You've had a lot to take in, and we haven't even gotten to contemporary yet."

Archer's stomach dropped. *Wow, he must think I'm absolute garbage. Didn't offer it to any of the Bs.* "Sure, I guess, if you think I need it."

"It's not that—we have a pas de deux in that show. Thought we could at least start blocking it out before the group rehearsal."

"What? We do?" Archer's brow furrowed. Why on earth would they give him a pas de deux with Mateo fucking Dixon?

Mateo read his confusion. "They were looking for a male ballet dancer at the audition specifically for this. They chose you."

"They were? They did?" The weirdest feeling blossomed in Archer's chest.

"Well, yeah." Something close to a smile threatened to creep over Mateo's face.

The words swirled around his brain. Why was Mateo being so nice to him? It was hard to swallow with the lump in his throat. "Thanks," he scratched out.

"So . . . do you want some extra rehearsal?"

"Yeah. Yes. Yes, please. Definitely."

Mateo's eyes softened. "If you want to watch Eva tonight, we can do it after the first show?"

"Sure. Where, though, if the theater is full?"

"Yeah, there's not really anywhere great, but if you find me at the cabin after, let's say at eight, I'll show you."

* * *

Shady Queens was at her sparkling best. The buildings glowed a fresh white in the afternoon sun. Brightly colored boats painted like different LGBTQ+ flags bobbed in the water along the main dock. The grass was green, the paths were neatly trimmed, the sand was raked smooth on the volleyball courts . . . Everything was ready for the guests.

Off-duty staff were generally not to be seen around the resort, but they had free rein of the staff dorms, dining hall, and cabin. They could even swim around the employee dock as long as they weren't loud or rowdy. Archer had definite plans to work on his tan this summer, but for now he had one thing on his mind: sleep.

He showered and crashed hard in his bed until Ben shook him awake a couple hours later at dinnertime. He realized he hadn't had much of a chance to talk to his other roommates the last few days, having spent most of his free time with Caleb.

"How's your week going, guys?" Archer asked, digging into his stir-fry.

"Good," Ben said at the same time Beau snipped, "Fine."

Archer glanced between them. "Okay?"

Beau's gaze shifted sideways at Ben. "Ben's having a great week."

Ben sighed, eyes rolling. "I was not checking him out."

Beau smiled a tight smile and patted Ben's leg. "Of course not, love."

"Um." Archer froze, fork hovering. "Checking who out?" He instantly regretted asking, of course, but it was too late.

Now Ben had a tight smile of his own. "Beau thinks I was checking out Gage."

"He's stone cold," Beau said, stabbing his chicken with a fork. "Why wouldn't you check him out?"

"Yeah, he's hot, but just because I happened to be looking at him—"

"So you admit he's hot?" Beau's eyebrow arched dangerously high.

"I—" Ben shut his mouth with a snap and gave Archer a desperate will-you-help-me-out-here? look.

Archer chewed slowly, looking between the two. "Nothing wrong with noticing someone is hot, right?" he ventured.

Beau studied him for a moment. "Of course not, Archer." He took a delicate bite.

"Speaking of hot," Archer continued, "I'm so excited for the show tonight." Sadly, in all his time in New York, focused as he was on auditioning and saving money, he hadn't seen much drag.

"Oh my God, we saw Eva in New York last fall!" Beau announced and, happily, the subject was changed.

Ben flashed Archer a grateful look.

* * *

Eva Stiff was a marvel. She was at least six foot eight with her platform heels and towering pink wig, wrapped neck to ankle in shimmering gold fabric. The dancers were allowed to watch the show from the wings, so Archer crowded in with the rest of the troupe, except Mateo, who was not there.

"Isn't she fierce?" Dominik whispered in awe as she took the stage to the utter delight of the crowd.

"Amazing."

Eva opened with a Cher song, and the audience ate it up. She was funny and smooth, pulling assorted guests up on stage as the show went on. The first participant was a small, delicate-looking elderly woman who was wearing a lilac dress with a matching hat, but she bounded up onto the stage with the alacrity of someone half her age and hugged Eva like they were old friends. She came up to the drag queen's rib cage.

"Give it up for Ms. Eileen Lamb!" Eva cried.

So they did know each other. "Who is Ms. Eileen Lamb?" Archer whispered to Caleb as Eva wrapped a feather boa around Eileen's shoulders.

"She's basically a resident guest, been coming for years and years," he replied. "She's here all summer, and she almost never misses a show. She hits on the other elderly lesbians."

"Oh, nice," Archer replied, watching Eileen shimmy along to the music.

Eva was fabulous—upbeat, whip-smart, and a little naughty. Archer could see why she was starting to make it big.

"Archer, you coming?" Betty asked when it was over. "We're gonna go grab a drink with Eva before the second show." She bobbed her head at the greenroom.

Mateo would be waiting for him. "Nah, I told my parents I'd call them."

For some reason, he didn't want Caleb to know where he was going. He ran back to his room to change and grab his duffel, then made his way down to the cabin.

Mateo was leaning on the railing, hands loosely clasped,

gazing out over the lake. There were a few employees drifting here and there, but most were either working or at the theater.

Mateo turned his head when the step creaked under Archer's foot.

"Hi," Archer said. "You didn't want to see Eva Stiff?"

"Nah. Not in the mood for a crowd." He turned back to the water.

"Hmm." Archer joined him at the railing and took in the view. "Nice night." The sun was just vanishing behind the trees, leaving the water a shimmering molten gold.

Mateo nodded, the light reflecting off his eyes. "It's beautiful."

"You feel ready for the week?" Archer asked. There were a few butterflies in his stomach, to be honest, after seeing how incredible Eva was. Shady Queens didn't mess around with amateurs.

Mateo half shrugged. "We'll pull it off. Helps that we're working on our pas de deux now."

Archer nodded. "So where are we going?"

Mateo grabbed a flashlight off the railing. "Follow me."

They thumped down the steps, but instead of heading back toward the resort like Archer expected, Mateo turned and went past the cabin, taking a shadowed path that led farther into the trees.

Archer hurried after him, following the patch of light at Mateo's feet.

They walked in silence, the trees swallowing up the resort behind them until it felt like they were the only two people on earth. Their path met up with a broader, smoother one, and they continued up a moderate incline.

"Where are we going?" Archer asked when his calves were starting to burn.

"Right . . . here," Mateo said, stopping and turning off the flashlight.

Archer blinked as his eyes adjusted to the dimmer light. They were in a clearing of packed grass ringed by small boulders and maples, white flowers winking at them from the shrubs below. It was lovely. "What's this place?"

"There are hiking trails all around the lake, and the resort does yoga and aerobics classes here sometimes when the weather's nice. It's not perfect, but since we're blocking and not en pointe or anything, it should work."

Archer nodded and dropped his bag. Guess he wouldn't need his ballet shoes. He kicked off his flip-flops. Bare feet, it was.

Mateo followed suit, and they stepped together into the center of the clearing.

"Alright, so . . ." Mateo started. "We're dancing to 'Dance of the Blessed Spirits,' from *Orfeo ed Euridice*. Do you know it?"

Archer nodded and grinned. "Did my first ballet recital to that song."

Mateo paused, blinking. "You did?"

He nodded again. "I was four."

"That's crazy." Mateo scratched his head. "I did, too."

A surprised laugh escaped Archer's lips. "What? No way."

They stood, smiling at each other, until Mateo cleared his throat and settled into position. "We start in third, and fondu . . ."

Mateo led him through the steps—entrechat, piqué en tournant, cabriole . . . He was patient and steady, hands sure against Archer's waist, supporting him exactly when required. It was weird for Archer because of course he'd always been the one supporting his partner, but now Mateo was there for him through lifts and pirouettes. It was an athletic number, too, with plenty of leaps and jumps, and even though they weren't going full out, it left Archer sweating.

"Then we finish with a pirouette into double tour"— Mateo demonstrated effortlessly, pirouetting before whirling through the air in a double turn, then landing on a knee, arms extended gracefully—"down to knee."

Damn. Seeing the muscle and power behind Mateo's dancing, right up close under the moonlight . . . Archer could barely swallow as his mouth dried out. "Got it. Water break?"

The silver light reflected the sweat glistening along Mateo's hairline. "Sure."

Across the path was a boulder, jutting out over a rise. The lake glimmered through a gap in the trees below them. Mateo sat and stretched his legs out. Archer climbed on next to him. The silence between them was thick, punctuated by the ever-present crickets.

"So . . . this is your first season at Shady Queens?" Archer asked.

Mateo looked at him sharply, eyebrow raised. "You know it is."

A few responses swarmed Archer's tongue—*I'm sorry, I don't mean to pry, just trying to get to know you better*—but before he could choose one, Mateo softened.

"Sorry." He looked back at the lake. "It's . . . I can only imagine what people say about me."

"They don't say that much." Archer studied Mateo's rugged profile. His brow was furrowed in his usual "don't bother me" manner.

Mateo snorted. "Sure they don't."

"Well . . ." Archer wiggled his earth-stained toes. "A little maybe."

Mateo didn't reply, only picked up a small twig and twirled it between his fingers.

"They say . . ." Archer ventured, ". . . the fame went to your head. Partying and . . . stuff."

"Stuff, hey?" Mateo blew a small, amused breath through his nose. "Yeah, I guess 'partying and stuff' about covers it." He tossed the twig into the brush.

Archer shrugged. "I'd party too if I was the star of a smash hit."

Mateo didn't reply for a full minute, and Archer simply waited.

"I've been sober since," Mateo said, voice low, then he glanced over at Archer, reading the confusion on his face. "I've been drinking nonalcoholic beer."

"That's great, Mateo." Archer reached over and rested his hand on Mateo's, just for a second.

Their eyes met. Mateo looked like he wanted to say something else, but he turned and slid off the rock and dusted off his sweats.

"Again?"

"Again."

They ran through it again, and again, until the moon was high, Archer's feet were black, and his water bottle empty.

"How did you get here?" Mateo asked on their way back down. "I'm surprised you're not dancing in a company somewhere."

"Oh." Archer captured the flutter in his heart at Mateo's words and tucked it away for later. "No, I—I was an accountant in Ohio until five months ago."

Mateo laughed, then stopped, seeing Archer's face. "You're serious?"

"Completely. Spent the last five months in New York auditioning, and I couldn't book a single gig."

"Oh, well . . ." Mateo waved a hand. "It's all politics, who they hire, or it's completely subjective. You know, the casting director just got dumped by a blond so they don't even look at you. Or their cousin's friend's little brother is auditioning so they pick him. Or they choose the guy they want to fuck. Not that you're not fuckable." He cleared his throat. "Not that you are. I mean—Fuck."

Archer tried not to laugh. "Thanks?"

"Anyway . . ." Mateo marched ahead without looking at him. "There are a million reasons someone might not pick you, and they have nothing to do with your dancing."

They had reached the cabin. They stopped.

"Thanks, Mateo. That was . . . really fun." Archer realized that this rehearsal had been the most fun he'd had so far at Shady Queens.

"You're welcome." Mateo's gaze was soft as it landed on Archer.

For a split second, it felt like the end of a date, and Archer's eyes went to Mateo's lips, before he scolded himself for being ridiculous. "I'll see you tomorrow?" he said, hoping Mateo couldn't see his blush in the dim light.

"You bet."

Archer fell asleep with the thought of Mateo's long, strong body lifting his as they moved in the moonlight.

7

I Like You

"Morning." Caleb plopped down next to Archer on the bench at breakfast. "Where'd you end up last night? Your bed was empty when we got back."

"Oh, I . . . went for a walk." His night with Mateo didn't feel like something he wanted to share. "Did you have fun with Eva?"

"Hell yeah, she's fucking hilarious. She told us this story about the time when she was just starting out and she lost her bra right before the show, so she had to borrow one from a waitress and stuff it with bar rags. But then the waitress's shift ended in the middle of her show, and she came *on stage* and demanded Eva give it back. Eva refused and the woman tackled her, and they ended up wrestling and everyone thought it was part of the show." The table cracked up around him, and Archer laughed with them. As cool as it would have been to hang out with Eva, he had no regrets.

They had time to kill before rehearsal at two, so they all headed down to the dock for a swim and sunbathing. Caleb didn't leave his side, touching his arm or thigh to get his attention, offering to get him a drink from the cabin, and even brushing a piece of wet hair off Archer's forehead when they climbed, dripping, out of the water.

When it was time to head to the theater, they traveled as a pack. Caleb slung an arm over Dominik's shoulders, laughing at one of his jokes, then took hold of Archer's hand.

"One sec, Archer." Caleb pulled him back when they arrived at the theater, while the rest of the crew tramped through the stage door.

"What's up?"

"Archer . . ." Caleb smiled up at him through his long eyelashes. "In case it isn't obvious, I like you."

"Oh." He was surprised to hear Caleb say it out loud, and his cheeks flushed. "I like you too."

Caleb smiled. "That's good." Then he leaned forward and kissed him.

Archer's mind spun. On the one hand, it felt nice to have lips pressed to his again. On the other . . . it was probably a bad idea to go down this road with a fellow dancer and roommate—it would be awkward as hell if things didn't go well. Then Caleb slipped his tongue into his mouth and Archer took a step back, ending the kiss. His jaw worked as he tried to think of something to say, but he didn't need to say anything at all.

"Excuse me," came the growl from behind them.

He whirled. Mateo. Mateo, looking angrier than ever, brow pulled down so far it almost met the tip of his nose. For some reason, Archer felt like a kid caught with his hand in the cookie jar.

"Sorry, Mateo," Caleb said smoothly, stepping aside and pulling Archer with him. "We'll be right in."

Mateo leveled his gaze at Archer for a half second longer before he stormed inside.

"Oh, good," Caleb said with an eye roll. "Mateo's gonna be a dick again today. Anyway . . ." He smiled at Archer and squeezed his hand, giving him another quick kiss. "Guess we'd better get inside."

"Yeah." Archer smiled back and let Caleb lead him through the door.

The stage was abuzz with stretching dancers and the tech crew up in the rigging, adjusting lights and speakers and doing sound checks. The performers were still in warm-up clothes, although Stewart was in a fancy-yet-rumpled eggplant-colored suit. Judy had a matching sequined bow on her collar.

Dominik came running down the center aisle from the lobby. "Our photos are up!" he announced.

The entire troupe went charging back up the aisle, busting through the swinging doors into the lobby and over to the display. It was quite impressive and took up most of the black wall along the entryway. There was a framed poster for each show, Sunday through Saturday, with the headshots with their names below, all around the outside. Archer's eyes went straight to the *Latin Flame* poster, and his lungs emptied.

Holy fuck.

Their picture . . .

Mateo was dangerously hot, of course, as expected, but Archer . . . he looked pretty hot, too. They were in their hold, Archer tipped back like they were mid-step. Mateo's gaze was boring into Archer, burning with longing. Archer's head was turned away flirtatiously, but his eyes were cast back at Mateo, lips curling in the faintest hint of a knowing smirk.

It was pure sex.

"Goddamn," Betty murmured, sidling up to him. "That's a great picture."

Archer jumped, realizing he was staring. "Oh, thanks. Yeah, the photographer did a great job." He waved at the display. "These are all great."

"Yeah?" Betty asked with a teasing smile. "You've looked at all of them, have you?"

He wanted to hiss at her to shut up, but then Mateo was next to him, studying their picture, too. He nodded once before moving on down the line.

Betty winked at Archer.

They did a full run-through of *Around the World* and *Retro*, then Stewart sent them all off to have a quick early dinner before they'd have to rush back for hair and makeup.

"It all happens tonight, my darlings!" Stewart cried. "Do not be late!"

"I'll catch up with you at dinner," Archer told Caleb, eyeing Mateo, who was over chatting with Francisco.

Caleb pecked his cheek. "Okay. See you there."

Archer waited patiently until Mateo began to make his way off the stage. "Hey, did you want to go over our pas de deux again tonight?" he asked.

"It's our opening night," Mateo muttered, walking past Archer down the stairs. "There's a party."

Archer followed him. "Oh. Tomorrow night, then?"

Mateo stopped, hand on the door. "I don't think so, Archer. We don't need it."

"Okay. I only thought—"

"You'd better go eat dinner," Mateo interrupted, before pushing his way out, leaving Archer standing alone in the darkened backstage, trying to process what had just happened. This Mateo was a completely different person from the one who had danced with him in the clearing the night before . . .

No . . . surely Mateo Dixon did not give a shit who he

kissed. Or maybe the kiss was simply Archer being unprofessional again? Maybe it cemented Mateo's belief that Archer was only here to party. He sighed. There were no rules about employees hooking up . . . in fact, he was pretty sure almost every employee *did* hook up somewhere along the way. He wasn't going to marry Caleb or anything, but he was cute and fun and . . . if he wanted to fool around with Caleb, there was nothing stopping him. Except the little voice in his head, but that was easy enough to ignore.

* * *

Archer was returning his dinner tray when Betty scurried up to him.

"You and Caleb been awfully cozy lately," she said with a knowing look. "Did I see him kiss your cheek on his way out?"

"Yes," Archer said sheepishly. "He, uh . . . well, we actually, like, *kiss* kissed right before rehearsal started."

Betty smacked his arm. "Shut up! That's awesome."

"Yeah." Archer shrugged. "I guess."

"What do you mean, you guess? Caleb's hot. And from what I hear, he likes to hook up with the hottest guy here, so"—she fired finger guns at him—"congrats."

Archer nudged her. "Are you saying I'm the hottest guy here?"

She studied him with a scrunched face. "You're okay."

When they got back to the theater, Dominik had poured a round of shots for everyone in the greenroom and handed one to Archer with a grin. "First show tradition!" he announced.

As Archer clinked glasses with Caleb and tossed back the fruity concoction, he noticed that Mateo wasn't there yet. It wasn't until the shot glasses were collected and tidied away that Mateo came in. He didn't so much as glance Archer's way.

They did their own hair and makeup—Betty helped with his, a bit of a stage makeup expert, it seemed—and got into their sparkly white *Retro* costumes. Archer examined his reflection in the mirror as a thrill raced through him. It might be a tiny cabaret in the Catskills, but he was proud of himself for being there and working hard the past week to learn so much choreography. The audience out there wouldn't care if anyone was experienced or learned the choreo that morning. They wanted a great show, and Archer was ready to give it to them. And maybe, just maybe, the right person would be in that audience who could give Archer a break.

With a few finishing touches left, Stewart appeared, eggplant suit even more crumpled than it had been that morning. "Gather round, ducklings," he said, waving his cane.

They shuffled together, arms around each other in a tight huddle. Somehow Archer ended up between Mateo and Caleb, both warm and solid under his hands, although Mateo was taller and bulkier. He could also smell Mateo's fresh, forest-y scent again. Then Caleb squeezed his waist. Archer turned to him and smiled, squeezing his shoulder back.

"My darlings," Stewart began. "The moment is upon us. The moment where you smile and shine and dance your fucking hearts out for the good guests of Shady Queens. It's like I said to Cooper Knox ten years ago before his first show on this very stage—"

Cooper Knox? Archer mouthed at Caleb. Caleb nodded. Cooper Knox was the understudy for Elder Price in *The Book of Mormon.* Archer had no idea that Cooper had danced at Shady Queens.

"—these guests want nothing less than your best, and nothing more than to *feel*." His gaze traveled around the circle. "Are we ready?"

"Ready!" they replied in a chorus.

"Hands in," Stewart said.

They threw their hands into the middle. Archer's heart was full as he scanned the smiling faces.

"Judy be with us," Stewart intoned. "Shady Queens!"

"Shady Queens!" they cheered.

Stewart nodded solemnly. "Places, please."

Archer took his spot in the wings next to Betty and rolled his neck, pulse racing. The audience hummed behind the curtain, a mass of excited voices. This was it.

Then Francisco's announcement boomed. "Welcome to Shady Queens Cabaret! We are so pleased to welcome you to this season's inaugural performance. Please sit back, relax, and let us entertain you as we travel back in time to the era of leisure suits and disco balls, Cher and Studio 54. We give you . . . *Club Retro!*"

"Disco Inferno" started blasting as the curtain rose. Archer let the smile stretch across his face, and he was on stage, following the chain of shimmying dancers. With the lights bright on him, he couldn't see the audience in the darkened theater but he could hear the cheering over the music. He took Betty's hand, and she whirled in front of him, her dress sparkling.

They discoed, they hustled, they spun and boogied and dolphined their way through the numbers, sequins flashing and smiles shining.

The audience roared when they struck their final pose. The dancers bowed and bowed again. It was the most fun he'd had performing since he was a kid, and Archer couldn't believe he got to do this twelve times per week for three more months.

The lights went up, and they waited for photo opportunities with the audience. The resort guests tended toward retirement age, but there were also families and other younger, child-free couples. Eileen Lamb was there, snapping pictures and waving at Mateo.

Once they made their way backstage and the theater emptied, they had time to grab a snack and stretch before the second show.

After the second performance, Stewart was waiting, eyes moist. He sniffled. "You have made this old director so proud. But . . ." He clapped his hands. "We have work to do! I'll see you all back here tomorrow morning at eight—"

A chorus of groans cut him off.

"Alright, alright . . . nine. But not one second later!"

Stewart hugged every one of them before departing, and then they milled around, hugging each other, celebrating their first night, not ready to change out of their costumes quite yet. Archer knew this was just a fun summer job for most of them, but that didn't lessen the sense of pride and accomplishment threatening to burst his heart in that sweaty crowd. He was a professional dancer. He was doing it.

"Hey." Caleb took Archer's hand, grinning at him. Beads of sweat glistened on Caleb's forehead. He leaned in and gently brushed his lips over Archer's. Archer's heart was pounding from the adrenaline still, and his body responded accordingly. He kissed Caleb back and shivered when Caleb's fingers trailed over the nape of his neck. "You did so great," Caleb whispered, now stroking Archer's cheek with his thumb. "How did that feel?"

"Amazing," Archer said, goose bumps stippling his skin. Caleb kissed him again. "Let's go party."

They peeled their costumes off and hung them up on their racks, then went back to the dorm to shower and change. When Archer got to his room after his shower, he was dripping and wrapped in a towel. He froze in the hallway at his door. There was a sock on the doorknob.

"What the . . . ?" he muttered. It had to be the B-Boys in there . . . unless Caleb wanted some alone time? Archer looked up and down the hall. *Well, now what?* He hadn't brought a change of clothes to the shower, and all he had with him was his sweaty rehearsal gear. He looked up and down the hallway again before dropping his toiletry bag and tank top. He eyed his dance belt. He really didn't want to put it back on again. But his only other option was to go commando under his tights. He stood there, holding his dance belt and tights and chewing his lip, when Caleb appeared. He was fresh from the shower and looked like a million bucks in slim-fitting white shorts and an unbuttoned blue striped shirt.

He cocked an eyebrow when he saw Archer standing there, then cackled at the doorknob. "Guess the Bs were horny after the show." He studied Archer. "But your clothes are in there, aren't they?"

Archer sighed. "Yes, except for these." He held up his belt and tights.

Caleb laughed again. "Come on, let's find you some other clothes."

They went down the hall to Dominik, Gage, River, and Harley's room, but there was no answer when they knocked. The dorm was otherwise quiet, most of the staff probably already at the cabin, working, or in bed for their early start.

Caleb clapped Archer on the shoulder. "We'll find you something at the cabin."

Archer groaned. He decided to wear the dance belt and slid it back on under his towel, followed by his tights and tank top. He left his toiletry bag and towel hanging in the bathroom.

Caleb smirked at him when he appeared back in the hallway. "Don't worry, you look hot."

Archer sighed and scratched at his tights.

They made the trek down to the cabin. The rest of the dancers were already there—even Mateo, but minus Beau and Ben, of course—celebrating their successful opening night. Betty and Seta were on the coffee table doing a rather dirty version of their "Ladies' Night" routine. Dominik and Harley were dancing around the coffee table.

"Perfect, there's Mateo," Caleb murmured in his ear. "Go ask him."

"I'm not gonna—" but Caleb had already pushed him toward Mateo.

"Um, hi," Archer said when Mateo looked at him with a raised eyebrow.

"Did someone steal your clothes again?" Mateo asked.

"No, this time I forgot them."

"Ah," Mateo said, as if that explained it. It was just that Archer was an idiot.

"See, I, uh—Ben and Beau . . ." Archer sighed. "Is there any chance I could borrow some clothes, please?"

Mateo's eyebrows shot up, and Archer was sure he was about to say no, when instead he nodded. "Sure. Come with me."

Archer followed Mateo down the hall and up the creaking stairs at the back. At the top was another hall. The first door was a bathroom, then Mateo led Archer to the last bedroom.

The room was small, being a single, but immaculate and . . . much cozier than Archer was expecting. A warm plaid blanket was thrown on top of the standard-issue beige comforter, and the dresser was lined with photos. Next to his bed sat a well-worn copy of *Beowulf*, stacked on top of a Tolkien biography, a bookmark halfway through. Archer was drawn to the photographs, and he wandered closer to examine them. The first showed a smiling family sitting at a picnic table—a mom, a dad, and a dark-haired boy. The second had to be Mateo in his late teens on stage in a ridiculously beautiful penché, leg extended far over his head. The third was Mateo standing on the sidewalk under the marquee for *Robin's Egg*, pointing up at it and smiling, with an older version of the couple from the first photo.

Archer realized he was lost in the images when Mateo cleared his throat.

"Sorry." Archer straightened, sheepish. "Those are lovely photos. Are those your parents?"

Mateo's face softened. "Yes."

"Where was the picture at the picnic table taken?"

"Here, actually."

"Really?"

"Yeah. I came here with my parents once when I was eight. I think they already knew I was gay."

"Wow, that's so cool." Archer studied the photograph again. "Your parents are beautiful." Archer remembered reading that his mom was from Mexico, and his dad's family had a Cuban background. They both had Mateo's black hair, bronze skin, and solid frame, but he had his dad's strong jaw and heavy brow. And his mom's smile.

"They were." Mateo examined the picture with him. "I really miss them."

"Oh, I'm so sorry. Are they . . . ?"

"Yes." The softness from Mateo's face was gone. He gripped the edge of the dresser. "My dad had a heart attack and Mom had a stroke not long after. About six years ago."

Archer did the math. "That was right around . . ."

"When *Robin's Egg* debuted. Yup." Mateo's hands flexed on the wood, then he blew out a breath and yanked a drawer open. "You need clothes?"

"Oh, yes. I—Yes, please."

Mateo dug through a few items, then offered Archer a T-shirt and a pair of shorts. "Here. These are a little on the small side for me."

Archer wondered if a joke might lighten the mood. "Maybe we should measure width now?"

The corner of Mateo's mouth twitched. "I'll leave you to get changed."

"Thanks. And, Mateo?"

Mateo paused, hand on the door. "Yes?"

"I'm really sorry about your parents."

Their eyes met. "Thank you. You'd better hurry up. Caleb will be waiting."

Archer changed quickly, then, with another glance at the pictures, bundled up his dance gear and headed back downstairs. The party was in full swing. River had joined the girls on the coffee table. Archer hoped the ancient piece of furniture would hold up.

"There you are!" Caleb cried, appearing at his side. "Mateo's clothes look good on you." He put his hands on Archer's waist and leaned in for a kiss.

"Thanks."

"Listen." Caleb whispered in his ear. "Those guys from

maintenance are back, and I think it's time we took the smug bastards down."

Archer didn't see Mateo the rest of the night, but he thought about him, the scent of forest and sunshine lingering in his nostrils.

No One Wants to Be the Stormtrooper

Archer woke up Tuesday and found his phone lit up with seventeen messages. He had lost it in the couch cushions at some point the night before, then was too drunk to bother with it once he found it again.

"Shit," he mumbled when he saw they were all from Lynn. That many messages had to mean the bar-in-the-alley proposal either went really well, or really, really bad. He began scrolling.

It's raining. Fuck.

Never mind, it stopped raining.
Okay, I'm doing this.

We're here, and there is a huge line.

Fuck, I heard someone say "y'all."
The tourists have found it.

Do we bail?

Okay, the line is going fast. We'll be
in soon. I should at least see what it
looks like, right?

Sasha just asked me who I keep
texting. I said you were having a
cute boy crisis.

Is it bad that I'm lying to Sasha
on the night I want to propose to
her?

We're in. Okay, the lights are
gorgeous but it smells like
vanilla-scented piss and garbage,
Archer.

I think they tried to use vanilla
air-fresheners.

I don't think I can do it.

Sasha looks so hot,
though.

The bartender wants $50 to use the
ring as garnish???

Aaaand it's raining again.

Welp, they're closing because of the
rain. They turned all the lights off.
So now we're just in a wet alley that
smells like vanilla piss and garbage.
Guess there's no proposal tonight! It
was a good try.

Hope the first show was amazing!
Tell me all about it!

Also tell me how Caleb was.

"Ah, fuck." Archer sat up and scrubbed his face before sending her a reply. **Wow, I really blew that one.**
Her answer popped up right away.

So Caleb was good?

Archer laughed. **Lol, you know what I meant, you saucy minx. But seriously, sorry the bar was a bust! No one wants their engagement to smell like vanilla piss and garbage.**

It's not your fault! I loved the idea.
Sasha would have looked so
pretty with all those lights
around her.

> **Aw. You would have too! Let's keep**
> **thinking. I'm sure we'll come up with**
> **something better.**

Thanks, Arch! I appreciate all your
help. I couldn't do this without you.

> **Happy to help! Gotta run now, though.**
> **Rehearsal. xo**

* * *

They would be working on the contemporary choreography today. Archer had learned their pas de deux at least, but the group hadn't even touched that show since he had arrived. After warm-up, they did a slow run-through, teaching the routines to the new members. The show highlighted the dancers with ballet training, no doubt, including jumps and pirouettes, but everyone had a chance to shine with graceful, fluid movements and long, elegant lines.

When they reached the pas de deux, Mateo put out his hand to lead Archer to the center. They would be performing this piece in only white tights, so for this rehearsal they both had taken their shirts off.

It was a beautiful piece, and dancing it now on the stage instead of a grassy clearing allowed them crisper movements and higher leaps. When they finished, the whole company burst into applause, even Stewart. Betty whooped.

"Exquisite!" Stewart chirped. "Mateo, Archer . . ." He threw a chef's kiss at them. "How fortunate we are to have found you two."

Archer looked at Mateo, expecting him to be smiling back, but he was not. He was looking at Stewart, face blank. Archer's chest ached, now that he was starting to understand a little of what might be going on behind Mateo's stormy facade. Still . . . it hurt the way Mateo gave him tiny glimpses of his inner workings, then slammed the door shut moments later.

"Wow," Caleb said when Archer approached. "When did you two work on that?"

"Oh, Mateo asked if I wanted some extra rehearsal time earlier," Archer said vaguely.

"Yeah? Some alone time with Mateo, hey? Should I be jealous?"

Archer snorted. "Not at all. He clearly hates me."

Caleb pecked him on the nose. "Don't worry, I'm kidding. He hates everyone."

Mateo didn't dance like he hated him, though. Their tango was as smoldering as ever when they debuted the *Latin* show that night. Every touch of Mateo's hands said *I've got you*—firm on Archer's back or thigh as he guided and lifted, reassuring and warm. When their eyes met, Mateo's said *I want you*, always fully committing himself to the fire the audience needed to see between them. Their hips slotted together in perfect sync—*I feel you*—not a foot out of place, the two of them melting a path across the stage with every chassé and pivot and lunge.

But when it was over, when they faced the audience together, chests heaving in equal measure, hands clasped as they took a small bow . . . there was nothing. Mateo turned it off.

"Gorgeous," Caleb said to him with a kiss when Archer came off the stage. "You two are so hot together. Makes me kinda . . . hot." He squeezed Archer's hips and gave him a meaningful look.

The swirl in Archer's stomach was more apprehension than excitement. "Thanks," he said. "But you'd better get out there."

"Okay, but I'll be thinking about you . . ." Caleb winked before taking Ben's hand and cha-cha-ing onto the stage. Archer turned to go find his water and saw Mateo watching him.

"So . . . you and Caleb?" Mateo asked, casting a sidelong glance around to make sure no one else was listening.

Archer blinked. "Me and Caleb what?"

Mateo rolled his eyes. "You know what I mean. You and Caleb are together?"

"Um . . ." Archer blinked some more. "Maybe? We haven't really talked about it."

Mateo nodded with pursed lips. "Be careful. You're here to work, not fuck around."

Irritation flared in Archer's chest. "I guess I can do whatever I want while I'm here, can't I, as long as I do my job?"

Mateo didn't get to treat him like he didn't exist, then tell him how to live his life a minute later.

"You think it's smart to get involved with someone you have to perform with every night for three months?"

"Your concern is not needed," Archer said crisply. "I'm a grown-up, and I can make my own decisions, thank you."

Mateo shrugged, giving cool indifference back. "Fine. Just don't say I didn't warn you."

Fuming, Archer ignored the voice that told him he didn't need to get the last word. "You're an expert in workplace relationships, are you?"

Hurt flashed over Mateo's face, and Archer instantly regretted it.

He stepped over to Archer and grabbed his hand.

"What are you—?" Archer started, but Mateo was pulling him onto the stage. Oh, right. Time to cha-cha.

After the show, Archer kissed Caleb hard, making sure Mateo saw. He was perfectly capable of making his own choices, thank you. And when Caleb smiled and slid his hands around Archer's waist and kissed him back, it was easy to feel like it was the right one.

The rest of the debut performances went as smoothly—*Urban Beat* Wednesday, *Around the World* Thursday, *Broadway Boulevard* Friday, and rounding out the week, the contemporary *From the Heart* on Saturday. The partying toned down after the first show, especially since they were still rehearsing every morning, making sure everything was locked up before Stewart left.

"Oh, my darlings," Stewart purred after the last show of the week, grabbing each dancer and kissing them on both cheeks. "You have made this old man happy. Look at you. Yes, even you, Dominik," he said, shaking his head affectionately. "You have already moved beyond the need for my guidance. I am irrelevant!"

"Noooo," they sang in chorus.

"We do this every year," Caleb whispered to Archer. "Stewart leaves 'early,' but we beg him to stay longer. He'll be out of here first thing tomorrow."

Archer was a little nervous about their director leaving already, but he had to assume they really were ready to keep it going on their own.

"Um, Stewart?" Archer asked as the others began to head out into the night. "Do you have a second?"

"I have many seconds for you, Archer," Stewart replied, gesturing to the front-row seat next to him. "Please sit."

"Before you go," Archer said as he settled, "I wanted to thank you for . . . for this opportunity."

Stewart waved his hand. "The pleasure is all mine, Archer. You are quite the dancer."

Archer flushed. "Thank you so much, but . . . that's just it. I—Well, I've been auditioning for shows in the city for months, and I haven't gotten anything yet . . ."

"Terrible business," Stewart agreed. "Talent has little to do with it, doesn't it? Not naming names, but there's a certain rising star known for pounding more than the boards, if you know what I mean." Stewart leaned forward and winked. "Not that there's anything wrong with putting a little Jesus Christ in one's Superstar, but one doesn't want to, er, go full Daniel Radcliffe, does one?"

"I . . ." Archer paused, wondering if he was still following Stewart's metaphor.

"Anyway . . ." Stewart whistled for Judy. "If Cooper Knox did it, I've no doubt you can, too, Archer. If everything stays as tight as it is now, and you all put on a flawless show, it will no doubt catch the eye of the right person."

What if it doesn't, Archer wanted to say, but Stewart had bent down to pick up Judy and was leaving little kisses on her tiny head. "Thanks," Archer said instead, getting to his feet. "I hope so."

After Archer's shower, Caleb pounced on him back in their room. "It's time to go!" he announced.

"Go where?" Archer asked, toweling his hair.

Caleb eyed Archer's bare chest under his unbuttoned shirt. "To the cabin. Saturday is Game Night," he said, as if it was obvious.

"Game Night? What kind of games?"

Caleb slid a finger into the waistband of Archer's shorts and pulled him closer for a kiss. "You know, games! Monopoly, Scattergories, charades . . . anything, really. The winner gets to pick next week's game. There's like a hundred of them in the cupboard in the cabin, plus Dominik brought a suitcase full."

Archer worked on his buttons, remembering Lynn's advice and leaving three open. "So what are we playing tonight?"

"Oh, we start every season with Monopoly, but we only play it the one time. After that, we get too annoyed with each other, and we can't even finish the game."

"Of course." Archer had somehow never played Monopoly. An only child, no cousins around his age . . . He never had the chance, although he felt like he had a pretty good idea how it went and doubted this bunch would make it through the whole game, even tonight.

When they got to the cabin, Archer was surprised to see all of the dancers there, including Mateo. The Monopoly board was set up on the battered coffee table with the mismatched furniture pulled around it and cushions scattered on the floor so there was enough seating for all sixteen of them. Ben and Beau were cuddled up in an armchair with Gage and River next to them on the ground. The couch on one side was full, as was the love seat. Betty sat at one end of the second sagging couch and Mateo at the other. The only seating left for Caleb and Archer was to squish in between them.

Archer sat next to Mateo, who was wearing loose-fitting black shorts and a soft berry blue T-shirt that turned his eyes to an inky midnight black.

"Didn't think I'd see you here," Archer said, trying to settle with an inch of space between them.

Mateo raised an eyebrow at him. "Why not?"

Archer wanted to snort. "You don't seem like the type to play board games."

"Oh, you're not allowed to miss Game Night," Mateo said seriously, but the corner of his mouth twitched.

Dominik stood. He had freshly shaved his head that morning and his mohawk was extra pointy. "Welcome to the first Game Night of the season! Listen up: You drink every time you buy a property. If you go to jail, you finish your drink. Free parking is a thing, and if you win it, everyone else drinks. Every time you build a hotel, you get to make someone else drink. Otherwise, you know what to do."

Now that Archer knew it was Drinking Monopoly, Game Night made more sense. Then he examined the game board more closely. "We're playing . . . Star Wars Monopoly?"

Dominik grinned. "Fuck yeah, we are. This is my board. Okay, so there's only eight pieces—I lost the Threepio—and since there's sixteen of us, we have to play with partners. Can we go in pairs like how we're sitting?" He pointed around the table, pairing them off . . . and Archer was with Mateo.

Caleb rumbled in annoyance. Archer sighed inwardly,

wondering what on earth possessed him to sit next to Mateo. Then again, Caleb and Mateo would probably have been a worse team.

"I'm Boba Fett," Dominik announced, lunging for that game piece.

"Whoa, whoa, whoa," Seta piped up. "Why do you get first pick of the pieces?"

"It's my board."

Rather than argue, a flurry of hands scrambled for the other pieces, but Mateo managed to snatch one right away.

"Leia, huh?" Archer wanted to smile.

"Yup." Mateo fiddled with the pewter princess in his hand.

"I figured you for more of a Han guy."

Mateo shrugged and placed Leia on Go but said no more about it.

"Alright, keep your secrets," Archer murmured. "Leia it is."

There was some tussling over the remaining pieces—no one wanted to be the stormtrooper—and Dominik started handing out the money. They rolled to see who would go first and the game began.

Harley and Grace—Mateo's curvy, redheaded *Retro* partner—were up. Harley moved their Darth Vader token the appointed seven spaces, making a weird, vacuum-type noise.

"What's that sound?" Seta asked, probably trying to be polite but not quite making it there.

Harley gave her a look of disdain. "A lightsaber, obviously."

"That's not a lightsaber sound!" Seta protested.

"Well, feel free to show me on your next turn—Oh, that's right you can't, because you can't use the Force."

The lightsaber bickering continued as Mateo leaned over to whisper in Archer's ear. "What are your tried-and-true Monopoly strategies?"

Mateo's breath tickled, and their thighs were now pressed together. It was . . . distracting. Of course, he knew Mateo's thigh well. It was between his during the tango. It supported him in their pas de deux. He knew each ridge, each rise, very well. But for some reason, seeing it flush against his on the couch . . . He was very aware it was touching him.

"I've actually never played before," he managed to reply.

"Really?"

"Really."

"Well, then"—Mateo leaned back, all sexy confidence—"don't worry. I've got this."

Mateo went after the red and orange properties, winning an auction for the Cloud City Reactor Control Room against Seta and Yuki, and snapping up the spaceships (which, Archer was informed, were normally railroads). He bought up cheaper property that others passed up, and didn't seem worried when Dominik crowed about buying the most expensive property (the Coruscant Imperial Palace). The game rolled on as all the properties got snatched up, and it didn't take long for more bickering to break out.

"We would like to build four houses, one each on our Tatooine—" Dominik began.

"It's not your turn," Caleb interrupted.

"Doesn't matter, you can build whenever you want," Dominik informed him.

"What? No, you can't."

Dominik rolled his eyes. "Pretty sure we had this argument last year—"

"Actually, you can build whenever you want," Mateo interjected.

"What?" Caleb turned to glare at Mateo over Archer's lap. "Bullshit!"

Mateo leaned forward and snatched the rules sheet from the box under the table. "Let's check, shall we?"

Archer swallowed a smile at the expression on Caleb's face. A rule follower himself, he was secretly delighted.

"Ahem." Mateo read. "'You may buy and erect *at any time*—'"

"Erect." Dominik snickered.

Mateo ignored him and continued. "'—as many houses as your judgment and financial standing will allow.'"

"Well, that's stupid. You should build when it's your turn," Caleb grumbled.

"That may be the case, however . . ." Mateo put the rules back in the box and smiled sweetly.

Archer had to bite his lip to keep from laughing.

Caleb sulked and took another sip of his beer.

Later on, with their Leia piece in jail and their beverages freshly drained, Mateo was quietly explaining to Archer how sometimes it was okay to be stuck in jail for a bit because then you didn't land on anyone else's property and have to pay them rent, when Caleb's voice grabbed Archer's attention.

"Archer? Hello?"

"Sorry?" Archer's cheeks flared, aware he was staring at Mateo's thigh again. He tore his gaze away and looked over at Caleb.

"I said, can I get you another drink?"

"Oh, that's fine, I'll get them." Archer hopped up, feeling the need for fresh air. He wandered over to the fridge, pausing for a moment to admire the view of the lake out the window. It was late now, the only people in sight a couple strolling along the curve of the shore. Then he dug three drinks out of the fridge—a beer each for him and Caleb, and one of Mateo's nonalcoholic beers. When he climbed over Mateo's legs and plopped back onto the couch, Caleb leaned over and planted a kiss on his cheek as he took his bottle.

"Thanks, babe," he said. "You're the best."

"No problem," Archer mumbled, cheeks heating at the attention. He handed Mateo's drink to him.

"Thanks, babe," Mateo said with crinkled eyes. "You're the best."

Caleb rolled his eyes as Archer's cheeks flushed even hotter. "You're welcome," Archer muttered.

"We're out of jail," Mateo nodded at the board. "But I had to pay rent to the Bs."

"I'll allow it," Archer said with a mock frown. "But try not to let it happen again."

Mateo's eyes crinkled further as he popped the top of his drink. "I'll do my best."

Archer turned his attention back to the game. His thigh was still against Mateo's.

"We want to build a house on—" Seta announced.

Dominik interrupted. "Sorry, the bank is out of houses."

"What?"

"Yeah, Mateo and Archer have them all."

"Do we?" Mateo was utterly nonplussed, taking another sip.

Archer had noticed that Mateo built all the houses they could, and almost all of their properties had four houses on them. They hadn't built a single hotel yet.

"Build some fucking hotels, man!" Caleb chirped. "Other people need houses, too."

"Hmm." Mateo studied the board with fake concentration. "No, I don't think I will."

"Well, Archer can decide to. You want to build some hotels, don't you, Archer?" Caleb turned to him. "You get to make everyone else drink."

"Um." Archer looked between Caleb's furrowed eyebrows and Mateo's barely contained smirk. "Sorry, I'm going to let Mateo be in charge. He knows what he's doing and I'm a rookie."

That was the beginning of the end. Caleb got sulkier and sulkier as he and Betty lost all their money, and the stack of bills in front of Mateo and Archer grew and grew. Most of the others were too drunk or busy making illegal trades to notice or care about Caleb's sulking. But when he had to mortgage his last property, he quit.

"Whatever," he fumed. "This is such a stupid game, anyway. Everyone always breaks the rules. I'm going to bed."

He was met with a chorus of boos and tossed cushions, but he flounced away anyway.

Archer sighed and saw Mateo watching him. "I guess I'd better go after him," Archer said.

There was a shift to Mateo's features that Archer couldn't quite read. "Guess so."

Archer followed Caleb out into the night, wishing he was still in the cozy circle around the coffee table.

9

Tea for Three

Archer couldn't find Caleb anywhere. He was not on the path ahead of him back to their dorm, and he wasn't in their room or the bathroom. So Archer shrugged and got ready for bed, figuring Caleb would show up when he was done pouting. He fell asleep quickly, the exhausting week and promise of a Sunday morning sleep-in pulling him down into a deep slumber.

When he woke to the sound of Beau and Ben stumbling off to breakfast in the morning, Archer allowed himself the luxury of rolling over and burrowing back under the blankets. The second time he blinked into consciousness, the room was empty. He soaked in the silence, stretching out each finger and toe, enjoying the shiver in his muscles. When he felt ready to face the world, he grabbed his phone and saw a message from Lynn: **How's things?**

Great! he replied. **We made it once through all the shows. Pretty smooth.**

Her reply popped up right away. **And Caleb?**

Yeah, we're still . . . hanging out.

Just hanging? No other "ing" verbs?

Not yet . . . I don't know . . . He's hot but it
doesn't feel quite right?

In the words of the divine
Ms. Natasha Lyonne, it's sex, not
a space shuttle launch.

Archer laughed at the *American Pie* reference. I know . . .
but I could very well be heading back to Ohio in the fall, so
no point in getting heavily involved with someone. Or what if
we break up before that and still have to dance together every
night?

True, true . . . or do you have your
eye on Mateo still?

Archer's cheeks reddened, remembering the heat of
Mateo's body pressed to his on the couch last night. Definitely not. So, any new proposal ideas?

Ugh, we are absolutely swamped
at work right now. We're in court in
two weeks for a huge case. Proposal
might have to wait a while.

Okay, I'll keep thinking.

Me too. Thanks, Arch. Talk soon.

It turned out he had slept right through breakfast and
was in danger of missing the lunch window, too. He had
a quick shower, threw on some sweats, and jogged up the
path to the dining hall. Most employees had already cleared

out, but he saw Caleb sitting alone at one of the long tables. Archer gripped his tray and went to sit next to him.

"Hey," he said, prepared for some frost, or at least some remnants of the sulk from last night.

But there was nothing. "Hey, you," Caleb chirped, leaning over to give Archer a kiss on his cheek. "Man, you were out cold when I got up this morning. Have a good sleep?"

"Yes, great sleep. Where did you go last night? I left right after you did but I couldn't catch up to you."

"Oh . . ." Caleb waved an airy hand. "You know, took a walk, cleared my head."

"Look, I'm sorry about the Monopoly, I—"

"It's fine," Caleb interrupted. "It's only a silly game. I think I was overtired."

"It was a crazy week, that's for sure."

Archer was glad Caleb wasn't mad, but he felt a little unsettled as they chatted over their sandwiches. They had to hurry, though, because after lunch, the dancers gathered at the theater.

"Well, my darlings," Stewart said, leaning on his cane, Judy wagging her tail at his feet. "You have no need of me anymore. Judy and I are off to other adventures, but we'll be back in a few weeks to check in on you. Now, Mateo . . ." He rested a hand on Mateo's broad shoulder. "You're in charge. I trust you to keep these whippersnappers in shape."

Mateo nodded and hugged him.

"Dominik, listen to Mateo. I know you think all of your ideas are good but . . ." He studied Dominik's mohawk. ". . . they are not."

Dominik sighed and hugged him. "Thanks, Stewart."

Stewart went down the line, imparting final words of wisdom for each dancer, until he reached Archer at the end. "And Archer, my boy. Remember, sex on the dance floor, yes?"

Archer's cheeks heated. "Right."

Stewart hugged him, scooped Judy up with a flourish and, with a final wave, tromped out the door.

The troupe looked at one another in silence for a minute.

"Swim and suntan?" Dominik suggested.

Swim and suntan.

Archer and Caleb were heading back to the dorm to change into their suits when a voice called to them. "Excuse me! Young man!"

Archer looked back and saw Ms. Eileen Lamb waving at him. She was wearing pink this time, another flowery dress with a matching hat.

She came puffing up to them. "Hello, loves. My goodness." She put her hand on her hips and leaned back to catch her breath for a moment. "It's already so hot, and it's not even June yet." A few silver curls had escaped from her cap.

"Ms. Lamb," Archer said, smiling.

She didn't seem surprised that he knew her name. "Yes, and you are . . . ?"

"Archer Read," he said as she shook his hand. "And you may already know Caleb?"

"Hi there," Caleb said with his seasoned performance smile.

"Hello, Caleb. I do remember you from years previous." But Eileen barely glanced at him. "I had to talk to you, Mr. Read, and let you know that the ballet duet you did with Mr. Dixon was breathtaking."

"Oh, thank you. And please, call me Archer."

"I'll meet you there," Caleb muttered to him.

"Okay," Archer replied, but Caleb was already several steps away.

"Well, Archer, it was just stunning," Eileen continued. "You two literally took my breath away. Those grand jetés at the end? Superb."

"Thank you so much, Ms. Lamb." Archer had never had anyone approach him in public about his dancing before, and he had to admit it was rather thrilling.

"You know, I used to be something of a dancer in my day," she informed him, patting a curl back into place.

"Oh? What kind of dancing?"

"Ballroom—the waltz was my favorite. But I was almost a Rockette, you know." She sighed. "That was another time, of course. Perhaps I could have you and Mr. Dixon for tea sometime and tell you all about it? We could talk dance?"

"That sounds great."

"That last cabin"—she turned to point along the east side of the lake, to the very last one perched by the shore with its own small dock—"is where I stay every summer. Been here for years."

"Oh, that's awesome. You must really love it here."

"I sure do. What about Wednesday?"

"Wednesday?"

"Would you and Mr. Dixon like to come to tea on Wednesday afternoon?"

"Oh, um . . ." Archer's brain whirred. "Let me ask Mateo."

"Thank you, Archer. I'd love to talk more."

"Me too. I'd better get going now, Ms. Lamb, but it was lovely to meet you."

"You too, Archer. I'll look forward to seeing that piece every week."

"Thank you. I look forward to dancing it."

* * *

On Monday, they were waiting offstage for Francisco's welcoming announcement for *Club Retro* when Archer heard the murmur of two voices arguing but trying to be quiet about it. He turned to see Ben and Beau facing off, arms crossed and glaring, anger in stark juxtaposition to their shimmering white costumes. The other dancers were turning to watch them, too.

"Are you fucking kidding me?" Ben hissed at his boyfriend. "You're going to pull this shit on me *now*? We go on in two minutes!"

"Oh, I'm sorry if my feelings are *inconvenient* for you," Beau snipped.

Ben threw his hands up. "For fuck's sake. I am not crushing on Gage!"

Gage's eyes widened. They tried not to stare at him.

"I'm so sorry, Gage," Ben continued, his voice growing louder. "But my insane boyfriend is jealous of you because, apparently, I happened to look at you one time."

"'Happened' to look at him, *please*." Beau rolled his eyes. "You were literally drooling over him on the dock yesterday."

"THAT'S NOT WHAT *LITERALLY* MEANS."

"Hey!" Mateo stormed over, brows bunched. "Get it the fuck together. They'll be able to hear you out there." He pointed through the masking draperies to where the audience waited.

Ben pressed his lips together, chagrined. "Sorry, Mateo. It's just . . . I don't know what else to say."

The room fell into awkward silence.

"Maybe this is a good time to tell you all," Gage interjected in a stage whisper, "that River and I are together."

All heads swiveled over to River, who froze, eyes wide, then offered an awkward grin. "Ummm," they said. River usually didn't say much.

The group turned back to Beau and Ben.

"Fine." Beau sniffed. "I believe you."

Ben shook his head. "You are—" But he noticed Mateo still glaring at them and took a calming breath. "Fine."

Mateo nodded. "Fine?" he asked Beau.

"Fine," Beau said, arms still crossed.

Mateo sighed, but it was drowned out by Francisco's announcement.

He caught Archer's eye and Archer shrugged. Hopefully that would be the last of the Bs drama . . . but somehow, he doubted it.

* * *

"Oh, hey," Archer said to Mateo after the first show. "I meant to ask you . . ."

It was hard to focus as Mateo peeled the top half of his jumpsuit down and began toweling off his glistening torso. "Yeah?" he asked.

"Um. So. Uh, yesterday I ran into Eileen Lamb, you know that resident guest who comes to every show? She's always wearing flowered dresses?"

"I think so?" Mateo said, now tipping his head back to chug from his water bottle.

"Well, she is a big fan of ours, I guess. She used to be a dancer. She stopped me to tell me how much she loved the pas de deux, and she invited us—like, you and me—to tea on Wednesday."

Mateo paused to cock an eyebrow. "Tea? In her cabin?"

"Yeah, I guess it's a little odd, but she seems really sweet and just looking to make friends. Relive her glory days."

Mateo shrugged. "Sure, I guess so."

"Great, I'll find her and let her know."

* * *

"Ready to go?" Mateo appeared at Archer's bedroom door Wednesday afternoon.

"Yup." Archer scrambled to his feet. *Shit*. Mateo was early. Archer had planned to meet him outside the dorm. Mateo looked amazing though—breezy white linen shorts and a matching shirt that made his tawny skin pop. His black hair was tousled perfectly over his forehead. Archer wondered if he looked nice enough in his faded raspberry T-shirt and khaki shorts.

"Ready to go?" Caleb looked up and frowned. "Go where?"

"Um, Ms. Lamb invited Mateo and me to have tea in her cabin."

"What?" Caleb scrunched his face. "That's weird."

"I guess, but . . . can't hurt, right?" Archer reached under his bed for his flip-flops, but then noticed Mateo had slate blue canvas loafers on and changed his mind, digging for his white slip-on sneakers.

Caleb's eyes narrowed. "So the two of you are just . . . going to have tea . . . with an old lady."

Archer nodded, eyes flicking to Mateo, who looked completely unbothered by Caleb's skepticism. A real talent of his.

"Whatever," Caleb shrugged, attention going back to his phone. "Have fun."

"Thanks. We'll be back for dinner."

Caleb nodded without looking up again.

Archer slipped his shoes on while Mateo hovered in the doorway, then they headed out into another beautiful day at Shady Queens. They walked in silence along the path toward the guest cabins and onto the grassy flat by the main beach. Archer smiled at a pigtailed toddler chasing after a ball, her moms following her, popsicles melting in their hands.

"Are you having a good time here?" Mateo asked as they took the next path toward Eileen's cabin.

"What? Oh, yeah. Definitely. I mean, a paying gig for almost four months, not having to pound the pavement in the city, getting rejected every couple days."

"Yeah . . ." Mateo nodded. "It's not really the same, though, is it? Performing at Shady Queens versus a stage in Manhattan?"

Archer stiffened. "Not all of us can land roles on Broad-way."

Mateo studied the lake and the ripples kicked up by a warm breeze. "That's not what I meant. I—"

"Helloooo!" They were interrupted by a distant trill.

Archer looked down the path, and there was Eileen, on her little front porch waving a scarf at them. Yellow, this time.

"Hello!" she called again, her smile growing the closer they got. "Thank you so much for coming!" she cried as they reached the path up to her door. She hopped down the steps and wrapped Archer in a hug.

"Hi, Ms. Lamb," Archer said, surprised at her wiry strength. Once he had his limbs back, he turned to Mateo. "Mateo, may I introduce you to Ms. Eileen Lamb?"

"Hello, Ms. Lamb," Mateo said smoothly, shaking her hand. "Thank you so much for having us. That's very kind of you."

"You're so welcome, and it is *such* a pleasure to meet you, Mr. Dixon. Please, please, come in." She ushered them up the steps and herded them into her cabin. It was one of the smallest guest cabins available, one bedroom and a combined seating area and kitchen, but other than that it bore absolutely no resemblance to the rest of the cabins. Almost every surface was covered with flowers or floral prints—curtains, throws, cushions, rugs—plus actual vases containing flowers, and pictures of flowers, and figurines of flowers. A lot of flowers.

Archer and Mateo stood in the doorway gaping as Eileen hurried over to the kitchen to grab the whistling kettle off the stove.

"Wow!" Archer exclaimed, eyes still jumping around, unable to focus on one particular bloom. "How did you . . . pack all this in here?"

"Oh!" Eileen laughed. "My flowers? Yes, I have a storage unit nearby and my assistant arranges it all for me before I arrive. I like to feel at home when I'm here. And really, it is my home for the summer."

"I like the . . ." Mateo's eyes drifted, too. "The bouquet of violets."

Eileen beamed as she poured the water into the teapot covered in pink roses. "I picked those myself on a walk this morning. Now . . ." She put the kettle down and waved at the couch draped with lavender throws and cushions. "Please, won't you have a seat?"

"Can I help with anything?" Archer asked, noting the rather massive three-tiered serving stand of tiny triangle sandwiches and mini scones on the counter.

"Not at all!" Eileen sang, staggering over with the thing and setting it on the coffee table. "I made these scones this morning myself, for you two."

"I can't believe you went to all this trouble!" Archer said, eyeing the piles of treats.

"Hmm . . ." She scooted back to the kitchen. "I have to admit, I do have a bit of an ulterior motive."

"You do?" Archer asked, sharing a glance with Mateo.

Eileen paused to pick up the heavily laden serving tray.

"Um . . ." Archer hopped up and took the shaking tray from her. "Please, let me."

"Thank you, dear." Eileen watched Archer fondly as he set it down next to the stand. "I'll pour, shall I? Please, help yourselves to the food."

Archer passed a dainty plate to Mateo and took one for himself before choosing two egg salad sandwich triangles and a blueberry scone. Mateo took the same for his plate.

"How do you two take your tea?" she asked.

"A bit of cream and sugar for me, please," Archer asked.

"Same for me," Mateo said.

Eileen poured and stirred and handed out their matching cups and saucers.

The first bite of the egg salad was mouthwatering, and Archer was about to devour the rest of it in one bite when Eileen set her saucer down.

"I have to tell you," she said, folding her hands together. "I couldn't believe it when I saw you on stage, Mr. Dixon."

"Oh?" Mateo said, scone halfway to his mouth. "And please, call me Mateo."

"Certainly, Mateo."

"You recognized me, you mean?"

She beamed, reaching for the shelf under the coffee table, and pulled up a Playbill. "I saw *Robin's Egg* twelve times. You were an absolute marvel."

Archer froze. Oh God. What had he walked Mateo into?

Mateo looked frozen too, and then he set his scone down. "Thank you."

"Would it be too much to ask if you signed my Playbill, please?" She held it out to him with a fancy pen.

"Sure," he said with a tight smile, reaching across the table. "How did this get here?"

"My assistant brought it for me when I saw you that first night."

"Ah."

Don't ask, don't ask, do not ask what happened, Archer chanted in his head at Eileen as Mateo scrawled his signature next to his face on the front and handed it back to her.

Eileen clutched it to her chest, eyes bright. "Thank you so much, Mateo. I will treasure this."

Mateo shifted. "You're welcome." He picked up his plate again. "This scone looks delicious."

"I certainly hope so! The oven here is so fussy . . ."

Archer let out the breath he didn't realize he had been holding. He hoped they could make it through the rest of the tea without Eileen bringing up *Robin's Egg* again, and they did. She asked about Archer's life, was shocked that he hadn't had any luck on the audition circuit, and complimented their dancing again.

Archer asked about her background, and she regaled them with stories from her youth about ballroom dance competitions and the time she made it to the final round of auditions for the Rockettes.

Archer kept a nervous eye on Mateo, worried that he would be furious, but he seemed relaxed, eating at least three mini scones and having a refill of tea.

When it was time for them to head back and get ready for that evening's performance, Eileen waved goodbye from the front porch with the promise to have them back soon.

"I'm *so sorry*," Archer said the moment they were back on the path toward the main beach and out of view of her cabin. "I had no idea she knew who you were. I never thought about her wanting your autograph and shit."

Mateo shrugged. "It's okay. She's sweet. And I had a good time, actually. She's got great stories."

Relief swept over Archer at Mateo's reassurance. "That's good. I did, too. I'm still really sorry, though." They crossed the grassy flat, watching the families squeezing out the last of their day at the beach before it was time to get ready for dinner. "So . . . can I have your autograph?" Archer hedged as the dorm came into view.

Mateo laughed, eyes crinkled against the dipping sun. "No."

10

Sweet as Pie

After the show the next night, on their way to hang out at the cabin for a bit, Caleb pulled Archer into the trees and pushed him up against a maple. "You looked so sexy tonight," he murmured before leaning in and brushing their lips together.

"Oh, yeah?" Archer asked, responding with a lip brush of his own. "Was it the line dancing that did it for you? Or the Irish step dancing?"

"The line dancing, actually. I have a thing for cowboys . . ."

Caleb was a good kisser, and a tingle swirled in Archer's stomach when Caleb's lower lip settled between his. Caleb pressed up against him, sliding his hands under Archer's T-shirt.

Archer laughed at the tickle. "Getting frisky in the woods?"

Caleb gave him a look with lidded eyes. "Maybe we go back to the dorm and put a sock on the doorknob?"

"Everyone's waiting for us," Archer demurred, softening the no with another kiss. "But . . . soon."

"Alright." Caleb took his hand and pulled him back into the path. "I can wait."

And Caleb did seem okay with waiting. The days passed, one show blurring into the next, and he hardly left Archer's side. Week two came to a close, with Drinking UNO for Game Night—much less contentious than Monopoly, although there was a disagreement over whether one had to pick up four if a pick-up-two was placed on a pick-up-two—then week three passed without incident.

Archer barely spoke to Mateo, with Caleb almost always attached to his hand or lips during their free time. When he did try to talk to Mateo, he got brusque replies, although their tango sizzled as usual. Game Night that Saturday was charades. There was no fighting over the rules this time, but Harley got super pissed at Daniella when she didn't immediately guess Michael Jackson after his moonwalk and crotch grab. Her excuse was that she was laughing too hard, but Harley didn't take the loss of that point well. It was a long, loud night, and Archer was really looking forward to sleeping in on Sunday when he and Caleb stumbled up the path in the wee hours of the morning. That was why it was extra rude when he woke up on Sunday to Caleb shaking him, much earlier than he would have liked.

"Wha . . . ?" Archer muttered, rolling over and blinking Caleb into focus.

"You want to head into town today?" Caleb sat back on his own bed to put his shoes on.

Archer sat up, rubbing his eyes. "Town?"

"Hallfield. It's like an hour's drive. Small, but they have a good general store, some cute shops, and a market on Sundays."

It had been nearly a month since they arrived at Shady Queens, and Archer had gotten pretty cozy in this world, blocking out the outside reality most of the time. But the idea of venturing away and leaving cranky Mateo behind for the day sounded like fun.

He stretched. "Sure, I'm in."

"Great, we leave in thirty. Let's go, princess!"

Mrs. C loaned them one of the resort shuttle vans for the day, charging them only for the gas. Betty volunteered to drive, and it looked like most of the dancers were loaded up when Archer arrived. He climbed in and was shocked to see Mateo sitting against the window in the first row.

"You like shopping?" Archer asked, settling next to him since the back was full.

"I consume products such as toothpaste and deodorant, and on occasion I need to buy more," Mateo said dryly.

"Okay, fine," Archer muttered.

"Why are you always surprised when I join in on group stuff?" Mateo asked after a pause.

Archer parsed words in his mind so his reply didn't sound too rude. "I don't know, it seems to me like you prefer to keep to yourself."

Mateo looked out the window. "True enough."

Dominik made them listen to Taylor Swift the whole drive, although Archer didn't mind. The music was loud enough that he didn't feel like he had to talk to Mateo, so he leaned his head back and enjoyed the girl-power anthems and fresh air from the rolled-down windows.

Hallfield was about what Archer expected for a quaint tourist trap town in the Catskills. There was a main street without a franchise in sight—all independent cafés and shops, freshly painted clapboard fronts and hand-lettered signs.

But at the end of the street, behind a big sign for a farmers market, was an entire carnival. A Ferris wheel soared above the nearest buildings, and they could see a haunted house, a carousel, and other assorted booths and striped tents. It buzzed with excitement, the street crowded with people flooding in and out of the grounds.

"A carnival!" Betty squealed when they saw it.

"Can we go to the carnival? Can we? Can we?" Dominik bounced up and down in his Converse high-tops.

For some reason, they were all looking at Mateo.

"We can go," he said. "We just have to have the van back by—"

But they were all gone, charging toward the ticket booth. Caleb grabbed Archer's hand. "This is going to be so fun!"

Archer agreed. He couldn't remember the last time he had been to a country carnival like this. They all bought tickets, even Mateo, then scattered once they got in.

"What do you want to do first?" Archer asked as he looked around.

"The haunted house!" Caleb announced.

Archer groaned. "I hate haunted houses!"

"Why?"

"I don't like being scared."

Caleb laughed. "Come on, you big baby. I'll protect you!"

Archer hated every minute of it. The haunted house was comprised of the same narrow, pitch-black hallways he remembered from when he was a kid, but now they were even more cramped and panic-inducing. Every jump-scare sent his heart crashing through his rib cage, even though he knew they were coming, and he clung to Caleb with his eyes screwed shut when the man in the Michael Myers mask started following them. Still, he had to admit, once safe in the sunshine again, the adrenaline coursing through his veins was kind of fun.

"What's next?" Caleb wondered, blinking in the bright light.

"The Ferris wheel!" Archer decided.

This time it was Caleb's turn to groan. "Nooo, I'm afraid of heights."

"I believe the phrase I'm looking for is 'Come on, you big baby. I'll protect you.'" Archer tugged Caleb toward the line up.

But once they got to the gate, Caleb looked up with huge eyes. "No. There's no way. I can't!"

"Okay," Archer sighed. "Let's go do something else, then. I don't really want to go by myself . . ."

"I'll go with you, Archer."

They turned at the deep voice. It was Mateo.

Archer's heart fluttered at the idea of being high above the crowd with Mateo. "Oh. Okay, thanks."

"Well, maybe I—" Caleb looked up again. "Okay, I can do it."

"Are you sure? You look a little pale—" Mateo said.

"It's fine. Let's go."

Caleb marched them into line, and they were able to get on when the wheel was next loaded. Archer sat in the middle of the narrow bench. The seats were designed to fit three people, but Archer and Mateo were both rather broad, and the three grown men were a snug fit. Once again, Archer was very aware of Mateo's body pressed to his.

Caleb flinched when the worker shut the restraining bar across them, and he gripped Archer's hand.

"Are you sure about this?" Archer asked. "You can still get off."

Caleb shook his head, lips forming a hard line.

"Get off." Mateo snickered under his breath.

Archer looked at him, eyebrows raised.

"Sorry." Mateo frowned. "I've been around Dominik too long."

Archer turned back to Caleb. "You're absolutely sure?"

Caleb squeezed his hand tighter, eyes closed. "I'm sure."

"Okay." Archer patted the back of his hand. "Here we go."

Caleb shrieked when the chair heaved forward, then took a deep breath. "Okay, this isn't so bad—" He cut himself off with another shriek when the chair lurched to a halt and began rocking back and forth. "What's wrong? Why did we stop? Is it broken? Are we trapped?"

"Shhh . . ." Archer patted Caleb's leg and ignored Mateo's eye roll. "We're just loading the next car. It'll start and stop at every car so they can unload and load the riders."

"Oh, God," Caleb moaned. "Can I get off now?"

Mateo stiffened as he held in a laugh.

"Not now, Caleb. But it's okay. You're going to be okay. Take some deep breaths and picture something happy in your mind."

"Like getting off," Mateo supplied.

Archer glared at him, trying not to smile. *You're not helping*, he mouthed.

Sorry, Mateo mouthed back, then he leaned over to look at Caleb. "Statistically, you're more likely to die in the van on the way home than you are on this Ferris wheel."

"Maybe don't bring up dying?" Archer said through clenched teeth as Caleb started to hyperventilate.

Sorry, Mateo mouthed again.

Archer spent most of the ride making soothing noises at Caleb, but there was a moment at the top where Caleb stilled, eyes screwed shut as he clutched the edge of the car. Archer took a slow breath looking around at the green rolling hills and flashes of blue water around tiny Hallfield. Mateo took a deep, contented breath at the same time.

"It's pretty," Mateo said. His knee bumped Archer's.

"Yeah," Archer agreed.

Then Caleb let out another squeak and Archer went back to soothing.

It was definitely the longest Ferris wheel ride Archer had ever been on. When they were finally done, Caleb staggered out of their seat and down the stairs, face green.

"You did it!" Archer informed him. "Look at that!"

Caleb clutched his chest. "Never. Again."

"Definitely never again," Archer agreed.

"Excuse me, gentlemen." A Black woman with a tight black bun and a frilly apron approached, clipboard in hand. "My name is Agnes, and I'm running the pie baking contest today. I was wondering if you three would be interested in judging for us?"

Caleb shook his head, face pinched as he pointed at himself. "Gluten-free."

"Hmm, not you, then." She turned to Archer and Mateo. "How about you two?"

Archer was awfully hungry, but . . . "How many pies do we have to eat, exactly?"

"You'll each be given a slice of six different pies, but you don't have to eat the whole thing. Just enough to rate them. Hallfield is famous for its pies, and I guarantee they will all be delicious."

Archer looked at Mateo while Caleb went to collapse onto a bench. "I am hungry . . . I'm game if you are?"

Mateo nodded. "Let's do it."

"Wonderful!" Agnes beamed. "Follow me!"

"Are you coming, Caleb?" Archer called over to the slumped figure on the bench.

He offered a meek wave. "Go on without me. I'm going to go find some booze."

"There was a pub back where we parked," Mateo told him.

Caleb flung his arm over his eyes, nodding. "Thanks. I'll head there in a minute."

Agnes led them to the center pavilion. A long table covered in red-checked tablecloths and dozens of absolutely delectable-looking pies was set up in front of a low stage.

"Oh, damn," Archer said. "These look so good!"

Agnes was pleased. "They will be! Now come on up here to the judges' table."

They climbed the few steps to the stage where they joined two women and another man already seated. "You can sit here," Agnes said, pointing to the open chairs at the end. "And we'll begin shortly!"

"Hope you really like pie," Archer said, as they watched an aproned swarm descend on the table below and begin piling thick slices onto labeled paper plates.

"I do, actually," Mateo said. "My mom was a baker. She used to make the most delicious key lime pie."

"Oh, yeah? I love key lime. I think my favorite is blueberry, though."

"Well, you're in luck," Mateo said, as a huge slice of blueberry and a scoresheet was placed in front of each of them. "Let's dig in."

* * *

"Oh my God, I'm so full," Archer said, half laughing, half groaning, leaning back in his chair. "But that was amazing."

"Sooo amazing," Mateo agreed, patting his stomach. "And so, so full. I'm not sure I needed to finish off every bite of that last key lime."

"Yes, you did," Archer assured him. "And the one before. But we should probably get going if we're going to do our shopping and get the shuttle back for Mrs. C."

Mateo moaned. "I don't know if I can get up. Thank God we don't have to dance tonight."

"No kidding." Archer stood and held out a hand to Mateo. "Come on, I'll help you."

Mateo took his hand and Archer hauled him to his feet and . . . neither of them let go. They held hands down the stairs and through the crowded pavilion until they reached the main thoroughfare and it felt like too much space around them to keep holding on.

Mateo paused outside the entrance, jamming his hands in his pockets and nodding at the nearby pharmacy. "I'm going to head in here."

"Okay." Archer realized he was mirroring Mateo's posture and took his hands out of his pockets. "I'd better go find Caleb."

"Right." Mateo turned to go.

"Right . . . Hey, Mateo?"

He paused again. "Yeah?"

"Thanks. That was fun."

"Yeah." Mateo nodded, eyes on a tuft of grass poking through the sidewalk crack. "It was."

Archer found Caleb in the pub with Betty and a few of the others, a pile of shopping bags at his feet.

"There you are!" he cried when he spotted Archer. "How was the pie?"

"Urgh," Archer moaned, slumping into the chair between Caleb and Betty. "Delicious, unfortunately, and plentiful. How are you feeling?"

"Amazing! The cutest boutique opened since last summer. It's all reclaimed, remade vintage stuff. Look at this hat I got . . ." Caleb turned to rummage through a bag.

Archer shook his head. Nothing ever threw off Caleb for long. He ordered a beer from the server and sipped it as he dutifully admired Caleb's purchases. Then, with Caleb safely a few drinks in and exceedingly cheerful, Archer made a quick solo trip to the general store. He cast a wistful look at the used bookstore on his way but didn't have time to check it out before they had to meet at the shuttle and head back.

Archer climbed into the van and settled into the back row with Caleb this time. He closed his eyes as Caleb chattered, smiling, the taste of blueberries still on his tongue.

11

Happy Birthday

The weight of Caleb's warm body climbing into bed with him wrenched Archer from his sleep early Tuesday morning. "Happy birthday, Archer!" Caleb whispered. "Are you awake?"

"Hmm?" Archer mumbled, rubbing his eyes. "I am now. And how the hell did you know it was my birthday?"

Caleb slid an arm around him and burrowed up against his side, the fresh scent of his shower gel settling over them. "Betty saw your ID on Sunday when you ordered your beer. She might have told everyone." He pecked Archer on the cheek. "Hope that's okay?"

Archer considered. He loved birthdays when he was younger, using them to wheedle more ice cream or musical soundtracks out of his parents. But birthdays became less fun as his twenties crept by. And if twenty-seven was maybe too old, twenty-eight *definitely* was. "It's okay," he decided. Better to let his friends distract him for the day.

"Great!" Caleb sat up and patted Archer's thigh. "Then get up! There's a surprise for you in ten minutes."

"Is it a surprise if you tell me it's a surprise?" Archer wondered out loud as he searched for a wearable shirt from his collection on the floor.

"Hmm, good point. Make sure you act surprised, okay?"

Caleb allowed him a minute to brush his teeth, then dragged him to the dining hall. He was nearly vibrating as Archer loaded his plate with eggs and bacon, then skipped ahead of him into the dining area.

An enthusiastic chorus of "surprise!" greeted Archer when he stepped through the doorway. He did his best to look surprised through the grin stretching over his face. The dancers were crowded around a table decorated with a white and sky-blue polka-dot tablecloth, matching napkins and paper plates, and a cake. The rest of the dining hall paused to clap and cheer for him, too.

"Happy birthday!" Betty squealed, darting out from behind the table and throwing her arms around him.

Archer laughed before giving her a stern look. "I hear you're the one that gave it away?"

"Don't be mad! I'm so sorry! I didn't mean to see your birthday, it just happened. And it was impossible to ignore since it was only two days away!"

"Are you mad?" Caleb slid his arms around Archer.

Archer kissed him. "Hard to be . . . I can't believe you did all this for me!"

Caleb waved at the chair at the head of the table. "Let's have some cake!"

They let Archer inhale his breakfast before Dominik led the entire hall in a loud, off-key "Happy Birthday to You." Archer tried not to visibly cringe—*why is the horrendous awkwardness of people singing to you a required part of birthdays?*—and avoided eye contact by studying the cake instead.

It was round and tall, with smooth, blue icing that matched the tablecloth dots exactly, and it had its own white fondant polka dots. It was beautiful, really—professional looking—and Archer wondered if maybe Caleb had talked the resort pastry chef into making it for him. And, mercifully, it had only a single white candle on it. They cheered when Archer blew it out. When he cut into the cake, he discovered that it was three layers, two chocolate with vanilla in the middle. Archer dished out the pieces and Betty helped pass the plates around the table.

Archer dug into his first bite with relish. "Oh my God . . . It's amazing," he mumbled through his mouthful.

"Mateo made it!" Betty said, giving Mateo's shoulder a squeeze. "Can you believe it?"

"You made this?" Archer repeated, dumbfounded. "How? When?"

Mateo blushed. "I think I mentioned my mom was a baker? I helped her all the time, since before I can even remember. I made this last night . . . well, I guess it was actually this morning. Chef let me use the kitchen after they closed, then I got up early to decorate it once it had cooled. They had some extra fondant and . . ." He trailed off, cheeks turning a darker pink.

Archer's heart fluttered, his face heating to what he figured was a matching shade. "That's . . . so sweet of you, I—Thank you so much, Mateo."

Mateo studied his plate, scooping up another bite onto his fork. "You're welcome."

"Yes, a man of many talents," Caleb chimed in. "I guess it helps that you've had a lot more time for baking these past few years."

An awkward silence fell over their end of the table.

"Caleb," Archer muttered. "That's—"

"No, it's fine," Mateo said quietly to Archer. Then he looked up at Caleb and smiled—the least friendly smile Archer had ever seen, eyes two black pools of disgust. "I heard you didn't have time to make your boyfriend's cake, so I was happy to step up."

Caleb's smirk faltered, lips pressing into a thin white line.

"I love the cake," Archer said before Caleb could respond. "Thank you so much for making it."

Chatter resumed around them as Mateo and Caleb continued to stare each other down.

"Did you enjoy the cake, Caleb?" Mateo asked.

Caleb sniffed. "You know I can't eat that."

"Shame." Mateo popped a bite into his mouth.

They glared for another beat before Betty cleared her throat. "Okay, so . . . we have to be out of here by nine, but let's go down to the cabin for presents."

"Presents?" Archer asked. "You guys, this is too much!"

Caleb gave him a warm smile, the chill of the moment gone. "Of course you need presents!"

Mateo muttered something under his breath that Archer couldn't quite catch.

They cleaned up their decorations and trooped down to the cabin, Archer carefully transporting the rest of the cake. "Why did you make that comment about Mateo having time to bake now?" Archer whispered when he and Caleb were mostly alone on the path.

Caleb rolled his eyes. "I was joking."

"But that's, like . . . not really something to joke about."

"Mateo is a big boy. He can take it and dish it out as good."

"Maybe, but—"

"Don't worry about Mateo, Archer." Caleb smiled at

him, the sunlight poking through the trees and giving his skin a burnished glow. "It's your birthday!"

They settled around the couches in their usual Game Night positions, and Betty presented Archer with a pair of vintage sunglasses from the boutique in Hallfield—large, square aviators with gold-tinged lenses.

"Those look amazing on you!" Betty announced when Archer tried them on. "The gold goes so well with your hair."

"Thank you, I love them," Archer told her.

The group put a wad of money into the beer fund to cover him for the next month, then Mateo handed him a small, flat paper bag stamped with purple flowers. "It's just something small," he said, shifting in his seat. "I saw it on Sunday when we were in town."

It felt like a book, but when Archer reached in, his fingers first brushed a smaller square of paper. He slid it out of the bag and unwrapped the purple tissue to reveal a fridge magnet—a little wedge of pie that said LIFE IS SWEET IN HALLFIELD in a round script.

His heart squeezed, emotion welling up his throat. "Aw, that's so cute, Mateo. Thank you."

Mateo shrugged. "I thought it would be a fun memento."

"It will be, thank you." Unexpected tears pricked Archer's eyes. He reached into the bag again, head down, and pulled out an old illustrated copy of *The Hobbit*. His jaw dropped.

"And I found that at the used bookstore, if you can believe it."

Archer blinked. "How did you . . ."

"I saw the copy you had in your room. It was falling apart."

"Thank you so much, Mateo." Archer shook his head. "I love it."

Mateo shrugged again, rubbing the back of his neck. "You're welcome."

"I—"

"And now my gift!" Caleb crowed, handing Archer a paper bag with the resort's logo on it. "I didn't know it was your birthday until we got back"—he shot a pointed look at Betty—"so this was the best I could do."

"You didn't have to get me anything," Archer insisted, peeking into the bag. It was an assortment of snacks from the gift shop, including his favorites. "Yum! Thank you, Caleb."

"And . . ." Caleb gave him a meaningful look with an eyebrow waggle. "I have something else for you later tonight."

"Um . . ." Archer flushed, for some reason looking over at Mateo, who was examining the armrest. "Okay. Thank you."

The gang scattered after that, some heading out to the dock to swim, others wandering back to the dorm. Archer's phone buzzed as he stood, and he smiled when he saw the caller ID. "I'll meet you out there," he told Caleb, and then he took the call out onto the deck and leaned on the railing overlooking the lake. "Lynnie!" he said when he answered.

"Happy birthday, Archer!" Lynn cried. "Oh my gosh, I miss you so much."

"Aw, thank you. I miss you too."

"Are you having a good day? I wish I could be there."

"I wish you could, too. But I'm having an awesome day. The dance crew threw a little party for me."

"Tell me all about it."

So he did, but she cut him off when he got to the part about Mateo's gift.

"Wait, wait, so . . . Mateo made you a cake *and* got you an incredibly thoughtful and personalized gift?"

". . . Yeah?"

"Archer . . . he totally likes you."

Archer opened his mouth to argue but it took his brain a second to come up with the argument. "I don't know, Lynn. I really doubt it. He's usually so grumpy."

"Is he?"

"Yeah, he's always barking orders and giving me shit."

"But always at work, right? When you're dancing?"

"Yeah, but—"

"No buts. I'm telling you."

"Well . . ." His brain was still spinning. "It doesn't matter, does it? I'm with Caleb."

"And what did Caleb get you?"

"Um. A bag of treats from the gift shop."

Her silence was deafening.

"It's not his fault! He didn't know it was my birthday until we got back from town."

"Mm-hmm."

"It's the thought that counts, Lynn! He didn't have to get me anything at all."

"He kind of does, if he's regularly making out with you."

But at Archer's noise of protest, she relented. "Okay. It was sweet of Caleb to get you a present. I'm just saying . . . Mateo likes you."

Archer's gaze landed on the dock. Caleb was laughing with Dominik, then they turned and tried to heave River and Gage into the lake. A scuffle ensued, and the four of them went tumbling into the water in a hollering mass of well-toned arms and legs.

Mateo was on the dock, too. He didn't join them often, and he had removed himself from the crowd a little now, stretched out on a red and white striped towel and watching the antics with a straight face.

Caleb was the obvious choice. He clearly liked Archer a lot, was fun and affectionate, and had the easy lightness that came with being only twenty-four . . . and it wasn't like Archer wanted anything serious that would last past the summer. But Mateo . . . Archer's gaze lingered over his thick, sculpted shoulders and long limbs . . . Yes, he was ideal teenage crush material, stupidly hot, and could set the dance floor on fire, but in person . . . mercurial, closed off, older, and overly serious . . . None of those things sounded like a good idea for a summer fling.

"I don't think he does," Archer said to Lynn. "He just likes to bake and . . . buy people stunningly perfect birthday presents."

Lynn laughed. "Okay, Archer. As long as you're happy."

He looked back at Caleb, who was now trying to drag Ben into the water. "I am."

"Good. Listen, when you're back, I'm going to take you out for the most incredible belated birthday dinner. There's this new, sort of over-the-top Italian-but-not-really place Sasha found in Brooklyn you have to try."

"Sounds amazing." Archer strolled along the porch toward the back of the cabin and a quieter view of the lake. "Hey, speaking of Sasha, have things slowed down at work? Any more proposal ideas?"

Lynn sighed. "Yes, they have, but not really."

"What if," Archer said with a flash of inspiration, "you did it old-school—baked the ring into a cake?"

She laughed. "You want me to bake a cake?"

Archer considered the sketchy old kitchen in their apartment. "Or hire someone else to do it?"

"Hmm . . . you know, that's so unexpected for me, I kind of love it. I *could* bake a cake! Maybe if we win the trial, I'll tell her we're celebrating. Or, I guess if we lose, moping."

"There you go! And get some champagne. A bottle of *nice* champagne, one that costs more than two-ninety-nine."

"Thanks so much, Archer! I have to run now, though. Hope the rest of your day is amazing!"

"You're welcome. Thanks for calling. Love you."

When he got down to the dock, he barely had time to pull off his T-shirt before Caleb hauled him into the lake. He surfaced, laughing and wiping water from his eyes, and he found Mateo watching him. Archer smiled and flicked a few drops at him. "You coming in?"

"Nah." Mateo lay back, a lazy smile on his face. "I like it up here."

"Come on, Mateo," Caleb called, sloshing him with a wave of water.

Mateo sat up, spluttering. "Fuck off, Caleb!"

Caleb rolled his eyes and splashed him again. "It's only water."

Mateo stood and, with another glare at Caleb, marched off down the dock.

"Okay, seriously, what's your problem with Mateo?" Archer asked, pulling himself onto the edge of the dock.

Caleb followed. "I'm sick of him acting like he's better than everyone else."

Archer sighed. There was no denying Mateo held himself at a distance from the rest of them.

"He's not that bad," River said from where they were reclined on the dock. "He's just . . . you know, a little older. Not into partying."

"Then why is he even here?" Caleb continued. "He was a fucking Broadway star. It's embarrassing."

Archer had no reply to that so he tried another angle. "Look, it's my birthday, and he made me a cake—"

Caleb rolled his eyes.

"—so can you give him a break? Please, for me?"

"Don't know why you like him so much," Caleb muttered.

"Hey . . ." Archer took Caleb's chin in his hand, then leaned in for a kiss. "I like *you*."

"Do you?" Caleb asked with a small smile sneaking onto his face.

"I do."

"Good. I like you too."

Their kiss was cut short by Dominik charging up behind them and shoving Caleb back into the lake. "Get a room!" he cried, and the brawl was back on.

The day ticked away in a pleasant haze of cool plunges and warm kisses. Archer had the last slice of cake for lunch, basking on the sunbaked dock. It was really, really hard when it was time to get moving for the night's show. "I should get the night off for my birthday," he grumbled as the rest of them began to gather their towels and other belongings.

"Let's go, princess," Caleb said fondly, threading his fingers with Archer's. "You can dance some of that cake off."

Archer patted his stomach. "Rude."

* * *

Archer was waiting in the wings before the six o'clock *Latin* show in his black pants and shimmery scarlet and purple shirt when Mateo approached.

"Hey," Archer smiled, feeling shy with Lynn's words ringing in his head. "Thanks again for the cake."

"It was no problem."

"And I'm sorry about Caleb. I don't know what his issue is."

Mateo grimaced. "People get weird when you get a little

famous. And I know I'm not . . . the friendliest person on earth."

"Still . . ." Archer looked up and saw Caleb watching him and Mateo from the other wing. "I'm sorry."

Mateo looked like he had more to say, but Francisco started his welcoming announcement, and he had to bolt to get around back to the other side for his entrance.

Archer turned his smolder on as he and Mateo began their walk toward each other at the start of their tango duet. When they met in hold, Mateo's hands were jolts of electricity on Archer's skin. Archer tilted his head, their lips closer than ever before. He breathed Mateo in, the scent sending sparks through his brain, and then they were dancing.

It was their hottest tango yet.

Mateo held him tighter, their bodies slotting together like they were one. Hips brushing, feet flicking in perfect sync, eyes locking at each pause. Archer's throat squeezed as the heat flooded through him.

When they finished, heart pounding, head dizzy, Archer swayed toward Mateo's lips, the urge to kiss him nearly overtaking him. But the roar from the audience was a douse of cold water, and he turned so they could take their bow as Caleb and Ben began their duet.

Archer couldn't find any words to say to Mateo when they got backstage. They drank their water in silence, mopped their brows, and got back out there.

The nine o'clock show was much the same—a dizzying, electrifying connection—except in their final pose, instead of his hand being on Archer's shoulder, Mateo's hand rested on the back of Archer's neck. He let out a whoosh of air as their eyes met. *Fuck. His hand is on my neck.* If they weren't in front of an audience right now, Archer didn't know what he might have done. They looked at each other another long moment, then took their bows.

After the show, Archer hurried to the greenroom to change, brain spinning with confusion and afraid of what he might say to Mateo. He was momentarily distracted when he checked his phone and found a missed call from his parents—*Nine thirty* P.M. *on my birthday, good job, guys*— but returning it would have to wait until morning.

"Wow, you were sizzling again tonight, sexy," Caleb said, peeling his shirt off and giving Archer a steamy kiss.

"Thanks, you too," Archer replied, trying to name the emotion that was settling in his gut. Anxiety? Guilt? Excitement?

When Archer and Caleb got back to their room after a shower, just in their towels, there was no sign of Beau and Ben. Archer slid his arms around Caleb and kissed him. "Thank you for an amazing birthday."

Caleb kissed him back and pulled Archer down onto his bed. "You're welcome."

Archer snuggled up against him, wiping at a drop of water trickling down Caleb's chest. "I can't believe you pulled it all together so quickly."

"Yeah, it was fast! We had to scramble a bit when we got back. It was lucky Betty thought to run and grab the decorations right away, but I wish she had let us know when we were still in town."

A thought clicked in Archer's brain. "So, no one knew until you got back here?"

"I don't think so . . . Why?"

"No reason." His stomach flipped. Was it really possible Mateo hadn't known about his birthday until they got back? No, Betty must have run into him in the store. Why would he have bought those things for him otherwise? But before he could puzzle it out further, Caleb's tongue was in his mouth.

The heat of the kiss grew until their bodies were pressed together, hands roaming, and the flames lapped at Archer's insides.

Caleb tugged Archer's towel loose. "Do you want to stay back here tonight?" he whispered.

Archer pulled Caleb's muscular body tighter against his. "Yeah."

"Good," Caleb said, teeth scraping at Archer's neck, then lips trailing down his chest. "I haven't given you the rest of your present yet."

12

Late

Archer woke up Wednesday morning wrapped around Caleb. The heat of his body and the sleepy scent of his sweat sent tendrils of warmth winding through his center. Memories of the night came back to him in snatches of curled toes and grasping hands, and the smoldering embers inside him sparked back to life. He glanced at the other beds to make sure there was still no sign of Beau and Ben. It seemed they had very kindly vacated the room for the night.

Archer smiled when he saw Caleb blinking at him with heavy eyes.

"Morning," Caleb mumbled. He brushed his lips over Archer's jaw.

"Morning." Archer pulled the blanket up around them.

"How are you?" Caleb asked, tracing his fingers over Archer's chest.

"Really good."

"Oh, yeah? I can tell." Caleb's hand slid between Archer's legs and took hold of him with a firm grasp.

Archer laughed. "Hold that thought." He slipped out of bed, pulled on some random clothes, and hurried to the bathroom to relieve himself and brush his teeth, Caleb following. Then they raced back, giggling and tossing their clothes before they tumbled into the bed and began engaging in a repeat performance of the night before.

A while later, the day now fully underway and his stomach growling, Archer sat up and stretched. "Come on. We're going to miss lunch, too."

"Noooo . . ." Caleb pulled Archer back under the covers. "Stay with me."

"I'm so hungry," Archer moaned, his stomach rumbling in agreement.

"Shhh." Caleb reached for the gift shop bag on the bedside table and dug into it. "Here you go!" He handed Archer a chocolate bar.

Archer furrowed his brow and frowned with mock seriousness. "I'm afraid that's not going to cut it."

"Okay, hear me out," Caleb laughed. "Eat this now, cuddle with me for, like, ten, fifteen—twenty more minutes, then we'll go grab a picnic and take it out in a boat. Yeah?"

"Hmm." It was a romantic idea, Archer had to admit, and Caleb's eyes were so big and beautiful when he was trying to be convincing. "Deal."

"Yesss." Caleb ripped open the chocolate bar and offered it to Archer, who took a big bite and then snuggled up with a contented sigh.

They cuddled and swapped chocolatey kisses until there was no more avoiding it. "Okay," Archer groaned. "I'm still hungry, and it's been thirty minutes."

"Fine," Caleb pouted. "Only because your stomach is growling so loud."

They had quick showers, Archer threw a beach bag

together, and they headed to the dining hall, where they packed up chicken sandwiches layered with extra avocado. They held hands on their way down to the main beach.

"We're allowed to take boats out?" Archer asked, watching the guests enjoying themselves along the shore, a few kids splashing in the shallows as their parents looked on.

"Yeah, they usually don't mind if staff have a boat or two out, as long as it's not too busy."

They clambered into a small rainbow-painted rowboat, laughing as they found their footing.

"When's the last time you were in one of these?" Caleb asked as Archer frowned at the oar.

"Couldn't even tell you," Archer replied, giving it an experimental wiggle. "And I've never rowed one."

"Never? Okay, the main thing is it's important we stroke in sync."

It took them a few lopsided circles, but it wasn't long before the little boat was propelling straight through the glassy green water, the sun hot on their heads, and chickadees calling from the shore.

When they reached the middle of the lake, Archer paused to catch his breath. "Look," he said, pointing up and shading his eyes. "A hawk."

Caleb looked up, squinting. "An osprey, I think."

"Beautiful." They sat in silence for a moment, awed by the nature around them, then right as Archer opened his mouth to speak, Caleb snickered.

"Let me guess—you're hungry?"

Archer chuckled. "You know me so well."

They dug into their sandwiches, laughing and chatting, pointing out other birds they spotted, until they had polished off all the food. Archer packed up their garbage, then laid out the towels on top of the life jackets on the bottom of the boat. They curled up together, leaning back against one of the seats.

Archer's eyes were just starting to close when his phone buzzed. A text from his dad. **Hello?** was all it said. He sighed.

"Who's that?" Caleb mumbled.

"My dad, in all his passive-aggressive glory."

Caleb took Archer's phone from him and stuffed it into his bag, followed by his own phone. "Let's relax for a bit." His fingers drifted down to Archer's waistband.

Archer let out a contented sigh and slid his hand under Caleb's shirt. Great idea.

The time passed by quite pleasantly—Archer had had more action in the last twenty-four hours than he'd had the entire five months in New York—and, with Caleb's head on his shoulder and a satisfaction deep in his bones, the gentle rocking lulled them both to sleep.

* * *

"Fuck!" Archer jolted awake in the boat and sat up in a panic, lurching Caleb off his shoulder. "Fuck! What time is it?" The sun flirted with the hilltops. He scrambled for his bag.

"Hmm?" Caleb rubbed his eyes.

"Shit, Caleb! It's five thirty!"

"What? Shit."

Archer scanned the shoreline. They had drifted even farther away from the resort, the white buildings barely visible in the distance. "Oh my God, we're going to be late for the show."

Caleb grimaced. "We can make it. Let's go."

Archer grabbed an oar and rowed as hard as he could. By the time they were halfway, his muscles ached and his brow dripped with sweat. It looked like they were closer to the theater than they were to the marina, which were on opposite ends of the beach.

"Forget the marina," Archer panted. "It'll be faster if we row straight to the theater."

They rammed the boat onto the little strip of sand, bemused patrons watching them from the deck, colorful summer cocktails in hand, as they scrambled out of the boat and around the back of the building.

It was 5:56 when they went tearing in the back door. Dominik started laughing when he saw them go flying by to the greenroom.

Mateo was pacing by Archer's costume rack, phone pressed to his ear. His face went from concern to anger when he saw them. "Where the fuck have you been? I've been calling you."

"I'm so sorry," Archer gasped, wrenching his sweaty clothes off and pulling on his hip-hop costume—fortunately the track pants and hoodie were forgiving of the rough treatment. "My phone was in the bottom of my bag, I guess. We've been rowing . . ."

"Rowing?"

"We took a boat out and fell asleep."

"You—"

"Relax, Dad," Caleb interjected, patting Mateo's cheek. "We're here."

Mateo pushed Caleb's hand away and opened his mouth to reply when Francisco's voice boomed from the front-of-house speakers. Mateo's eyes were laser beams. "Places," he hissed.

They ran from the greenroom right onto the stage, Archer's heart pounding before he even began dancing.

It was not his best show. He knew it. But he made it

through, hit all his cues, remembered all the steps, and he doubted the audience could even tell he was dragging a little.

Mateo noticed, of course. He glared at them after the first show. "Grab some food, catch your breath, and get your shit together by nine."

"Hey . . ." Caleb hooked his fingers around Archer's hip, pointedly ignoring Mateo. He pulled Archer closer and kissed him. "I thought you were hot out there. But save some sexy for me, yeah? I want some more of what I got last night . . . and this morning . . . and on the boat."

Archer flushed while Mateo glowered.

"Glad to see you're feeling bad about almost missing the fucking show," Mateo snapped.

"We're really sorry, Mateo—" Archer started.

"Look," Caleb interrupted. "If we *had* missed it, sure, be pissed. But we didn't. So calm the fuck down."

Mateo clenched his jaw. His eyes shifted to Archer and, for one heart-stopping second, gave him a look so plaintive and searching that Archer almost stepped toward him. Then it was gone, replaced with stone. "Whatever," he muttered. "Do whatever the fuck you want." And he turned and marched off.

Caleb made a face at Mateo's retreating back. "Ugh, I'm getting so sick of him." He mopped at his brow with a towel and gave Archer a smile. "Let's go grab some dinner."

Archer sighed. "We have to return our boat."

"Nah." Caleb waved a hand. "It's fine. The marina is closed now, anyway. We can bring it back in the morning."

Archer paused. "I don't feel right about letting it sit there. Plus, our stuff is still in it."

"Okay, well, if you want to go now, I'll meet you at the dining hall. I'm *starving*." Caleb changed back into his clothes and gave Archer a kiss before he strolled out the door with Ben and Beau and the others.

Archer shivered as he shrugged back into his damp shorts and tank top, then headed out into the evening by himself. He slipped down the small, sandy embankment and back into the boat, arms screaming in protest as he rowed along the beach. The water was dark now, reflecting the last rays of light in rippled yellow stripes. The marina was indeed closed, so he tied their boat to the dock, neatly stacked the life jackets on the seat, and gathered up their belongings. It was a long walk back across the length of the beach and down the path to the employee dorms. He stopped by their room to change and drop off their stuff, then made the hike up to the dining hall. He wanted to jog to save some time, but there wasn't enough gas left in the tank.

"There you are!" Caleb said when Archer sat next to him with a tuna melt. "You'd better hurry up. We need to head back in a minute." Caleb was already finished and had his chin propped up on one hand, drinking a milkshake and deep in conversation with Ben.

"A romantic boating adventure, hey?" Dominik chuckled on Archer's other side. "Hope it was worth it. I haven't seen Mateo that pissed before."

Archer sighed and stared at his sandwich, the knot of guilt in his stomach growing.

"He actually wasn't mad till you got back," Betty added. "He was just worried at first."

"I do not need some washed-up old man overseeing my every move," Caleb said loudly, joining the conversation. "I mean, Mateo isn't my boss, or my father. He can fuck right off, actually."

Stewart said Mateo was in charge, Archer thought, but he

didn't have the energy to argue about it right now. Instead, he stood. "We'd better get back." He took his food with him and nibbled on the way.

The second show was worse. His muscles were rubber, and lifting his arms over his head was painful. He knew his dancing was sloppy. He couldn't even look at Mateo afterward and hurried out of there as fast as he could, without waiting for Caleb. All he wanted to do was curl up and sleep this day off.

He had a quick shower and was settled into bed almost asleep when Caleb came back from his shower.

"You want to head down to the cabin?" Caleb asked, smoothing on some aftershave in the mirror.

"Not tonight," Archer mumbled.

"Oh." Caleb turned to frown at him. "You want me to stay with you?"

"No, it's fine. I'm exhausted. I'll be asleep in a minute."

"Okay . . ." Caleb patted his pockets and looked around the room. "Fuck, I think I left my phone at the theater. Did you see it anywhere?"

Archer shook his head. "Sorry, no."

"Alright." Caleb leaned over to leave a kiss on Archer's forehead. "Get some sleep then, princess. I'll see you in the morning."

"'Kay. Have fun."

Caleb shut the door quietly behind him and Archer was starting to drift when the thought of his dad's text bubbled up to the surface of his brain.

"Fuck," he muttered, sitting up and reaching for his duffel. His parents would already be cranky about him not calling back, and then if he ignored the text, too—better send a reply promising to talk in the morning. But when his hand closed over a phone in the bottom of his bag, it was Caleb's, not his. He groaned. Guess it wasn't bedtime quite yet. If he hurried, he could catch Caleb before he schlepped all the way to the theater looking for a phone that wasn't there.

Archer pulled on some sweats and was halfway down the path when he came upon two people kissing under a maple tree. Two men. One of them looked a lot like Caleb.

One of them was Caleb.

Archer's feet screeched to a halt at the same time his heart did. Pebbles clattered around his shoes.

Caleb looked around and saw him. Worry flashed over his face. "Archer!" He said something quick and low to the other man—a big, solid guy—who trundled off down the path. Archer thought he recognized him from maintenance. Caleb hurried up to him. "What are you doing here?"

"Your phone," Archer said dumbly, holding it out.

"Oh, thanks." Caleb took it, chewing on his lip.

"You . . . you've been seeing someone else?" Archer's head was spinning.

"I'm sorry. I should have told you. But we never said we were exclusive or anything. We weren't even sleeping together."

"Yes, we are!"

"Well, yeah, now we are! Look, I was just telling Steve it was over, anyway. It's been super casual. We only make out sometimes. I haven't fucked him or anything."

Archer opened and closed his mouth. True, they had never had a relationship talk or even used the word *boyfriend* yet . . .

"Archer, I really like you." Caleb took his hand. "A lot. Yes, I should have told you. I just wasn't sure you were that into me, to be honest. But after last night and our amazing day on the boat . . ." The boat. It was a distant memory now. "I want to be with you."

A hundred thoughts swirled through Archer's brain. "You were kissing him."

Caleb squeezed Archer's hands. "It was a goodbye kiss, I swear."

Admittedly, from what he had seen, it was a very brief kiss. Archer sighed. "Okay."

A tentative smile slid onto Caleb's face. "Okay?"

"Okay."

Caleb heaved a sigh of relief. "Thank you for trusting me. I would never do anything to hurt you. You know that, right?" He wrapped his arms around Archer and pulled him in for a hug.

"I know."

"Let's head back to the dorm, okay?"

"No, it's fine. You go ahead. I'm so tired, I just want to pass out."

"You sure?"

"I'm sure."

Caleb kissed him. "Okay. I'll see you in the morning."

Archer trudged back up the path, trying to make sense of the situation. Yes, Caleb should have told him earlier, but he could also see Caleb's point that it hadn't been anything serious until last night, and Caleb told Steve it was over the first chance he got.

His brain was grinding to a halt and crying out for the sweet oblivion of sleep when he opened the door to his room. But instead of blissful silence, he heard angry voices suddenly hush.

Ben and Beau stared at him from where they stood in the middle of the room.

"Sorry to interrupt," Archer said, swaying on his feet. "I really need to go to bed."

"It's fine," Ben said wearily. "You're not interrupting."

Beau glared. "Yes, once again, my feelings are unimportant."

"You know what?" Ben shrieked, going from zero to sixty, clearly a man at the end of his rope. "Maybe we *should* break up! Because you obviously don't trust me!"

Archer eyed his bed as Beau's face crumpled.

"I mean honestly, Beau! What more do you need me to say? I'm with *you*, I love *you*. I don't want anyone else here, or anywhere!"

Beau nodded and wiped at a tear. "I'm sorry, my love. You're right."

Ben sagged. "Am I? Because I can't keep having this same fight."

Archer eased into the room, avoiding eye contact with them, and crawled under his covers, nearly weeping with relief as his body sank into the mattress.

"You are." Beau's words were muffled.

"Then please, trust me. There is no one else for me."

Trust . . . The word throbbed through Archer's head. *Do I trust Caleb?* He tried to give himself over to sleep, but sounds and images from the day played in his brain like a television recap—being late for the show, Mateo's seething anger, Ben and Beau's fight, Caleb with Steve . . . It took Archer a long time to fall asleep, despite his exhaustion.

13

Cheating

Archer woke up feeling hungover Thursday morning, shoulders screaming in protest when he stretched. In an unusual turn of events, his three roommates were still quiet lumps under rumpled blankets. Archer studied Caleb in the bed next to him, long lashes resting on his smooth cheeks, plump lips parted as his chest rose and fell in the steady rhythm of a deep sleep.

The image of Caleb kissing Steve under the tree flashed in his mind again. *It was a goodbye kiss, I swear . . .* Archer's chest throbbed. He was no lovesick kid; he knew the realities of dating. They hadn't had any sort of conversation about their relationship status, and Caleb hadn't broken any promises. Still . . . Archer's shoulders weren't the only thing hurting a little this morning.

Looking for a distraction, he grabbed his phone and saw the **Hello?** text from his dad again. *Shit, totally forgot.* His parents would be stewing by now, but it would only get worse if he waited longer. He forced himself to tap out a reply.

Hey, Dad. Sorry, yesterday was crazy. I meant to get back to you.

A reply came right away. **Busy day dancing? We called on your birthday.**

Yeah, at nine thirty, Archer thought. **Yes, thanks, I saw that after my late show. Do you guys have time for a call now?**

Your mother's out.

Okay . . . Do you want to call me when she gets home?

Three dots, but no reply. Archer rubbed his eyes and looked over at Caleb again. He would have to wait and see, he decided. Give Caleb a chance to prove himself, but be careful not to get hurt. It was only for the summer, after all. No need to be so precious about it.

With another futile glance at the unanswered message to his dad, he sat up. He didn't often get up early enough to catch the staff breakfast window, and his stomach rumbled at the thought of a huge plate of waffles. He eased off the bed, rummaged in his drawer for clothes, and snuck out to go shower.

He was starting up the path to the dining hall when he heard the dorm door *thunk* shut followed by another pair of feet pattering down the steps. "Archer!" Caleb jogged up to him and slid his arms around him. "You should have woken me up."

Archer hugged him back. Caleb smelled the same as ever—fresh and light, like the breeze off a meadow on a spring day. "You looked like you were fast asleep, so I didn't want to disturb you."

Caleb pulled back, big brown eyes wide, and squeezed

Archer's forearms. "I wanted to say again that I'm sorry. It was stupid of me to keep messing around with Steve."

"It's okay." Archer gave Caleb a quick kiss. "I mean it."

"Yeah? You're amazing." Caleb pulled Archer in tight for another hug. "I'm all yours now. I want you to know that."

"I know."

"We still have almost three months together. It's going to be so fun."

Three months, Archer thought. The summer, nothing more. And that was fine. That was exactly what he had been thinking. Archer took Caleb's hand and started walking again. "Absolutely."

* * *

As the six o'clock show approached, Archer and Caleb were lounging together on Archer's bed, sharing a bag of gummy bears and watching ballet reels, when Archer's phone rang.

"Fuck," he muttered when he saw his mom's name. "I have to take this."

"Okay, but be quick, or I can't promise there will be any gummies left," Caleb warned, popping another red bear into his mouth.

"No red ones, anyway." Archer smiled and gave Caleb a quick kiss on his forehead before he headed down the hall and out the door.

"Hi, Mom. Hi, Dad," he said when he answered.

"Oh, there he is," his mom replied. "We called you on your birthday, you know."

"I know, Mom." Archer leaned against the railing, tilting his head back to take in the leafy green patterns, vibrant against snatches of blue sky. "Thanks. It was just really late when I got your message."

"Hmm. How are things? Did you get a birthday cake?"

Archer told them about the trip into town, the surprise party, and the sweet gifts his friends had given him.

"Beer fund?" was his dad's reply. "I hope you aren't drinking too much."

"What? Dad, I'm . . . It's fine."

"I was talking to Lulu Hammond, who works at the bank?" Archer's mom said, as if this was a normal direction for the conversation to go. "And she said her brother-in-law is looking to add another accountant to their practice. You know, that big one in the building across from the courthouse?"

Archer rubbed his forehead. "I still have three months to go here, Mom."

"Of course, but I'm just saying, you won't have many chances to get a job at a firm like that."

"I have to get going," Archer said, the words bursting out of him from the pinching in his lungs. "I need to grab some dinner before the show."

"Okay," his mom said. "Great to hear from you. Take care, hon."

Archer hung up and stood blinking at the quiet green cathedral around him and, for a second, considered hurling his phone as far as he could into its mossy depths. Then he sighed and went back inside to see if there were any red gummy bears left.

* * *

"I hope Mateo isn't still mad," Archer said on their way down to the theater.

"Fuck him," Caleb snorted. "I don't know why you care so much about his opinion."

"I know, it's just . . . It's Mateo Dixon! I worshipped him when I was a kid."

"You did?"

Archer kicked at a rock and shrugged. "Yeah."

"Well . . . he's just Mateo now, some grumpy asshole you have to work with. Honestly, don't worry about him for one second. It doesn't matter what he thinks."

So Archer tried not to worry about him. But his stomach curdled when he offered Mateo a friendly smile in the greenroom, and Mateo looked right through him.

Mateo managed to avoid eye contact the rest of the week, in fact, except where necessary for the pas de deux in Saturday's show. But there was nothing in his eyes beyond cold professionalism, and that came through in their dance. Usually, Archer could feel the audience breathing with them, but tonight the theater may as well have been empty.

Caleb's right, Archer told himself as he changed after the show. *It doesn't matter what Mateo thinks. Obviously, I blew any chance we had to be friends, so now I just have to dance the best I can and try not to fuck up anymore.*

I can do that.

I hope.

He packed up his bag and was about to leave the greenroom when someone approached him from behind. "Archer, can I have a minute?" It was Mateo.

"Of course, sure." Archer steeled himself for more criticism or another tongue-lashing.

"Tonight, while we were dancing, I had a thought."

"Oh?"

Mateo stepped close to him and grabbed his waist. "I was thinking here, when I hold you . . ."

Archer's mouth dried out. He was not expecting this. Their noses were nearly touching. He inhaled Mateo, sweat and moss.

"What if," Mateo murmured, "we paused, for four counts. Just letting it simmer."

"Simmer," Archer repeated, like an idiot, trying not to stare at Mateo's lips. That was a mistake because then their eyes met. Mateo's were dark and intense, and they drilled down into Archer's very core. He feared every molecule in his body was about to disintegrate.

"I thought it would add some tension." Now Mateo's gaze darted to Archer's lips, then back up. "Then we go into the lift. We can remove the turn at the end to make up the four count."

They were still nose to nose. "Um." Archer breathed. "Yeah. Yes. Sure. Sounds good."

Another pause. Mateo had not let go of his waist. Surely Mateo could hear his pounding heart.

"Good." Mateo stepped away. The corner of his mouth twitched. "Let's do that then."

Then he was gone, leaving Archer's body bereft and mind spinning.

* * *

"What game are we playing tonight?" Archer asked Caleb as they flopped onto the less lumpy of the two couches in the cabin.

"I'll give you a hint," Caleb said, shifting closer and sliding a finger under Archer's waistband. "It was Archer"—he kissed Archer's nose—"in the cabin"—he kissed his chin—"with the killer body." He planted another kiss on his lips.

Archer laughed. "I haven't a *clue*."

Caleb grinned. "Promise you'll be my partner tonight anyway?"

"Of course."

"We are, in fact, playing *The Simpsons* Clue," Dominik said, nudging his way past them and dropping the bright yellow box onto the coffee table before bouncing into the armchair.

"Simpsons Clue? How do you even have all these crazy games?" Archer asked as Ben and Beau took their spots on the floor next to them, and the others gathered around. Mateo wasn't there, and neither were Gage and River.

"'Cause I'm awesome," Dominik replied, opening the box and pulling out the character pieces. "I'm Homer–slash–Mr. Green."

Seta rolled her eyes as she settled on the other couch with her drink. "I'd argue about why you get to choose your character first, but honestly, it's not worth it."

Dominik looked smug as he started handing out the detective notepads. "Glad you're learning."

The game proceeded pretty much as Archer remembered—first, three cards were hidden in an envelope that would reveal the murderer, location, and weapon. The rest of the cards were dealt out, then the players moved around the board and made suggestions when they had a who-dunnit guess. The other players would prove them wrong by showing if they had one of those cards in their hand, so the guesser would cross those options off their notepad until, by process of elimination, someone had enough information to make an actual accusation.

It should take a while to rule out all the other suspects, so it was surprising when Dominik announced he wanted to make an official accusation very early in the game.

"What? Already?" Seta frowned. A player could only accuse once, and if they were wrong, they were out, so they had to be pretty sure.

Dominik cleared his throat. "Krusty the Clown, in the nuclear power plant, with the poisoned donut." Dominik pulled the three cards out of the envelope, peeked at them, then, with a flourish, triumphantly laid them out for everyone to show he was right.

There was a pause. "How did you figure it out so quickly?" Seta asked, eyebrow quirked. "I don't even have half the boxes crossed off yet."

"Me neither," Harley chimed in. "Highly suspicious."

"I didn't cheat, if that's what you're implying," Dominik said primly.

"You must have, though," Harley insisted. "Like, it's literally impossible for you to have gotten it so fast."

"I have a strategy," Dominik allowed, shrugging and collecting the cards.

"'Strategy'?" Seta repeated, with air quotes.

"I can't tell you," Dominik said, "or else I won't be able to use it anymore."

"Right." Harley nodded. "Because it's cheating."

"It is not!"

Archer sighed and took a pull of his beer. He glanced at Caleb, wanting to share an eye roll, but Caleb was talking to Ben on the floor next to him.

"You're going to have to tell us your strategy," Betty waded in. "Or else it seems like you cheated."

"Fine," Dominik relented, wounded at the lack of trust.

The group waited, breath held.

"When someone makes a suggestion and then someone else proves them wrong," Dominik explained, "I can tell what they're crossing off by *where* they mark their detective sheet."

Seta blinked at him. "What?"

Dominik rubbed at the fuzz on his head. "Like, if you guessed Bart and someone shows you one of their cards to prove you wrong, then you mark off something at the *top* of your sheet where the suspects are, I know the murderer isn't Bart. So, I can cross him off, too."

There was silence around the table for a good five seconds before everyone began yelling at once. "That's totally cheating!"

"No, it's not!"

"Yes, it is!"

"It doesn't say you can't in the rules!"

"Oh my God, are you for real?"

"It's a good strategy!"

"That is the cheat-iest cheating *I have ever heard of!*"

Archer watched the fighting, wondering what Mateo would have said. It was better with his calm, steadying presence here.

"Fine! I won't play anymore!" Dominik announced. He got up and stormed off toward the back door.

"Don't be a baby!" Seta called after him. "We can play again for real now that we all know how you cheat."

The screen door slammed.

Seta snorted. "Ridiculous."

"So . . ." Caleb hedged into the awkward silence. "Who wants to go for a midnight swim?"

"Yeah, sure," Seta agreed, starting to clean up the game.

"Bedtime for me," Beau yawned.

At the same time, Ben hopped up. "I'm in for a swim."

Beau frowned. "You were saying you were tired, earlier."

"Well, I'm not now." Ben narrowed his eyes at Beau in a challenge.

Caleb smiled and took Archer's hand. "You in?"

Archer watched the B-Boys silently fighting and vowed to keep things nice and light with Caleb. "Sounds great." He winked. "As long as it's swimsuit-optional."

* * *

They had a late night, and when Archer finally cracked his eyes open Sunday morning, he was alone in their room. He saw that Lynn had texted **Call me!** and wasted no time dialing her number.

"So . . . I baked a cake yesterday," she said as soon as he answered.

His heart leaped. "And?"

Lynn groaned.

His heart sank right back down. "Did she say no?"

"I didn't get to ask! I went for a shower when it was in the oven and when I got out, I smelled smoke."

"Oh my God!"

"Then the smoke alarm went off, then the sprinklers."

"Holy shit, Lynn."

"It wasn't for very long, but . . . part of the ceiling fell in."

His jaw dropped. "What?"

"Not too bad, just where Leak Perry was." She gave a weak laugh. "Now it's a 9021-hole."

Archer half laughed, half moaned. "Oh, Lynn! Are you okay?"

"Yeah." She sighed. "I mean, I'm still a bit shaky, but I'm staying with Sasha for now, while it gets repaired."

"Well, that's good. And how are my plants?"

"Er, extra watered?"

"Perfect. How long are repairs supposed to take?"

There was a pause. "Fletcher said a month, but . . ."

Fletcher was an unreliable asshole. Archer gulped. "Let's hope it's less than three, anyway."

"Oh, don't worry, Archer, I'm sure it will be! Worst case, you can always crash with me and Sasha while you work things out."

Right. "Work things out" while unemployed and homeless in the most expensive city in the world. He could picture the glee on his mom's face when he arrived back in Ohio. "I'm sure it will."

* * *

As the week went on, Archer's guilty feelings about almost missing the hip-hop show lingered, especially since Mateo was still clearly pissed about it. He and Caleb barely existed, as far as Mateo was concerned, except for the odd time Archer would feel eyes on him and turn to see Mateo glaring.

But as that week passed, then another, he noticed that some of the other dancers were showing up closer and closer to showtime. What used to be a good hour of hushed backstage chatter over warm-up and careful makeup application was now down to about ten minutes of cursory stretching and a slapdash stop at the makeup table.

"We're on in five minutes, Grace," Mateo said to his *Retro* partner when she rolled in before the show Monday night and began peeling her clothes off.

Grace looked unconcerned as she flipped through her costume rack. "So?"

"What happened to warm-up?"

She shrugged and pulled her jumpsuit off the hanger. "Don't need long."

Betty came over, brow furrowed. "Grace?"

"Yeah?" She zipped up her suit and fluffed her red hair out.

Betty frowned. "I thought I saw . . ." She turned Grace around and nodded. "Yeah. You have a ripped seam. Right here." She pointed at Grace's side.

"Shit." Grace craned her neck to look.

"Four minutes," Mateo snipped.

"I've got this," Betty said, digging into a drawer for a sewing kit. She pulled out white thread and a needle and got to work.

"Three minutes," Mateo muttered, arms crossed.

"You're not helping," she replied evenly, drawing the thread through the fabric.

The time ticked away. She was rushing through the finishing stitches when Francisco began his welcome announcement.

"Shit, sorry." Betty snipped the extra thread off. "I hope that holds."

"Thanks, hon. It'll be fine." Grace squeezed Betty's arm as they raced to their places in the wings.

It didn't hold. Halfway through the show, it came open again. A patch of skin appeared during their particularly rigorous hustle, with Grace up in the air on Mateo's shoulder, and only continued to grow as she spun around him. She did her best to fix it with duct tape when she had a few minutes off stage, Mateo watching, lips pressed together.

After the show, as they were getting changed, Mateo slammed the door to the greenroom. "Listen," he barked in the silence. "I need everyone in this room *one hour* before showtime. Warm-up, hair and makeup, costume checks all done with ten minutes to spare. Got it?"

There were a few murmurs of agreement but Caleb

rolled his eyes and threw a cheeky salute. "You got it, drill sergeant."

Grace and a few others tittered.

Mateo's eyes flashed but his lips curled in a smirk. "You can be a dick, Caleb, just be a dick in this room one hour before showtime."

Archer fought the smile threatening to creep across his face.

Mateo's eyes held his for a second, the hard edges maybe softening.

Caleb tilted his chin. "You realize no one actually gives a shit about a tiny rip in a costume?"

Mateo took a step closer to Caleb, his voice quieting to a near-whisper. "That's fine, Caleb. I just need you in this room not giving a shit one hour before showtime."

Caleb glowered. "Can we go eat now, or are you going to control that, too?" He took Archer's hand and pulled him toward the door.

"Just be back—"

"Yeah, I know, *one hour* before showtime. Jesus."

Archer thought he heard the low rumble of Mateo's laugh as the door closed behind them.

"What an asshole," Caleb muttered as he marched up the path.

"Mmm," Archer said, smile now free in the long evening shadows.

14

Things Fall Apart

The next day, Archer was making his way down to the cabin after lunch when he spotted Eileen Lamb waving at him from the expanse of grass by the beach, glowing in her yellow dress. He turned toward her, smiling and waving back.

"Hi, Ms. Lamb!" he called when he got closer. "How are you?"

"Hello, Archer," she said. "I'm fine, thank you. But . . . what I want to know is, how are *you*?"

Archer frowned. "What do you mean?"

"I'm a bit worried about you. The show has seemed a little . . . er . . . ragged the last week or so, hasn't it? Is everything going okay?"

"Oh." A stone dropped into Archer's stomach. He didn't think the audience would have been able to tell things were getting a touch sloppy. "I guess it has. But, you know, maybe we're getting a bit too comfortable. We probably won't ever look as sharp as we did the first week."

"Hmm." Her lower lip poked out. "For most of the

guests, that will be the one and only show they'll see, won't it? It probably should look just as sharp." She was being kind, but Archer felt terrible. Maybe they hadn't just been disappointing guests—his Broadway career could hang in the balance. An amateurish resort show wasn't going to impress any potential connections.

He was trying to muster up a response when she continued. "And is everything okay with Mateo?"

His cheeks flushed. "Er . . . I guess. We're not exactly friends, but—"

She cleared her throat politely. "I meant *for* him . . . Is he alright? He seems distant. Or, I don't know, unhappy in some way."

Archer didn't know what to say to that, either.

Eileen tilted her head and smiled. "I wonder if you might want to come for tea with Mateo again? Perhaps I can help."

"Oh . . ."

"I don't mean to stick my nose in, you understand." She patted Archer's arm. "But I've been around the block a few times. I know a thing or two."

"Thank you for the invitation. Let me ask him," Archer said, not expecting it to go well.

It went worse.

Archer arrived nice and early for warm-up. As he'd hoped, Mateo was the only one in the greenroom. He was at the barre stretching to soft classical piano music. Archer took a deep breath as he pulled his ballroom shoes out of his locker. "Eileen invited us for tea again," he said, approaching like a wildlife photographer creeping up on a skittish fawn.

Mateo's jaw clenched as he arched his back and extended an arm behind him. "Us?"

"Yes."

Mateo snorted, straightening out again, leg and arm gliding to the side. "Why don't you bring Caleb?"

Archer admired the long, powerful lines of Mateo's muscled body. "She didn't invite Caleb. She invited you."

Mateo turned to face Archer. "Why?"

Archer studied his shoes, brushing off an invisible scuff mark. "She said the show was getting a little ragged."

"That's putting it mildly." Mateo huffed, turning back and sinking into a demi-plié.

"And . . . she asked if you were okay. She said you seemed . . . unhappy, and she offered to help."

Mateo froze for a second, then continued, sliding a foot out into fourth. "I'm the same as always. I don't know what she thinks she could possibly do, besides get me to sign some more shit for her."

Archer blinked. "You said you didn't mind that."

"Well, I mind." Mateo turned to face him again, dark, flashing eyes a stark contrast to the lilting piano music. "I fucking mind, Archer. I don't want to be reminded about that time in my life, and I can't fucking escape it, even here, goddamnit."

"You—" Archer started, but Mateo put a hand up.

"Don't. Just . . . don't."

The back door swung open. They stared at each other, the sounds of laughing and chatting crescendoing around them.

"I'm sorry," Archer said helplessly as Betty and a handful of others trooped in.

Mateo reached for his headphones and shook his head. "Go warm up," was all he said.

Archer swallowed the lump in his throat and did just that.

Their tango was ice-cold that night. There was no heat in Mateo's touch, no fire in his eyes. Stewart likely would have been horrified and brought the entire performance to a screeching halt if he had seen it. What made it even worse was knowing that the audience could see it too. He pictured Eileen out there in the crowd, pursing her lips and shaking her head. Archer slouched into the greenroom after the second show, more wretched than ever.

It was much the same on Wednesday, and Archer couldn't shake the sense that everything was going horribly wrong.

"What's up?" Caleb asked after the second show, dropping next to him on the bench. "You seem sad." He leaned forward for a kiss.

"I'm fine. Just tired, I guess."

"Listen, Ben had such a fun idea. He said we should go on a hike tomorrow, take a picnic with us. Something a little different."

Archer smiled as best he could. "That does sound fun, but . . . I might take it easy tomorrow."

"What? You have to come."

"I don't know . . . Maybe I'm coming down with something."

"Oh no." Caleb frowned. "I hope not."

"But you go," Archer said, squeezing Caleb's knee. "Have fun."

* * *

Archer woke early Thursday to the sound of his roommates getting up. Once they had cleared out, he fell back asleep and had the most bizarre dream. He was in the rowboat with Caleb again, drifting in a lake filled with flowering lily pads. Dragonflies droned over their heads, and the sun drenched everything in a hazy, golden light. Totally content, Archer leaned in to kiss Caleb, but when he pulled away, he found himself an inch away from the dark flame of Mateo's eyes.

"Oh my God, I'm so sorry!" Archer yelped, pulling back so violently the boat began to tip.

Mateo gripped the sides as the boat swayed. "Why did you do that?" he asked, his tone sharp and accusatory. The boat continued to rock as he glared at Archer, until it dumped Mateo right over into the water without a sound.

"Mateo!" Archer screamed, scrambling to reach for him.

But Mateo popped back above the water, smiling, shining droplets dripping from his perfect locks. "Get in here," he said. "The water is amazing."

"What?" Archer blinked and looked down at his clothes. He was wearing his white *Retro* jumpsuit. "In this?"

"Take it off first, of course." Mateo winked. "Take it all off."

Archer woke up with a gasp, sweaty and tangled up in his sheet. "Fuck." He rested a hand on his racing heart and rolled over to check the time. It was two o'clock. "Holy shit." He rubbed his face. "Maybe I am getting sick." He had even missed the lunch window.

He closed his eyes again, grasping at the threads of his dream before they drifted away. Mateo's face, sparkling and smiling, floated behind his eyelids. But it quickly dissolved into the more familiar scowl when he remembered the way Mateo had shut down Eileen's invitation and yelled at him about the autograph. Archer sighed and stretched until his growling stomach forced him to forage in his bag for an extra muffin he had stashed at lunch the day before.

He was sitting up in bed, trying not to leave crumbs, and scrolling his phone when Beau came in.

"Oh, hey. Back from the hike?" Archer asked.

"I didn't go," Beau said, hanging his beach towel on a hook. "Ben knows I hate hiking." He flashed Archer a sympathetic look. "I see Caleb abandoned you, too."

Archer swallowed the last bit of muffin. "He didn't abandon me. I wasn't feeling up for it today."

"Ah. So he went anyway."

"I told him to."

Beau gave him a *sure, Jan* look. "Shouldn't your partner want to be with you?"

Archer shrugged. "A lot of the time, yeah. But not *all* of the time."

"Very well." Beau's smile was small and tight. "I'm glad it doesn't bother you that your boyfriend is off alone in the forest all day with mine."

"Alone? Didn't a bunch of people go?"

"Did they? Who else went?"

"I don't know." Archer blinked, confused. "I was sleeping, but I assume . . ."

He trailed off when he saw the expression on Beau's face. This time it was more *oh, my sweet summer child*.

"You know what they say about assuming, Archer. Don't be an ass."

* * *

Archer went for dinner as soon as the dining hall opened, still with no sign of Caleb, and he was early for warm-up again—some sad attempt to make Mateo like him, he supposed. But Mateo ignored him, headphones firmly embedded in his ears when Archer arrived. The greenroom slowly filled up, until Archer realized that, in fact, only Caleb and Ben were missing.

He sent Caleb another message—**Hey, where are you? Everything okay?**—but it joined the other unanswered texts.

"Have you heard from Ben at all?" he asked Beau.

"No. I'm a little worried, actually. It's not like Ben to be late."

Archer frowned and found Betty powdering her face at the makeup table. "Did you go on the hike?" he asked.

"What hike?" she replied, leaning forward to examine her work in the mirror.

"Never mind," Archer mumbled. He eased over to Dominik at his costume rack. "Did you go on the hike today?"

"Nope," Dominik replied. "I was gonna, but my hamstring has been bugging me. I think it ended up being only Ben and Caleb."

"Oh."

"Speaking of . . ." Dominik looked around. ". . . where are they?"

"I don't know. It's five forty-five, though. And they haven't answered any texts."

Dominik cringed. "Has Mateo noticed yet?"

They swiveled to look at him just as he strode over to Harley.

"Harley," Mateo said, mildly annoyed.

"What?" Harley replied without looking up from his phone.

"It's Thursday."

Harley blinked up at him. "Yeah?"

Mateo rubbed his forehead. "Thursday is *Around the World*."

"Oh." Harley looked down at his *Broadway* costume. "Right."

Mateo muttered something, pinching the bridge of his nose. "Look," he said, teeth clenched. "I need you to get it the fuck together."

"Yeah, yeah, I'm on it," Harley muttered. "Geez."

"I don't think he's noticed yet," Archer whispered to Dominik.

Right then, Mateo's head snapped over, staring right at Archer.

Archer widened his gaze, trying to look innocent.

Mateo's eyes narrowed, and then he began looking around the room.

"Shit, he's onto it," Dominik muttered. "He's gonna fucking lose it on Caleb."

Then the door to the greenroom banged open. Archer breathed a sigh of relief and turned to grab Caleb's costume for him.

But when Archer looked over, Caleb was not standing in the doorway.

The man who was in the doorway was wearing a turquoise suit, brandishing a cane, and carrying a small dog.

"Stewart!" Betty cried.

He threw his arms out. "I'm back, darlings!"

Betty and a few others rushed over for hugs.

"You didn't tell us you were coming back tonight," Mateo said, his stare slightly wild.

"I wanted it to be a surprise!" Stewart proclaimed, smoothing Judy's fur. She yipped.

"Oh, it's a surprise, alright," Archer murmured. *Fuck.* Where was Caleb?

There was no more avoiding it. They would need some

sort of plan if Caleb and Ben were going to miss the show. Archer sidled up to Mateo.

But Stewart saw him. "Archer, my boy!" he cried. "How lovely to see you." He grabbed Archer and kissed both of his cheeks.

"Stewart!" Archer was, of course, genuinely happy to see Stewart, but there were more pressing matters at hand. "So great to see you too, of course, but I actually need to talk to—"

"How is your tango, young Archer? As sizzling as ever?"

"Er, well, I—"

"I meant to get back on Tuesday to see the *Latin* show, you see, but Judy needed to get her toenails clipped and her regular groomer was on holiday—"

"That's great, Stewart, but I just—"

"—and would you believe that the first place I called couldn't get her in for two weeks? Two weeks! Insanity."

Archer tried to nod politely, eyes flicking to Mateo and back.

"So I started calling around and there was one place that had an opening before that . . ."

Mateo was surveying the faces in the room, then he looked at Archer, eyebrow raised.

Archer nodded meekly as Stewart rambled.

"Fuck!" Mateo said.

"Er . . ." Stewart trailed off. "Is everything alright, Mateo?"

"Not really," Mateo said. "*Fuck.*"

"It's okay!" Archer said. "We can figure this out."

"What's wrong?" Stewart asked.

"Well, the show is in ten minutes, and Caleb and Ben are not here," Mateo growled.

"What do you mean, they are not here?"

Archer laid a calming hand on Mateo's arm before he

could erupt all over Stewart. "Caleb and Ben went for a hike and they aren't back yet, and they aren't answering texts."

"Oh my." Judy whimpered and Stewart patted her head.

Beau sucked in a breath and sank onto a chair. "What if something happened to them?"

Betty perched next to him and put an arm around his shoulders. "I'm sure they're fine! Those trails go for miles and there's no cell reception past the resort. They probably went too far and couldn't get back in time."

Archer's stomach twinged. It had never even occurred to him that something was wrong. He was sure it was just Caleb being Caleb and still mostly expected him to come running in breathless any minute.

"Alright," Mateo barked. "Let's make a plan." He stalked over to the whiteboard and began writing down all the different *Around the World* numbers. "Okay, Western first. Line dance, then the two-step . . ."

Archer joined him. "The line dance is fine, no partner work, we can fill in the gaps."

Mateo nodded. "Now, the two-step . . . Seta and Beau, can you dance together instead of with Caleb and Ben?"

Beau shrugged. "I suppose, but I'll have to dance Ben's part."

"Right. Shit." Mateo started scribbling down all the partners.

"It's fine, I can do it." Beau stood and began miming the choreo in place, brow furrowed in concentration.

"Are you sure?"

"I'm sure."

"Okay, next is Ukrainian . . ."

They went through the rest of the numbers and did their best to cover Caleb and Ben's absence, re-pairing duos, or having some dance twice, or not at all. The clock ticked away until there was nothing to do but make a wish on Judy's collar—which Stewart made them do because it contained rhinestones that allegedly once adorned a Liza Minnelli costume—and take their places in the wings.

"Get Stewart out of here," Mateo murmured into Archer's ear as the greenroom emptied. "I don't want him to see the mess backstage."

Archer paused. "You want him seeing what the audience sees, then?"

Mateo rubbed his forehead. "Fuck. Which is worse?"

Archer blew out a breath. "God. I don't know."

"Put him in the audience, I guess. I'm not sure what I'll do when they roll in, and I don't want Stewart to see that."

"Something might have gone wrong, you know. They could be hurt," Archer protested.

Mateo gave him a sardonic look. "Caleb's fine."

Archer bit his lip, then turned on a smile for Stewart. "Stewart! There's a special seat out there for you. You don't want to miss this show."

15

Leave Your Shit at the Door

"Welcome to Shady Queens!" Francisco's voice boomed. "We hope your passports are up-to-date, because tonight, we take you around the world! Our first stop is the land of snow and Tim Hortons, poutine and Celine Dion, cowboys and Shania Twain—our friendly neighbors to the north. Welcome to Canada!" "Man! I Feel Like a Woman!" began blasting. It was time to line dance. Archer straightened his bandana, and off they went.

The first song went . . . okay. A few awkward gaps in the lines, though he doubted anyone in the audience could tell. Beau and Seta's two-step was bumpy in places, but hopefully there were enough twirling, bedazzled dancers all around that no one noticed.

The Ukrainian dancing went smoothly; they only had to space out more in their circles where Ben and Caleb would have been, and those two weren't in the cancan at all, so that went according to plan.

Capoeira was tricky—Archer was used to facing off against Caleb, but instead it was Dominik, and they weren't quite in sync. The number was fast-paced, with dancers darting off and onto the stage, and when Archer spun into the wings, he found himself face-to-face with the missing hikers.

"Oh my God, you're alright!" He grabbed Caleb for a hug.

Caleb hugged tightly back. He smelled like dust and sweat. "I'm so sorry. We went too far and got a little lost."

"But you're okay?" Archer pulled back to examine him.

"I'm okay . . . or rather, I will be until Mateo kills me. How mad is he?"

"You asshole!" Mateo growled as he leaped offstage.

"Pretty mad," Archer said.

"I swear to God, Caleb," Mateo spat, "you'd better have been fucking kidnapped—"

"We got lost, Mateo. I'm really sorry—"

"Ben!" Beau twirled up. "Do you have any idea how worried I've been? What happened?"

"We got a bit turned around—" Ben began.

"Ah. You've been 'lost' in the woods with Caleb all day, then? How nice for you!"

Ben's eyes widened. "What?"

Archer heard his cue so he danced back out, smiling, the sounds of the argument swallowed by the music.

At the end of the capoeira routine, there was a belly dancing number that only Seta, Grace, Iris, and Nijah performed. Archer hustled to the greenroom. Caleb and Ben were changing into their jive costumes.

". . . unbelievably thoughtless," Mateo was ranting, face red. "You said I could be pissed if you missed the show, and guess what? I'm pissed! I asked one thing of you—one fucking thing—and you fucked it up. You had to go traipsing off into the woods like a pair of selfish—"

"Mateo," Archer interrupted. "It was just a mistake."

"I know it was a mistake, Archer!" Mateo cried, rounding on him. "I'm sick of mistakes! Am I the only one who cares?"

"I care," Archer said. "We all care. But mistakes happen."

"You should know all about that, Mateo," Caleb sneered.

"Caleb," Archer snapped. "Now is not the time."

Caleb turned to the mirror, examining his vest, feigning indifference.

Archer looked back and forth between Caleb and Mateo, who was red-faced and seething. "Can we dance for now, and talk about this after?"

"Fine," Mateo growled. "Let's go fucking jive."

Archer rubbed his forehead. "Sounds like a plan."

It was not the most lighthearted jive Archer had ever danced. The performers' smiles were strained at best. Beau barely bothered to attempt one, Mateo's looked a little manic, and Caleb flat-out sulked throughout.

Bollywood, the final number, wasn't any better. What was meant to be a joyful dance filled with love and acceptance was more a simmering mess of bitterness and resentment. It was no surprise that the argument picked up right where it left off when the show ended.

"I cannot believe you think I *chose* to be late!" Ben began the instant they were backstage.

"You *chose* to spend the day alone in the forest with Caleb and—oops—totally lost track of time!"

"We looked like a bunch of fucking amateurs out there," Mateo seethed, wrenching off his translucent shoulder wrap. Archer normally would have let his eyes linger on Mateo's deltoids, but not now.

"Look," Betty said, placing her hands on Mateo's and Beau's arms. "Tempers are obviously high right now. Why doesn't everyone go take a breather, grab some food, and come back feeling a little better? By eight on the nose!" she added, seeing the words forming on Mateo's lips.

"Fine," Mateo sniffed.

"Fine," Caleb huffed.

"Fine. Fine. Fine," everyone else agreed.

After they had changed, Caleb took Archer's hand and pulled him out the door, but not before he got a glimpse of Mateo huddling in the corner with Stewart.

"Fuck," Caleb sighed once they got outside. "We really didn't mean to be late."

"I know," Archer said.

"We were fucking *running* the last hour trying to make it. My legs are done."

"You must have gone really far."

"I guess." Caleb shrugged. "It was such a nice day. We just walked and talked."

"Well, hopefully you had a good time."

"We did."

The feeling that something was going unsaid nagged at Archer, but he had no idea what it might be. "Wonder what Mateo and Stewart are talking about?" he asked instead.

"Undoubtedly, what horrible slackers we all are," Caleb said, rolling his eyes.

"Don't you think Mateo has a point, though?"

Caleb made a noise of derision. "This is your first summer, Archer. Mateo's too. Trust me when I say, things are going fine. The audience is a bunch of drunk people on vacation. They're happy no matter what."

"Why do you come back here every year?" Archer wondered, the question falling out unplanned. Archer knew Caleb was on his fourth season at Shady Queens, taught dance in the Bronx the rest of the year, and had been in the chorus of a few unsuccessful Off Broadway shows. But Caleb gave vague answers to most other questions about his life and didn't share an abundance of inner thoughts. In many ways, Archer felt like he barely knew him.

Caleb shrugged. "It's fun. Hot guys." He grinned at Archer. "Decent money for all the partying we do. Why, aren't you having fun?"

"Yeah, I'm having fun, it's just . . ." Without warning, tears sprang to his eyes. He was thankful they were walking and not looking at each other. "This is sort of it for me." *For my dream.* He couldn't get those last words to come out. "I want to do well."

"Aw." Caleb slid his arm around Archer. "Don't be so hard on yourself. You are doing well, and, I promise, it's nothing to get worked up about."

It is, though he wanted to say, but Caleb clearly didn't understand. "Thanks," he managed instead in a strangled voice.

"I wish Mateo would get off my back, though," Caleb griped. "He's practically ruining the summer."

"He has high standards."

"What, I'm not up to Mateo's standards?"

Archer shook his head, throat still tight. "That's not what I'm saying, I mean—"

"It's fine." Caleb cut him off and gave him an apologetic smile. "Sorry. I'm hungry and tired. I need to sit down and eat like five steaks."

"Okay. Let's get you those steaks."

Dinner was a subdued affair—they occupied their usual table and didn't talk much, with no sign of Ben or Beau. When they filtered back into the theater right on time, raised voices carried to them from the greenroom.

"That's it! I'm done!" It was Ben's words they could make out first.

"Uh oh," Archer muttered. They followed the sound of the shouting and inched into the greenroom. The B-Boys were facing off next to a makeup table in their cowboy gear.

"Looks like there's about to be a shootout," Dominik whispered behind his hand.

"Shut up!" Betty hissed, jabbing her elbow into his side.

"I'm *done!*" Ben repeated, ignoring the audience entirely. "I can't do this anymore, Beau! You either trust me, or you don't, and clearly you don't. It's over! *We* are over."

Archer was embarrassed that he gasped aloud until he realized they all had.

"Oh, shit," Dominik murmured.

Beau bit his lip and cast his eyes up to the ceiling, shaking his head. "You can't mean it."

"I mean it." Ben made a slashing motion with his hand. "It's over."

Beau burst into tears and ran from the room.

"Ah, fuck," Mateo said.

Betty and Grace hurried after Beau.

"I am not dancing with him!" Beau shrieked from the hall.

"I'm not dancing with him, either!" Ben yelled back.

Mateo threw his hands up. "I fucking quit."

"It's okay," Archer said, taking a deep breath. "Let's get back to the whiteboard."

Mateo didn't budge, shaking his head.

"Come on." Archer tugged at his arm. "We figured it out once. We can do it again."

Or so he hoped.

* * *

Archer's buzzing phone pulled him out of his sleep late the next morning. It was a text from Betty. He had missed a few messages in the group chat, too. **You'd better get down to the theater.**

Fuck. Last night's late show came back to him like a nightmare. The crying and sniping backstage. The red eyes and glaring onstage. The collision between Grace and Betty. Caleb tired after his day lost on the mountain, missing several cues, and jumping half the height he normally did. They had pulled off the show, Archer supposed, but it wasn't pretty. No one said much when it was over, melting away to their respective bedrooms to lick their wounds. Beau didn't come back to their room at all, and Ben refused to say a word to anyone. Archer didn't know what was waiting at the theater now, but it couldn't be good.

Still, he was not expecting to find Stewart in the same turquoise suit he'd had on last night, sprawled like a sea star in the middle of the stage. Judy sniffed his hand and wagged her tail. He was making a low groaning noise. Archer joined the dancers standing in a loose circle around him. There was no panic on anyone's face, only resignation.

"What's wrong?" Archer murmured to Mateo.

Mateo scrubbed a hand through his hair. "We got a bad review."

"We—A review? People review this show?"

"Well, not really. I guess someone posted about *Around the World* last night. Said it was, uh . . . sloppy, stale—"

"Sloppy!" Stewart wailed at the rafters. "And *stale*."

"And—"

"—*not worth the ten-dollar cocktail.*"

Archer cringed. "Oof."

"That's it, my darlings!" Stewart continued. "I've had it. Time to put old Stewart Harpham-Lale out to pasture. I'm sorry, Judy, I'm no good to you now. You'll need to find your own way."

Judy let out a plaintive yip.

"It's not your fault, Stewart," Mateo sighed. "It's mine."

"It's not your fault, Mateo—" Archer started.

"Why are you so nice to him?" Caleb cut in from across the circle. "He's such a dick to you."

"He's not a dick," Archer started to say at the same time Mateo protested.

"No one asked you, Caleb."

Caleb glared back, hands on hips. "Oh, but someone asked you?"

Mateo's chest inflated. "Stewart did, actually."

"Give me a break. You're not the boss here!"

Mateo laughed, a humorless bark. "You're really going to go with 'you're not the boss of me'?"

"Alright!" Archer yelled, cutting off the arguing. "We can all agree that the show last night sucked. Right? It *was* sloppy. We know we can do better. As far as stale goes— what if we made some changes?"

Stewart flopped his head over toward Archer. "What kind of changes?" he asked in a small voice. "Please, tell me, sweet Archer."

"What if we . . . put in some acro? Cirque du Soleil–type stuff. You know, from Canada, maybe instead of the line dancing."

Stewart sat up.

"I did a lot of acro as a kid, and I think Caleb did, too. Anyone else?" he asked the troupe. About half of the hands went up, including Ben's and Beau's, as they sulked.

"We don't need to change anything." Mateo stepped forward, glowering. "The show is fine. It's gotten messy, is all, which I've been saying for weeks. And one person with too much time on their hands didn't like the choreo. We don't need to do anything drastic."

"Hmm." Stewart sniffled.

"What we need is for everyone to show up on time, leave their personal shit at the door, and give it their all every night."

There was some awkward shuffling as the group studied their feet. Archer's ego stung a little at the way Mateo had shut him down, but otherwise it was hard to argue.

Mateo helped Stewart clamber to his feet. "Everyone back here for a rehearsal at one," he announced, trying to brush the wrinkles out of Stewart's suit.

"Yes, Mateo. You're absolutely right." Stewart sighed. He bent to pick up Judy and stroked her shiny fur. "Let's see if we can't tidy some things up."

They mumbled their agreement. Beau and Ben studiously ignored each other while Caleb and Mateo glared across the circle. It was going to be a long day.

Archer slipped out of the theater on his own, not really feeling up for conversing with anyone yet. But he was only a few steps up the path when someone called his name.

Eileen waved at him from a bench down a branching pathway. "Archer!" she said as he approached. "Good morning."

"Morning, Ms. Lamb." In the silence that followed, he knew they were both thinking about the shit show last night.

But Eileen just cocked her head and smiled from under her peach-colored sun hat. "Did you ask Mateo about coming for tea?"

"Oh, um . . . yeah, things have been kind of crazy the past few days."

"Hmm, yes, I noticed the missing bodies last night, and all the new partners. Not to mention the unhappy faces."

Yup, Eileen really didn't miss a thing. "Yes, er . . . Mateo said he would check his schedule . . ." Archer trailed off lamely.

She nodded. "I understand. If he changes his mind, I'm always available. Even if you don't want to talk dance, I'd love to whip up some raspberry scones for you."

Archer's heart warmed. "Thank you, Ms. Lamb. You're too kind."

She patted his hand. "I know how it is, when things don't quite work out how you planned."

"What do you mean?" he asked her.

She gave him a knowing look. "Another time, perhaps. I saw Mr. Harpham-Lale in the audience last night, so I imagine you have rehearsal to get to. You have a good day, Archer."

* * *

Archer grabbed a salad to go from the dining hall and took it down to the lake to eat by himself. There was a small sandy patch tucked into a copse of trees not far from the theater where he could flop onto a log and have a few moments of quiet. He studied the lake as he chewed, sunlight jumping off its surface in sharp white sparkles, the distant happy shouts from the main beach and chattering birds washing over him in a soothing medley. He closed his eyes and took a deep breath while the warm summer breeze played with his hair. *Breathe*, he reminded himself.

Things had felt off with Caleb since the hike, but he chalked it up to the mess the show had been last night. Archer figured once things settled down, it would feel normal with Caleb again. After all, their relationship was meant to be light and fun, not something to stress over. He finished his salad and took a few more deep breaths before gathering himself and heading back to the theater.

The whiteboard was out when Archer got back early, and it looked like Mateo and Stewart had mapped out all six of their shows with new partners so Beau and Ben wouldn't have to dance together. Mateo was standing back, gaze flitting over the board.

"Did you get a chance to eat?" Archer asked him, studying the names for tonight's show.

Mateo nodded. "I had an apple."

"Okay. Make sure you have a proper dinner before we go on, though."

Mateo sighed, idly popping the cap off and on a whiteboard marker. "I don't need you to look after me, Archer."

Archer blinked. "I'm not looking after you, I just . . ." The words *care about you* died on his tongue. "I'm only trying to help."

Mateo plunked the marker down on the ledge and ran a hand over his hair. "I know. Sorry."

Archer opened his mouth to say it was okay, but Mateo turned on his heel and marched off, saying something about needing to talk to Stewart. Archer watched him go. *Okay. He really doesn't like me. Time to let it go, Arch.*

Caleb popped up beside him and planted a kiss on his cheek. "Hey. I didn't see you at lunch."

"Hi. Yeah, I needed a little quiet time. Things have been . . ." He looked around, shrugging.

"I get it," Caleb said, taking his hand and kissing his knuckles. "It's going to be okay."

They were startled by a gasp from Betty. Her eyes were wide as she gaped at the backstage door.

Archer whirled. *What now?*

Ben and Beau stood in the door. Holding hands.

Archer's jaw dropped.

"Yeah . . ." Ben said. "We're back together."

Beau grimaced. "Sorry."

There was a thump as Mateo dropped a box of medical tape. "Are you f—" he started.

"We know," Ben said sheepishly. "We are so sorry for all the drama."

Beau slid his arm around Ben's waist. "We had a good talk and worked some things out. And we're *really* sorry."

There was a beat of shocked silence, then another.

"Excellent!" Stewart said. "Well, we have things figured out for the next time you break up, don't we? Mateo, did you write down our plan? In the meantime"—he breezed right over Ben and Beau's protests—"let's run through tonight's show, shall we? From the top!"

16

Rainy Day

Archer woke on the second Sunday of July to the gentle drumming of rain on the window. He wiggled back under his blanket with a contented sigh, letting the sound lull him back to sleep. Or rather, that was the plan, but the staccato whispers of Beau and Ben sniping at each other drowned out the raindrop patter. Archer pressed his pillow over his ear and swallowed a groan.

It was wonderful that they got back together, of course— all Mateo and Stewart's frantic work to rearrange the partnerships aside. With things patched up between the B-Boys, and everyone on their best behavior, Stewart had tightened up their shows with a few long days of rehearsal. Everything seemed to be back in order before he left again, citing Judy's upcoming birthday celebrations and all the work there was to be done in advance—especially because the caterers didn't understand Judy's specific dietary needs.

But now . . . Archer peeked out from under his pillow. The LIFE IS SWEET pie magnet Mateo had given him for his birthday caught his eye. It was stuck to the base of his bedside lamp, and it was the first thing he saw every morning. He looked past that to Caleb's empty bed—gone already, as usual. The man was religious about his work-out regime. Ben and Beau's whispers grew more frantic as Archer rolled over.

"I'm awake," Archer mumbled. "You can stop whispering."

"Sorry, Archer." Ben sighed.

"What, so it's all my fault?" Beau glared daggers at Ben.

Archer sat up, raking his fingers through his hair. "Don't mind me. I'll get out of your way." He collected a pair of sweatpants and a hoodie from the floor and pulled them on, ignoring their feeble protests. On a whim, he grabbed his new copy of *The Hobbit* and tucked it under his shirt, pulled up his hood, and ventured out into the rain. It was a welcome relief from the heat of July, and he took deep, moss-scented breaths on his way up the path.

He stopped by the dining hall for a late coffee and a breakfast sandwich, then, instead of heading back to the dorm, took the other path that went down to the center green. He was certainly not going to wade back into the hostile waters of his room, and he didn't want to go down to the cabin, knowing all of the off-duty staff would be packed in there.

Archer stood under a tree and took in the scope of the re-sort laid out before him. Shady Queens was quiet on rainy days. The beach was deserted, the volleyball courts empty. Some guests would stay in their cabins for a cozy day of reading or board games, and the rest would head up to the main building for a craft or movie.

He was thinking about finding a sheltered bench some-where when it hit him—the theater. The covered porch had padded seating, and no one would be there this far before showtime. He ducked his head and hustled over the slick grass. Shaking drops of water from his hood, Archer clambered up the theater stairs and pulled his book from his sweater. He came up short when he saw another figure who had had the same thought curled up on a bench with a view of the rippled lake.

"Oh. Hi." Archer stopped, feeling like a big fat intruder.

Mateo looked up. "Hi." His face was soft, no sign of irritation at being interrupted.

"Sorry, I—"

"Don't be sorry." Mateo nodded at Archer's book. "Looks like we had the same idea."

"I can find somewhere else . . ."

"Archer. It's fine. There's lots of room here."

Archer hesitated a split second before he took the bench next to Mateo with the same view of the lake and sat facing him. "You needed to escape, too?"

Mateo grimaced. "Yeah, there was a beer pong tournament in the cabin. You can imagine the noise."

"I sure can. What are you reading?"

Mateo held up the Tolkien translation of *Beowulf* that Archer had seen on his bedside table. "I reread Beowulf every few years."

"Nice." Archer showed him *The Hobbit*. "Every summer for me, since I was a kid. That's why my other copy was falling apart."

A faint smile flickered over Mateo's lips. "Well . . . Enjoy. This is a great reading spot."

"Except for the interruption, right?" Archer chuckled awkwardly.

Mateo tilted his head, eyes crinkling. "I don't mind just the one."

Archer smiled, an unexpected heat flushing his cheeks, as he settled and flipped to his bookmark. He couldn't resist sneaking the odd peek at Mateo as he read, making sure he wasn't irritated, but Mateo was lost in his book.

They read in silence for a while, cocooned by the sound of the pattering rain, until Archer's leg started to tingle. He stopped reading to stretch it out.

Mateo caught his eye. "The rain is nice, isn't it?"

Archer looked out at the lake again, a shimmering blue and gray stretch ringed by impossible green. "I love it, actually. It makes everything else feel extra warm and cozy. When I was little, my mom would tuck me under a blanket on the porch, and I'd sit there watching rainstorms for hours."

Mateo blinked, then held Archer's gaze a moment. "Yeah. I love it, too."

Something bubbled up Archer's throat—something old and familiar . . . something hopeful and new. It was a little overwhelming. "So . . . feeling better about things lately?"

Mateo looked back down, fingers smoothing over the cover of his book. He shrugged. "We've been keeping it together, anyway. But . . . I can't help but feel like something is still missing, or . . . or was never there." His eyes flipped back up. "What do you think?"

"I mean . . . it's been better than it was."

"Yeah." Mateo looked disappointed for a second, then he stood. "I'm going to get some lunch."

Archer deflated as Mateo strode by him, feeling like he did something wrong, but . . . Mateo stopped at the top of the stairs and looked back. "Do you want to come?"

He snapped his book shut. "Yes."

The rain faded into a light misting as they walked in a comfortable silence. They were approaching the dining hall when Caleb ran up.

"Archer! Hey." He threw his arms around Archer and kissed him soundly, not even sparing a glance for Mateo. "I missed you. Where have you been?"

"I was reading on the theater porch. With Mateo."

Now Caleb looked over at him. "You trying to steal my boyfriend, Mateo?" Neither his tone nor his eyes suggested he was the slightest bit kidding.

Archer's face flushed. "He wasn't—I—"

Mateo cocked his eyebrow. "Are your boyfriends stealable, Caleb?"

Archer tried again. "I'm not—"

But Caleb ignored Archer's protests and took a step closer to Mateo, mouth in an ugly curl. "You think you're hot shit, don't you?"

Mateo rolled his eyes. "Jesus, Caleb. I don't have time for this. I'm getting lunch." He pushed past Caleb and yanked open one of the doors to the dining hall.

"God, I can't fucking *stand* him," Caleb muttered once the door closed behind him. "I don't know how you put up with that ego."

"I don't know if it's ego—" Archer started to reply, but Caleb cut him off.

"Can we just not talk about Mateo right now? He puts me in such a bad mood." He scrubbed his hair. "Come on, let's go eat."

* * *

Ben and Beau getting back together had solved one problem—sort of, Archer supposed—but it had done nothing to repair the animosity Caleb had for Mateo. Caleb had been mostly quiet about it with Stewart around, but the cracks were showing again, only a few days after Stewart left, when he and Grace showed up only half an hour before *Retro*.

"I asked you to be here an hour early," Mateo said to them, but there was no heat to it, only resignation.

Caleb clapped Mateo on the shoulder as he sauntered by. "Don't worry about it, Matty. We're here."

"Don't call me Matty."

"Don't tell me what to do, Matty."

Somehow Mateo managed to swallow it down and roll his eyes, but Archer sank onto a chair, watching Caleb smirk and giggle with Grace, and he didn't like the sense of wrongness settling in his gut. Their behavior was straight out of high school, and he was too old for that shit.

And of course, the more Mateo swallowed down, the tighter it wound him up. He was short and sharp with everyone, snipping instructions, and not bothering to sugarcoat anything, and his patience for the B-Boys' drama had worn thin to the point of nonexistence.

Beau and Ben were fighting over their *Latin* routine that week, of all things. Ben had nearly dropped Beau in a lift in the early show.

"You missed the count. I always go up on four," Beau snapped, throwing his towel onto a chair.

Ben could barely deign to respond. "I have been lifting you on five this entire summer."

"You absolutely have not."

"Let me know," Mateo interrupted at full volume, so the entire greenroom could hear, "if you're breaking up again with as much advance notice as you can, yeah?"

"We are not breaking up, Mateo," Beau informed him, offended. "We are just discussing our choreo."

"Sure," Mateo said, shaking his head.

"Rude," Beau muttered.

"So rude," Ben agreed. "And it was on five."

"Four."

"Christ." Mateo stormed off.

Archer wondered if the troupe would even be able to make it through the summer without bloodshed. Everything probably looked fine to the average guest, but nothing felt fine. After the show, Archer was off. His skin itched, his eyes were dry, and he was somehow bone-tired and jittery at the same time. He ignored calls of *see you at the cabin*, slow to peel off his costume and pack up his bag, and he was the last one out when he left. Halfway back to his dorm, he realized he had left the backstage lights on. He swore and turned around.

When he swung the stage door open, he was surprised to see that all of the lights were off, except for the red light of the exit sign and a white glow coming from the stage. Then he heard the music, quiet and somber, a piece he recognized but couldn't quite put his finger on. He crept through the wings toward the stage, illuminated by a single spotlight.

Mateo was dancing.

He was wearing only his black tights, as black as the shadows that ridged his every visible muscle. Archer froze, hidden in the dark. Mateo whipped around in tight fouettés, until he slowed and came out of the last one in a leisurely stretch, leg rigid, arm extended overhead in an aching curve. His face burned with emotion, eyes closed, features gleaming in the light.

Archer knew he was watching something personal, something private, and yet he couldn't look away.

Mateo's limbs were soft and hard at the same time, each fingertip screaming with joy and agony. He leaped and turned, stretched and filled the space with beauty and fire, passion and despair. Archer's jaw dropped when Mateo's grand jeté spanned what seemed like the length of the entire stage. Then another and another.

When the music stopped, Mateo did too, chest heaving and glistening with sweat, eyes wet. Then he turned and looked right at Archer. "Did you enjoy the show?"

Archer jolted, hastily wiping the tear from his cheek he didn't realize had fallen. "I'm sorry. I didn't mean to spy . . . But that was incredible, Mateo."

Mateo grunted in reply, head dropping to stare at his feet. "It was nothing."

Archer took a few steps closer. "It took my breath away. You—You're . . . Mateo, why are you here? Why aren't you still on Broadway?"

Mateo stiffened, his face closing off. He turned and stalked over to the AV equipment, snatching a T-shirt off the ground and yanking it over his head before jamming a few buttons on the panel. The stage plunged into darkness. "None of your business."

Archer blinked as his eyes adjusted. "I'm sorry, I— Mateo, please . . ." He put out a hand as Mateo stormed past.

Mateo shook off Archer's touch and blazed down the stairs toward the exit. "Don't."

"I think people would love to see you again—"

"No, they wouldn't, Archer." He stopped at the door. "You just had this dumb childhood obsession with me. No one else misses me. No one else wants to watch me dance."

"Mateo." There was enough in Archer's voice to get Mateo to pause with his hand on the door. "Have you not seen and heard the audience when you dance? Are you kidding me? They love you, Mateo. They fucking adore you. So you were partying too much five years ago. No one cares. Celebrities can get high, crash a car, apologize, and book a new job the next day. You didn't hurt anyone."

"I hurt Abby," he said softly, hand falling to his side. He turned to face Archer.

"Do you want to talk about it?" Archer asked.

Mateo's eyes were wet. "I didn't mean to," he said in a rush. "There was one night I got drunk after the show, and Abby asked me if I was doing okay. We were friends and she was only worried about me, but I—I lashed out at her. Told her to mind her own business, that we weren't friends at all, we just worked together, and then . . . I told her she only got the role because she was trans."

"Oh."

"Yeah." He swiped an escaping tear. "Which is ridiculous. She's so talented, and she *was* my friend, but I . . . Fuck, I was such an asshole, Archer. I think I wanted to hurt her because I was hurting. I was a mess. My parents had just died and . . . everything felt so wrong. The fame and attention felt wrong, I felt wrong, and . . . I ruined it all. She barely spoke to me after that, and I kept being a jerk. Then I got fired, and I haven't said a word to her since."

He slid down against the door and sat there, wiping his tears.

"Mateo." Archer came over and sat next to him. "Being an asshole for a brief moment in your life doesn't mean you ruined anything. It doesn't mean you aren't a good person, that you don't deserve to be a star. You're so fucking talented. I completely understand that was a hard time for you, but . . . you could have it again, if you wanted."

Mateo sniffled. "I don't think so."

"I know so. I went to thirty-seven auditions over the last few months, and you are better than anyone I saw. You should at least try, if it's something that you want."

There was a beat of silence. "Thank you, Archer."

"Of course."

"You've been amazing all summer. I don't know if I would have made it this far without you."

"Oh." Archer flushed, then was further distracted by Mateo putting his hand on his knee and squeezing before he stood. "I'm glad I could help."

Archer stood too, and they faced each other in the shadows.

"Um," Archer said at the same time Mateo pointed at the greenroom.

"I actually left my bag . . . but it would have slowed down my dramatic exit."

Archer laughed. "I'll wait if you want to grab it."

Mateo collected his bag, then they headed out into the night together, but their paths split before long, one heading up the slope, one down.

"I'll see you tomorrow," Mateo said when they paused at the fork. "Thanks again, Archer."

"You're welcome."

Archer's steps were light on his way up to his dorm. Things suddenly felt a little bit more right. He slept like a log that night.

17

Shifting

Archer toweled his hair dry after his shower, relishing the quiet of his room. He had passed on going down to the cabin tonight—didn't feel much like partying with the others after another Caleb-Mateo showdown at the theater. Caleb had thought it would be a good idea to break from the choreo during the Bollywood finale of *Around the World* to go dance through the audience. The guests loved it. Mateo, not so much.

"What the fuck, Caleb?" he had growled as soon as they were in the greenroom.

Caleb rolled his eyes. "Here we go."

"Here we go? Sorry for not being on board The Caleb Train, I guess!"

Caleb laughed. "Wow, you went ahead and said it right out loud. Can't do anything that takes attention away from Mateo Dixon, Broadway star!" he said, punctuating his words with jazz hands.

"Give me a fucking break." Mateo jabbed a finger at him. "This is not about me, this is about you continuing to do whatever the fuck you want, including leaving your fellow dancers hanging out to dry while you strut around the theater like a goddamn folk hero."

"The audience loved it, Mateo," Grace chimed in. She shrugged and began to peel her sari off. "What's the big deal?"

There were a few murmurs of agreement around the room.

Mateo's jaw flapped. His eyes met Archer's.

"It's not the choreography, Caleb," Archer said tiredly. "It's hard for the rest of us when we don't know what's going on up there."

Caleb narrowed his eyes at Mateo, ignoring Archer completely. "The crowd was eating it up. Maybe it *should* be in the choreo."

Mateo threw his arms out. "Then let's fucking talk about it and plan for it, and not spring it on everyone in the middle of the show!"

"Oh, right, talk about it, as if you'd listen to a word I said."

"For God's sake, fine, let's have a fucking meeting about it tomorrow, then."

"And who's going to make the final decision at this 'meeting'?"

So it went, back and forth, around and around, on and on.

Then Caleb pulled the same stunt at the second show. This time, Grace joined him.

Mateo didn't say a word to anyone after, slamming his locker shut and stomping out of the greenroom.

Caleb had spent the entire walk back to the dorm bitching about Mateo. "He is such a dick! Why did they even hire him here anyway, after what he did to Abby? Who would even want to work with him?"

Archer suddenly couldn't listen to Caleb trashing Mateo

for another second. "It's not true, you know." The words
burst out of him.

"What's not true?"

"What you told me earlier. You said he was horrible to
her, but that's not really what happened. They were friends."

"They were?"

"Yeah, they got along great. He just lashed out at her one
time when he was—when she confronted him about something. They had a fight and he told her she only got the role
because she was trans."

"Is that what Mateo says happened?" Caleb asked,
skeptical.

"Yes."

Caleb considered a moment. "Still a dick move."

"Mateo would completely agree with you, and he felt
terrible about it. He still does. And, you know what, his
parents had both just died and he was dealing with being
this huge star. That's a lot for someone to take."

"I guess." Caleb shrugged. "Doesn't mean he's not a total douche."

Back at the dorm, Archer needed time to himself—the
role of peacekeeper-slash-doormat was really beginning to
wear on him, and he'd had enough of the fucking drama.
He took a long shower, dawdling until he knew Caleb and
the B-Boys would be gone, then headed back to the room
and its solitude.

Unfortunately, the events of the night continued to loop
through his brain, so it was a welcome distraction when his
phone buzzed with a message from Lynn. **Archerrrrr! How
are you? How are things?**

He flopped onto his pillow, considering. His moment
with Mateo felt too private to share, and he really didn't
want to rehash all the mind-numbing dance troupe

dramatics. **Hey! They're okay . . . but what about you? How's living with Sasha going?**

Lynn had reported earlier that the transition was fairly seamless, although Sasha was not happy with the way Lynn hand-washed her delicates and hung them up to dry around the apartment, and they could not agree on what brand of coffee to brew at home.

It's good! Lynn replied. **Really good. That's actually sort of what I wanted to talk to you about. Sasha said I should move in permanently. So . . . I don't think I'm going to renew the lease on my apartment.**

Archer's stomach curdled.

I'm really sorry, Lynn continued. **It doesn't make sense to keep living in that shithole when I'm proposing to Sasha anyway, you know? And who can say when it will even get fixed. My lease is up in three months and I'm not going to renew it.**

Archer cursed himself for not seeing this coming. Of course, Lynn was going to go live in Sasha's much nicer apartment. With the impending proposal on top of the 9021-hole . . . Lynn had no reason to stick around. **That makes sense,** Archer replied. **Thanks for letting me know.**

But you can still crash with us until you find a place.

Thanks, but I wouldn't want to impose on the newly engaged! Speaking of which, do you have a new proposal plan?

Yes! Okay, I was thinking we should go away somewhere! For like a weekend, a mini-vacation, something romantic and not too far.

Love that idea! Archer dutifully helped Lynn brainstorm ideas—the Hamptons? Cape Cod?—but his stomach was swirling. Homeless. Jobless. Hopeless.

Okay, I'll keep you posted if I book anything, Lynn said as their brainstorming wound down. **And don't worry, your plants are doing great! They love Sasha's. Lots more light. You should see the grin on little Spot's face.**

Good to hear. Thanks, Lynnie. Night. He was putting his phone down when there was a sharp knock at his door. He jumped a mile. "Come in?"

The door pushed open. It was Mateo.

Archer's stomach swirled in an entirely different way. He had never gotten over how handsome Mateo was, and seeing him tonight, framed in the doorway, with wet hair and loose gray sweats . . . He was even hotter than normal. "Oh, hey." Archer's cheeks heated. "What's up?"

Mateo's brow furrowed. "What's wrong?"

"Nothing," Archer said quickly, wondering what his face had been showing.

"Are you sure?"

"Yeah, it's only . . . my roommate in Manhattan. She's moving in with her girlfriend and I guess I'm officially homeless now." The panic fluttered in his chest. "Although my mom would disagree."

"Oh, shit. I'm sorry." Mateo came in and perched on the chair at the desk.

"Yeah."

"But you'll find something, right? Someone in Manhattan has to need a roommate."

"Maybe." Archer sighed. "Or maybe this is the final sign that I should give up and go back to Ohio."

"I don't know all the details, of course, but . . . you're talented, Archer. I don't think you should give up."

Archer shrugged, cheeks flushing hotter. "I don't know."

"What if . . ." Mateo straightened a pad of paper so it lined up with the edge of the desk. "What if we auditioned together?"

"What?" Archer laughed. "I love that you're thinking about auditioning again, really, that's so great, but . . . not with me!"

Mateo gave him a sharp look. "Why not?"

"Because you're Mateo Dixon!" Archer could imagine his Mateo poster on the wall behind where he was sitting. "Your agent will get you auditions. You don't need to do open calls like me."

Mateo rolled his eyes. "Okay, one, stop calling me *Mateo Dixon* like it's a thing. And two, I haven't had an agent since everything went to shit."

"You could get one again like *that*. Any agent who watched this show would be clamoring to sign you."

"No agents are watching this show."

"They could be! I heard that lots of people from the business vacation here. You never know who's in the audience."

"Well . . . I still think we should audition together. It would be fun."

Archer imagined how it would feel when Mateo inevitably booked the role at audition one, while he chalked up rejection number thirty-eight. He decided to change the subject back to whatever had brought Mateo here so late. "So . . . what's up?"

"Oh, I was wondering, do you think Eileen's invitation for tea is still open?"

Archer blinked. "I'm sure it is."

"Great. The sooner the better."

* * *

"Now." Eileen settled across from them in her floral armchair, eyes wide with concern. "Tell me what's been going on."

Archer and Mateo were on her couch, saucers in hand, coffee table laden with finger sandwiches and still-warm baked goods.

"I don't know," Mateo said. "Everything is a mess. We're so sloppy, and no one seems to care about the show."

"What makes you think they don't care?"

"It feels like the job is not a priority for them, that they aren't taking it seriously. I try to keep them in line, but . . . that only makes things worse."

"Well." She tilted her head. "Perhaps this crew needs a leader."

Archer took a sip of his tea, eyes darting between Eileen's wispy frame and Mateo's bulk on the dainty couch.

"Maybe." Mateo shrugged. "But Stewart's gone again, so . . ."

"Yes, Stewart is certainly a wonderful director, but, as you said, he's not here. *You* are the leader, Mateo."

"Me? I'm not a leader."

"Archer said that Stewart put you in charge when he left. That was for a reason."

Mateo snorted. "Clearly the wrong reason. Caleb hates me, and everything is a disaster."

"Caleb doesn't hate you," Archer cut in.

Mateo threw a side-eyed glance at Archer. "He hates me."

Archer paused and took a muffin. "Okay, he hates you a little."

"What would you say your leadership style is, Mateo?" Eileen asked, leaning forward and studying him.

"I don't have one."

"Hmm." Eileen took a sip of tea. "What do you think, Archer?"

Archer turned and narrowed his eyes at Mateo. "I would say he's a lead-by-example type. Responsible. Methodical. Dedicated to his craft. He does what others should do."

Mateo met Archer's eye. Archer smiled, sure he could detect a faint blush to Mateo's cheeks.

Eileen nodded. "That sounds right, from what I can tell. And it's admirable. But maybe it's not the most effective style for this group? Maybe they need a leader they can connect with."

Mateo shifted. "Connect? Not really my thing."

"Nonsense. Of course, you can connect. You've connected with Archer, haven't you?"

"Um—I—"

Archer wanted to melt into the cushions while Mateo floundered.

"Yes, it can be difficult to connect with *everyone*," Eileen continued, much to Archer's relief, "but I think, Mateo, some of them can sense the wall you have up."

Mateo bristled. "I don't have a wall."

"Er . . ." Archer shared a glance with Eileen. "There might be a tiny wall, Mateo."

Mateo looked between Archer and Eileen. "I don't, I—" He slumped back against the couch. "Fuck."

Archer placed a reassuring hand on his knee. "Look, it's not just you. Caleb is a lot, and the B-Boys clearly have their own . . . issues. But I know you have what it takes to get everyone together."

"Something to think about," Eileen said, raising her cup to her lips. "Now, have one of these muffins before they cool, won't you?"

* * *

The next afternoon, Archer was lounging on the dock with Caleb, Gage, River, and a handful of other dancers, baking in the scorching July heat, when a shadow fell over his face. He cracked an eye open against the glare and saw the dark shape of Mateo against the bright blue sky. "Hey!" Archer smiled up at him. Mateo hadn't hung out on the dock with them in weeks.

"Deigning to join us, are you?" Caleb drawled from his towel.

Mateo squinted. "Seems that way."

Archer shuffled his towel over to make room for Mateo's. "Welcome."

Caleb leaned back, folding his arms under his head. "Careful, Mateo. You wouldn't want to accidentally relax and have fun."

Archer shook his head. "Jesus, Caleb. Give him a break."

There was a silence on the dock. A few of the others exchanged glances.

"I was just joking," Caleb said with a pout.

Something inside Archer snapped—the growing feeling of wrongness burst out from wherever he had been stuffing it down. He got to his feet. "Caleb," he said. "Can we talk for a minute?"

"Um, sure?"

Heart racing, Archer turned and walked down the dock and up the steps of the cabin porch, Caleb following. Archer led him around the side, where they had at least a modicum of privacy.

"What is it?" Caleb said when Archer stopped and turned to face him.

Archer rubbed the back of his neck. "Listen . . . I've had a lot of fun with you this summer."

"I've had fun, too, Archer." Caleb took Archer's hand.

Archer blew out a breath and took his hand back. "But . . ."

Caleb's face fell. "But . . . ?"

"But I . . . I don't think I can be in a relationship with you anymore."

Caleb's eyes grew impossibly wide, searching Archer's face. "You're serious?"

Archer nodded. "Yes. I'm sorry."

"But why?"

Fuck. Archer struggled to find the words for the wrongness that had become impossible to ignore and was, in fact, growing by the minute, now that he had freed it. "I don't think that, ultimately, we are compatible."

"Compatible? What are you talking about? We get along great!"

"Yes, we do, but . . ."

Caleb's huge brown eyes were breaking Archer's heart a little. "Just say it, Archer."

"Sometimes, when I see the way you treat other people, I wonder if we are a good fit."

"Other people?" Caleb frowned, then it dawned on him. His face hardened and he let out a sardonic chuckle. "You're talking about Mateo, aren't you?"

"I guess . . . mostly."

"Unbelievable." Sad Caleb was gone. Angry Caleb was in his place. "I knew you had a thing for him."

"I do not!"

"Oh, please. You've wanted Mateo from the second you arrived here. Should have known you were settling for me."

Archer took a step back, off balance from the turn this conversation had taken. "I wasn't settling, Caleb. I liked you—"

"You just like Mateo better."

Archer rubbed his forehead. "Well, right now I kind of do!"

Caleb gasped.

"You've been so awful to him, showing up late on purpose, criticizing his every move, when all he's tried to do is what's best for the show—"

"Oh, the show, the show, the show! I am so sick of hearing about the show!"

"It's the entire reason we're here, Caleb!"

"Yeah, it's really not, Archer. That's what I've been trying to tell you! Nobody cares!"

"You should care! I care! And M—" He stopped.

"And Mateo cares," Caleb finished in a singsong. "What a perfect little couple the two of you will make."

"Look"—Archer sighed—"I hope we can still be fr—"

"Fuck off, Archer." Caleb smiled and waggled his fingers in a wave as he backed away. "Fuck right off." He whirled and bolted. Archer started to follow, but Caleb paused when he got to the bottom of the stairs and turned to the gang on the dock, who were watching, wide-eyed.

"HAVE FUN FUCKING ARCHER!" Caleb shrieked to Mateo. "YOU TWO CAN HAVE THE PERFECT SEX THAT'S RIGHT ON TIME AND ACCORDING TO PLAN! DON'T FORGET TO BE ONE HOUR EARLY!"

The kitchen crew who were halfway up the stairs snickered behind their hands as Caleb stalked up the path. Everyone in the cabin had no doubt heard the screeching, too. Archer considered throwing himself into the lake. But first, he looked at Mateo.

Mateo was horrified. Dominik and Gage clearly thought Caleb's outburst was hilarious and were doing a very poor job pretending they weren't laughing. Betty, Daniella, and

River watched Archer with concern etched across their faces.

Archer's feet were frozen to the deck, cheeks burning hotter than the sun. *Oh God, oh God, oh God.* He considered bolting up the path, under the pretense of chasing Caleb, but no. He couldn't avoid them forever. They'd all be dancing together in a couple hours anyway.

He sucked it up and trudged along the dock, eyes on his feet.

"So . . . not a good breakup?" Betty greeted him.

"I'm really sorry you guys had to see that," Archer said, avoiding Mateo's stare. "That was . . . Caleb . . ." He scrubbed a hand through his hair. "I didn't say anything like that, Mateo, he was angry and I—"

"It's okay," Mateo rumbled. "I figured that was Caleb being Caleb. What an ass."

The guffaw Dominik had been trying to hold in burst out. "According to plan, though! Classic!" He dissolved into a fit of giggles.

"Shut up, Dominik." Betty glared at him and gave Archer a hug. "You okay?"

"I guess, but . . . that sucked," Archer muttered into her shoulder.

"Yeah, breakups suck, but still better than dragging something out that doesn't feel right, right?"

Archer's eyes flicked over to Mateo. Mateo was watching him back. "Yes," Archer said. "Right." He cleared his throat. "Guess we'd better get moving. Show's in a couple hours."

Mateo's face pinched with concern. "Are you going to be okay dancing with Caleb? You guys aren't paired much, but—"

Archer shook his head. "No, I'll be fine. You don't need to change anything for me. I'm with you tonight for *Latin* anyway. I'm sure Caleb will be able to handle sharing the stage with me."

Mateo cocked an eyebrow. "Are you, now?"

18

It Teeters and It Totters

Caleb was huddled in the corner of the greenroom with Ben and Grace when Archer and Betty came in after dinner. The three heads whipped over, each giving Archer their own version of a death glare.

"Shit," he murmured under his breath.

Betty patted his arm. "It'll be fine. This isn't high school, remember?"

"Sure feels that way." About half of the troupe were apparently Team Caleb and had gone full-on silent treatment, when they weren't whispering behind their hands as he walked by.

"It's okay, Caleb," Grace said loudly enough for Archer to hear when he went over to his locker. "You deserve someone who treats you right."

Archer flipped through his costumes with a heavy sigh. He would just have to rise above the histrionics. He had a job to do. Time to shake it off.

Mateo came over. "You okay?"

Archer shrugged. "I suppose."

"Do you mind if I ask . . ." Mateo leaned in and dropped his voice. ". . . what happened?"

Archer bit his lip as he considered how much to say. "Something was off, and I couldn't ignore it anymore."

"What was he so mad about? When he yelled that . . . stuff?"

"Oh." Archer gave an awkward chuckle and pulled his *Latin* costume off its hanger. "Nothing. It was—I told him I didn't like the way he treated other people." He flushed. "You, that is."

"Oh."

"So he took the leap to . . . Well, you heard him."

"Oh." Mateo said again. He fiddled with the hangers on the rack, ensuring they were evenly spaced out. "I appreciate you standing up for me, but I hope you didn't . . ."

"I didn't break up with him for you, if that's what you're saying."

"No, of course not."

Archer's face heated. "Caleb and I weren't the right fit. That's all."

"Okay, good." The hangers could not have been more perfectly spaced.

"Good."

"Good. I'd better get dressed."

Archer watched him go. The glares of Team Caleb followed Mateo, too. "Ugh." He looked over at Betty at the makeup table, acting like she wasn't listening. "What were you saying about high school?"

"Sorry." She cringed. "It'll get better?"

"Right."

By the time they were due in the wings for their tango, Archer's head was all over the place. He had to focus. He could not afford to waste any more time being substandard on that stage. Someone important could be in the audience any night, and he'd lost sight of that. As Francisco's announcement reverberated, Archer blew out a breath and looked across the stage to where Mateo waited, searching for his steadying gaze. And there it was. Their eyes locked. Mateo's chest rose and fell in a deep breath as he nodded. *You've got this.*

Archer copied him, the burst of oxygen helping steady his pulse. *I've got this.*

Their music started. Archer began his slow walk out. Mateo's eyes were twin black coals, burning at him across the stage. As their hands met in the first hold, a pulse of electricity swept over him—a charge he hadn't felt with Mateo in weeks. Goose bumps prickled every inch of his skin.

Their chemistry was back. Their duet simmered with a new intensity—the turns were sharper than ever, each hold tighter, each foot and hand caress oozing with seduction. Mateo's scent surrounded him, a heady cloud of man and forest. A flame of arousal flickered in Archer's gut. Sweat beaded on his skin as they approached the tango's climax.

They struck their finishing pose as the next duet began downstage, and Archer had never before wanted so badly to keep dancing. But there was nothing to do but tango offstage, heart pounding, mouth dry. Betty gave him a knowing smirk from where she waited for her entrance.

"That felt good," Archer said to Mateo after chugging from his water bottle. "The dance, I mean. It felt good. We were good. At dancing."

"Yeah." Mateo wiped his forehead with a towel. "That was really good."

Their second show was even better. Archer smiled at

Mateo after, feeling a million times lighter than he had before. "Thank you," he said to Mateo.

"For what?" Mateo asked, pausing his towel to meet Archer's gaze.

Archer resisted the urge to lean in and kiss Mateo's cheek. "For being there for me."

Mateo's eyes flashed with an unnamed emotion. "Always."

"Please, could you two be any more obvious?" Caleb's voice cut in from behind him, dripping with derision.

Archer whirled.

"For fuck's sake, Caleb," Mateo said, before Archer could say anything.

Caleb smirked. "Defending your boyfriend? Cute."

"Archer is not my boyfriend, but yes, I am defending him, because you're acting like a child."

Caleb rolled his eyes. "Oh no, am I in trouble again, Father?"

"Caleb—" Archer tried.

Caleb narrowed his eyes at Archer. "What part of 'fuck off' were you having trouble with? Don't even talk to me."

"I can hardly blame Archer for breaking up with someone as petty and immature as you," Mateo snarled. "I'm only surprised it took him as long as it did."

Caleb's face crumpled. He turned and all but ran away.

"Fuck." Mateo put his hands on his hips, expression twisted with regret. "I'm supposed to be connecting with him."

A laugh burst out of Archer.

Mateo's lips quirked. "What? What's so funny?"

But Archer was already laughing too hard to reply.

Mateo started to chuckle, then guffaw along with Archer. It wasn't long until the two of them were roaring.

"Oh, shit," Archer gasped when he was able to speak again. "I'm so sorry. It's not funny."

"It's a little funny."

Archer gave up, and they laughed and laughed until they were breathless.

* * *

By the time Archer and Mateo got back to the greenroom, Team Caleb had cleared out. It was a nice break from the suffocating contempt, but he wondered what he would find when he got back to the dorm. An image flashed to mind of all of his belongings strewn about the lawn.

Fortunately, the lawn was as tidy as ever when he trudged up the path, but his room was even tidier—Caleb's stuff had been cleared out. Ben and Beau were there getting ready to head out.

"Where did he go?" Archer asked. He was expecting ice from Ben, so he directed his question at Beau, but Ben replied without any animosity.

"His friend Steve has an extra bed in his room."

"Ah, yes. Good old Steve." Archer sighed, wondering why that hadn't been a huge red flag six weeks ago, and how much of an idiot he actually was. He flopped on his bed and pulled out his phone. A message from Lynn waited—just a lawyer meme. Archer sent a laughing emoji, then figured he might as well tell her. **Caleb and I broke up,** he sent. **He was being such a dick about Mateo. I couldn't keep ignoring it.**

She replied right away. **Aw, shit. I'm sorry, Arch. You doing okay?**

Yeah . . . Caleb's pretty pissed though.
Might be awkward for a while.

**Hopefully he gets over it quickly.
Now what were you saying about
Mateo?**

                    Nothing! Nothing about Mateo.

**If you say so. Seems like he might
help you get over the breakup, just
saying.**

He could just imagine the sly expression on Lynn's face.
How's Sasha?

**She is THE BEST. So amazing,
in fact, that now I'm even more
nervous to propose to her!**

Archer sighed and leaned back against his pillow. He
was so happy for Lynn, but her happiness only served to
highlight the shit he was mired in, and, tonight at least, he
couldn't deal.

"You okay?" Beau asked. "Breakups are hard."

"I will be. I only wish Caleb wasn't so upset."

"He'll be fine," Ben said. "He just needs a couple days
to get over it."

                         * * *

"Is five days still 'a couple'?" Archer asked tiredly. He was
sprawled on his bed after Saturday's show. It had been an
exceedingly long week, Caleb's vitriol only growing each
day.

"I think he's feeling better," Ben said, combing his hair
in the mirror.

"Do you?" Archer propped himself up on an elbow.

"Yesterday he kicked me—literally *kicked* me—in the capoeira, plus I'm sure he hid my greaser jacket, and today he knocked my water onto my plate at dinner."

"Those could have been accidents."

"Yeah? He also flipped me off when I complimented his cabriole."

"Oh."

"Yeah. 'Oh.'" Archer flopped back onto his pillow.

"Look, he was really upset. It's hard getting dumped, especially when you can't escape the other person at all. Maybe he needs a bit more time."

"God, I hope so."

"And, worst case, we're only here for another five weeks."

"Right." Archer rubbed his eyes. That sounded like a really long fucking time to him.

A blond head poked into the room. "Archer!" Betty sang.

"Oh, there is no way in *hell* I'm going to Game Night." He pulled his pillow over his head.

She laughed and yanked the pillow away. "Come on! What are you going to do, hide in your room the rest of the summer? If you can dance with him, you can play a game with him."

"He *kicked* me!"

"I saw," she admitted.

"So in what world is Caleb going to sit there and happily play a game with me?"

She shrugged and tugged at Archer's hand. "That's his problem, then."

"No, it will undoubtedly be mine."

Betty gave him her best puppy dog eyes.

Archer groaned. "What's the game?"

"It's the Jenga tournament."

He sat up. "Sorry, the Jenga . . . tournament?"

"Yeah, it's super fun! You have to come! Everyone will be there."

"Fine," he moaned. "But I'm only going for you."

She kissed him on the cheek. "That'll do."

* * *

"Listen up!" Dominik waved his arms at the four waiting Jenga towers. "Standard Jenga rules apply. You may use only one hand at a time to remove the blocks, and if you were the last one to touch the tower before it falls, you lose. We start in four random pools of four players. You knock the tower over, you get a point. After an hour, the pools are reshuffled into top four, next four, et cetera, based on points. Then you play again in your new group, same rules, then each pool has a winner. Any questions? Didn't think so. Play nice, children."

Dominik had everyone's names ready in a hat to make the groups, and Archer was somehow not surprised in the least when he ended up in a pool with Mateo and Caleb. He glared at Betty when their group was called.

Sorry, she mouthed.

Archer sighed and sat next to their assigned tower.

Dominik was their fourth and was chuckling and shaking his head as he joined them. "Well, well. What a group. Can you guys handle this?"

Archer, Mateo, and Caleb all glared at Dominik.

"Perfect," he smiled. "I'll go first."

Dominik kept up most of the easy chatter at first, and, despite himself, Archer started to enjoy the game. Jenga was simple yet fun, and smiles slowly started to crack through the cranky facades each time the tower fell. Even

Mateo seemed to be enjoying himself, chuckles escaping at Dominik's antics, and he even winked at Archer when Caleb knocked the tower down.

They had been playing for almost an hour and the Jenga intensity had ramped up. Each person had three or four points, so everything was hinging on the last game.

Caleb was taking his turn, tongue poking out as he removed a piece from near the very bottom with great precision.

Archer held his breath as the tower swayed, then steadied.

"Alright, let's see what you've got, Dominik," Caleb crowed. "You—and this tower—are about to go down."

Archer grinned, waiting for Dominik's joke about going down, but Dominik was staring at this phone.

"Dom! It's your turn!" Caleb prodded.

Dominik frowned without tearing his eyes away from the screen. "One sec."

"Excuse me, judges," Archer joked, "what's the rule about stalling? The tower isn't going to get any less wobbly while you wait!"

Dominik's eyes grew wider as he read. "What the fuck . . ." he muttered.

"What is it?" Archer asked.

"My friend sent me this . . . It's a link to *The Broadway Broad*."

"Ugh, that garbage?" Even relatively new to the scene, Archer knew *The Broadway Broad* was a trashy gossip site that posted mostly sensationalized news and sketchy rumors about Broadway shows and their stars. It was very popular in the industry, even though no one wanted to admit that they read it.

"Oh, shit." Dominik swallowed hard and looked up. "I'm sorry, Mateo."

Mateo stiffened. "Just tell me."

Betty noticed the serious faces, and her group turned to listen, too.

Dominik began to read. "'Mateo Dixon, disgraced star of *Robin's Egg* and all-around terrible person, has been spotted center stage at Shady Queens, the premier upstate LGBTQ+ resort and perennial favorite of this publication's readers.'"

Archer's stomach dropped. Mateo sat frozen, face unreadable, hands clutching his thighs. The group on the other side of them was listening now, too.

Dominik continued. "'A source tells us he's up to his old tricks, being rude to castmates and thinking he's all that, but, wait until you hear what *really* went down with him and Abby Hodge before he firebombed his career.'"

Archer's jaw dropped.

Mateo's eyes swung over to meet his.

"'Our source informed us that Mateo told Abby she was a terrible actress and only got the role because she was trans.'"

"What . . . ?" Archer's brain raced to make sense of what was happening.

"'And,'" Dominik read on, "'to this day, he blames all of his horrifying behavior on the death of his parents. Way to avoid taking any responsibility at all, Mateo! No wonder you got fired. Who would want to work with you?'"

"Stop." Mateo's command was flat and low. But his face . . . the look of utter devastation—it was a knife to Archer's gut. Every eye in the room was on Mateo now. He stood and took a slow step away from the couch, then another, like he wasn't sure his legs were going to continue holding him up.

Archer stood too, his stomach trying to claw its way up his throat. "It wasn't me! I didn't talk to them!"

Mateo continued his measured walk to the back stairs.

"Mateo, please! I would never—" Archer followed, desperate to make Mateo understand. "I didn't tell anyone, I—" It hit him. He did, though. He did tell someone.

He swept his gaze over to Caleb. Caleb met it head-on, defiant.

"You? Caleb . . . how could you?" Archer's stomach heaved like it was considering unloading its contents.

Caleb's face was stone.

Archer turned and chased Mateo to the bottom of the stairs. "I'm so sorry, Mateo. I didn't mean to, I was—"

Mateo paused halfway up. He turned around. Their eyes met again, and the hurt Archer saw in them broke his heart. "Stop, Archer. Please . . . stop." Then he turned back, and was gone, swallowed by the darkness above.

Tears flooded Archer's eyes. His brain pinwheeled in a hundred directions while his stomach twisted into a thousand knots. A tear spilled down his cheek, then he spun and bolted out the back door, letting his feet take him wherever they wanted to go.

19

Caught

Archer's feet wanted to climb, up and away, far from the lights, from the people, from *The Broadway Broad*. They climbed until he found himself at the grassy clearing high above the lake, short of breath and staring at the rock he and Mateo had rested on after blocking out their pas de deux.

"Fuck. Fuck fuck FUCK," he spat. How could he have messed up so badly? Mateo had trusted him, confided in him. And now . . . Archer shuddered to think.

He slumped onto the rock and sat there long enough that he started to shiver as his sweat cooled, but he still had no desire to move. He wished he had never come to Shady Queens. That he had never even come to Manhattan, chasing his stupid dream. If he hadn't signed a contract for the summer, he would have packed his bag and gone back to Ohio at that moment.

He sat there longer still until his phone buzzed.

You alright? It was Betty.

He sighed and wanted to ignore it, but also didn't want Betty to send out a search party. **No.**

> **It's okay, Archer. Everyone can see that Caleb was clearly the shitty person here. We're all super pissed at him.**

> **Well, Mateo is pissed at me.**

> **He'll be okay once he has time to process it.**

> **That's what you said about Caleb. Now they both hate me.**

Three dots, then no reply. Archer waited. Betty couldn't argue with that. Then she started typing again. **Please come back. It's late. Get some sleep and we can sort it out in the morning.**

> **I'll be back soon. I just need a bit more time.**

> **Promise?**

> **Promise.**

The moon crept above the hills, so distant and tranquil, while words careened through his head. Angry words for Caleb. Ugly, furious words. And words for Mateo— anything for his forgiveness. Pathetic words. Inadequate words. When he ran out of words, he could do nothing but trudge back down the mountain.

* * *

Archer woke up Sunday morning after a few scant hours of shut-eye, remembered everything that had happened, then buried his head under his pillow and fell back asleep. The next time his eyes cracked open, it was Sunday afternoon. He ignored Betty's texts, other than to let her know he was alive and safe in his bed. But he did stare at his phone a long while still, all those goddamn words back and crashing around in his head.

I'm so sorry, Mateo.

It's all my fault. How can I make it up to you?

I never should have said anything to Caleb. I don't blame you for being angry.

Please don't hate me.

He finally sent a message around three o'clock, heart pounding as he typed. **Mateo, I want you to know how sorry I am. I shouldn't have told Caleb anything. He was saying all this stuff that wasn't true and I only wanted to explain. I realize now that I totally fucked up. I'm so, so sorry.**

There was no reply.

Archer didn't leave his room the entire day, except to use the bathroom, surviving on water, granola bars, and a bruised apple from his bag. Some silly phone games and a few YouTube rabbit holes kept him at least a little distracted. Ben and Beau tried unsuccessfully to engage him in conversation—they reported that Mateo and Caleb appeared to be hiding in their rooms all day, too—and otherwise let him be.

His sleep was racked with unsettling dreams that night. They were snatches of his New York life—walking the streets of Hell's Kitchen, running to catch a train in Grand Central, at The Fiddler with Lynn—but Mateo was there in all of them, a dark, brooding presence, hovering just behind him. Judging. Blaming. Every time Archer jolted awake, sweaty and pulse racing, it was like Mateo was still in the room with him.

He was completely exhausted when he woke up Monday, and the idea of facing Mateo at the theater made him want to vomit. Never mind what he wanted to say to Caleb—Archer didn't know if he would end up yelling or crying. Or both.

Groaning, Archer sat up, then reached for his phone on the off chance that maybe—maybe—Mateo had replied.

He had not.

There were several texts from Betty, though. **Archer! Come on, bud. You have to leave your room eventually. I'm coming to pick you up at noon and we're getting lunch.**

Okay? Okay!

Seriously, are you awake?

I'm on my way. Get your ass out of bed.

There was a sharp rap at his door. It was noon on the dot.

"I'm sleeping!" he called.

"And I'm coming in," Betty replied. She cracked the door open, then pushed it all the way when he didn't protest. "Hey," she said when she saw him. "You okay?"

He almost wanted to laugh. "Still no."

She sat on the desk chair. "Look, Caleb is the problem here. *You* slipped up, *he* was a malicious asshole."

"Doesn't matter." Archer sighed. "Mateo got hurt because of me."

"Intentions matter, Archer. They matter a lot."

"The outcome is the same."

She tilted her head and studied him, as if she were searching for something heartening to say but couldn't come up with a thing.

Curiosity got the better of Archer in the silence. "Have you talked to Mateo?"

She shook her head. "No. But I am sure he won't be as mad as you think. And you have to face him eventually." She stood. "Come on, let's go eat."

"I'm not hungry."

"Yes, you are."

"I need to shower."

"I'll wait."

"I hate you."

"No, you don't, you love me. Now go clean up. You look like hell."

* * *

Admittedly, he did feel a little better after a shower and a proper meal. But that feeling vanished when he walked into the greenroom early, and there was Mateo.

Mateo saw him and turned to walk away, but not before Archer saw his face darken.

Archer's insides clenched. "Mateo?" Only a couple of the others were already there, and they were sitting across the room chatting. He had to say it now before he lost his nerve.

Mateo paused, shoulders tensed.

Archer swallowed hard and continued in a low voice. "I'm sure you got my text, and I know you don't want to talk to me, but . . . fuck, I'm so sorry. Caleb was way off base, saying all these things that weren't true, so I only tried to explain . . ." He trailed off, knowing exactly how pathetic it sounded out loud. "Mateo, I would never—"

"Never what?" Mateo snapped, whipping around to face him, voice raw and rough. "Hurt me? Betray me? Humiliate me? Because you did all three. Christ, I told you about my parents—" He took a step backward, shaking his head. "Leave me alone, Archer. We are not friends."

The blood drained from Archer's head. Dizzy, he reached for a chair to steady himself. "That's fair, but . . . I want you to know I'll never mess up like this again, I swear. You can trust me."

Mateo's mouth twisted into a bitter smile. "You know, it's my own fault for believing that in the first place. Turns out you and Caleb are perfect for each other."

It was a knife through Archer's heart. He nodded, holding back a fresh wave of tears, tongue thick in his mouth. "Okay. Got it."

Betty had come in behind him, and the sympathetic look she gave was enough to send Archer fleeing. He turned and crashed directly into Caleb in the doorway. The shock of hitting him was nothing compared to the wave of anger that swamped his senses.

"How could you do that?" The words exploded out of Archer at the same time as his tears. "How could you sell out Mateo like that?"

He realized he was shouting in a silent room. Mateo watched from his locker.

"I only told them things that were true." Caleb's reply was quiet, and his eyes stayed on his feet.

"But it was no one's business!" Archer yelled. "Why would you go out of your way to hurt someone like that?"

Caleb's head snapped up. "Hurt someone? You wouldn't know anything about that, would you, Archer?"

Archer blinked as he processed, the anger fading as rapidly as it had exploded. "Was this . . . was this whole thing about getting back at me?"

The silence between them stretched on. Caleb looked away.

"Look," Mateo interjected, voice weary. "We have a show to do. Can we be professionals and just . . . fucking dance?"

Archer wiped at a tear and nodded. Caleb nodded too, at least having the decency to look a little ashamed. You could hear a pin drop backstage as they got ready. Most of them were mad at Caleb, some seemed to be mad at Archer, and in general, Mateo, Caleb, and Archer were given a wide berth.

Unsurprisingly, it was another terrible show. Archer couldn't even look at Mateo or Caleb, and he was on the verge of tears half the time. He knew his dancing was substandard—heavy and joyless.

After the second show, he threw his *Retro* jumpsuit in the approximate direction of his costume rack and hightailed it out of there. He had already showered and buried himself under his blankets by the time Beau and Ben came back.

A few hours later, once he had mentally tortured himself to the point of exhaustion, he fell asleep, wondering how he could possibly do this for another five weeks.

He was still in bed the next afternoon when Beau suggested going for a swim.

"Yes," Archer said, attempting to muster up some enthusiasm. "That sounds great." The idea of plunging into the cool depths of murky green water was actually appealing. Anything to shut the world out for a few minutes.

"Not me," Ben said with a yawn. "I'm going to grab a nap before the show."

"Okay, love." Beau gave him a quick kiss. "See you in a bit."

They found Dominik, River, and Gage down at the dock, too, and Archer was happy to be distracted by their antics in between deep, refreshing dives. He held his breath until his lungs burned, then pulled himself back up toward the sunshine.

The afternoon was winding down when Archer climbed out of the water and his shorts snagged on a wayward nail, leaving a long, ragged tear down the front panel.

"Shit!" he said, examining the damage. He held the fabric together with one hand over the expanse of exposed thigh.

"Oh man, that sucks," Beau said, but he was distracted by his phone. "Message from Betty in the group chat," he told Archer.

Archer dried his hands on his towel and retrieved his phone from his bag to check. **Meeting at 4:30, everyone! Stewart's back! Let me know you got this.**

Archer sent a quick **Got it**. Stewart. Hopefully that meant everyone would be better behaved again, although he wasn't sure there was any coming back from the current disaster. Mateo would probably never forgive him. Archer's throat squeezed as the guilt that had been washed away by the lake water came flooding back.

"Ben hasn't replied." Beau frowned at his phone. "He's probably still asleep. I'd better go wake him up."

"It's fine," Archer said. "I'm going to head up now anyway to change. I'll make sure he's up."

"Okay, thanks. I'll meet you guys at the theater then."

Archer wrapped his towel around his torn shorts and made the trek back up to the dorm. He unlocked their door and, as he pushed it open, was met with a mass of moving flesh and blankets. It took him a second to realize what he was looking at. "Oh, shit, sorry . . ." He started to back out when he realized . . . that was not Beau and Ben. Beau was down at the dock. And one of the people in the bed had brown skin . . . It was Caleb. And Ben.

Archer's heart stopped. The two naked men scrambled to separate and cover themselves with sheets. "What the fuck?"

"Archer! It's not what it looks like!" Ben's eyes were wide and frantic.

Archer blinked. "I'm pretty sure it's exactly what it looks like."

"Fuck, please don't tell Beau!" Ben begged.

Archer shook his head. "Holy shit, Ben. You can't ask me to keep that secret." Then he looked back and forth between the two of them as a thought occurred. "How long has this been going on?"

Ben and Caleb shared a look.

"Only a couple days," Caleb replied. Archer didn't miss the guilt that flashed across his face.

Ben reached onto the floor for his clothes. "Please, please, please, Archer. You cannot tell Beau!"

"Either you tell him, or I do."

"Okay, yes." Ben nodded and yanked a T-shirt on. "I will absolutely tell him tomorrow."

"No deal. You have to tell him tonight. Now. He's on his way to the theater. Stewart's back and we have a meeting in a few minutes."

"Fuuuuck," Ben moaned.

Caleb squeezed his hand. "It'll be okay. Just tell him what you told me."

"It's not that simple, Caleb." Ben dragged his hand through his hair.

"You made it sound pretty simple."

"Shit," Ben muttered. "We'd better go."

It was a quiet march down to the theater, each person lost in their own thoughts. Archer's mind whirred. He wasn't sure he believed Caleb about how long it had been going on, and that opened up a whole new can of worms he did not have the mental energy for.

When the three of them hurried into the greenroom, it looked like everyone else was already there, lounging in a rough circle.

Stewart stood, glowing when he saw them. "Brilliant! Now that we're all here—" he began.

"I'm really sorry," Ben said, voice brittle, "but I need to talk to Beau."

"We're about to start a meeting—" Mateo protested.

Archer interrupted. "He *really* needs to talk to Beau. Right now."

Beau stood, his face a mask of confusion. "Is everything okay?"

"Can you come with me for a second?" Ben led Beau out of the room.

Caleb awkwardly slid into the nearest chair, eyes down, hands fiddling with the strap on his bag.

Archer took an empty spot next to Mateo.

Mateo leaned over to murmur, "What's up?"

Archer opened his mouth when a bloodcurdling shriek reached them from the hallway.

"YOU'RE FUCKING CALEB?"

20

Chaos

Every jaw in the room dropped, except for Caleb's and Archer's. Caleb let out a groan and buried his face in his hands.

"Oh my," Stewart said, eyes wide.

Mateo stared at Archer. "What—"

Beau came streaking through the door in a beeline. "You asshole!" he screamed, throwing himself at Caleb. They went down in a heap of thrashing limbs, the metal chair crashing to the floor.

The rest of the room exploded as everyone started yelling and swarming the pile, trying to pull Beau off Caleb.

Ben had raced in after Beau. "Beau, I'm sorry, it was—"

Beau's fist went flying back as he wound up to hit Caleb, but he connected with Dominik's face instead.

"Ow! Fuck!" Dominik yelled, falling backward and tripping over Ben. The two of them hit the ground, blood streaming from Dominik's nose.

"Oh God, I hate blood." Betty clutched at Archer's arm as she started to tip over.

"Shit." Archer helped her into a chair. "Put your head between your legs."

"Beau!" Ben tried to explain from underneath a bleeding Dominik. "Can we please talk?"

It was unlikely Beau could hear a word anyone was saying as he attempted to pummel Caleb amid the chaos. It looked like he managed to land a few hits before Mateo and Archer got him around the waist and dragged him away.

"You piece of shit! You fucking asshole!" Beau let loose a stream of French curses as he flailed in Caleb's direction. Archer took an elbow in the eye for his efforts at keeping them separated, but maintained his hold on Beau's waist.

Caleb was curled up in a ball on the floor, arms over his head. Grace helped him up while Mateo tried to calm Beau.

"Easy, Beau. Easy," Mateo breathed. "Deep breaths."

Ben and Dominik disentangled themselves, and someone found Dominik a box of tissues, which he plastered to his face in handfuls. Betty still had her head between her legs.

Beau let Mateo guide him into a chair, eyes wet as he gasped for air.

Archer sat next to him and rubbed his knee. "That's good. Keep breathing."

Beau still glared daggers at Caleb.

"Seems to me, Caleb's not the one you should be mad at," Dominik pointed out helpfully, muffled through the tissue.

Beau nodded. "You're so right." He launched himself at Ben.

By the time everyone had calmed down the second time, Dominik's nose was still bleeding, Ben and Archer had the beginnings of black eyes, Betty was still woozy, and the B-Boys were both crying.

"Well," Stewart said, straightening his aqua-blue vest as he stood. "That was . . ."

"What did you want to meet about?" Mateo asked, eyes closed and pinching the bridge of his nose.

The sound of Beau's sobs filled the room.

"Er . . . perhaps it should wait?" Stewart said.

"How could you do this to me?" Beau wailed.

Ben was across the circle, ice pack to his eye. "Beau, come on. We haven't been happy all summer."

"But with *Caleb*?"

Caleb bristled. "That's rude. Ben—"

"I'll kindly ask you to shut the fuck up right now, Caleb," Mateo said through gritted teeth.

"Stop telling me what to do!" Caleb screeched at him. He charged at Mateo.

"Oh, fuck," Archer had time to gasp, before he threw himself between the two.

But Mateo was having none of it. He growled and launched himself back at Caleb. "What the fuck is wrong with you?" Mateo yelled. "Who does shit like this?"

"I'm sorry I'm not as perfect as you!" Caleb screamed back, trying to dodge around Archer.

"Perfect?" Mateo reached for him. "*Perfect?* You've done nothing all summer but tell me how shitty I am!"

"Boo-hoo, Broadway star!"

"Stop!" Archer cried amid the wheeling fists. "Please, stop, both of you." He worried what might happen to Caleb if Mateo landed a solid hit, but Mateo was mostly only trying to hold Caleb's wrists to keep him from landing a punch.

Caleb's panted gasps turned into sobs once Mateo had a firm grip on him, then he slumped against Archer, the fight gone.

"Sit down, Caleb," Archer said, easing him into a chair. "It's okay."

"No, it's not," he wept.

Archer met Mateo's eyes over a sobbing Caleb. *What now?* he asked.

Mateo shrugged. "Nice shiner," he said, mouth twitching.

Archer felt only slightly insane when he laughed. "Thanks."

"Uh, guys?" Betty swayed in her chair. "We go on in twenty minutes."

"Oh, God," Mateo groaned, checking his watch.

"Okay." Archer stood. "We can do this. Beau, do you think you—" He stopped when he saw Beau's chair was empty. And so was Ben's. "Er . . ."

"They left," Dominik said from behind his bloody tissue. "When Mateo and Caleb were swatting at each other. Beau took off and Ben went after him."

"Why didn't you stop them?" Archer asked, exasperated.

"Oh, excuse me for not solving the world's problems while bleeding from my *head*."

"Please. It's barely a trickle now," Mateo snapped. "Suck it up."

"And where's Stewart?" Archer asked, realizing his chair was empty, too. He wondered if now was an appropriate time to start panicking.

"He got a call, said something about Judy," Yuki informed them. "He said he had to go."

Another giddy laugh bubbled up Archer's throat. It came out as a hiccup.

Mateo stood, eyes determined, jaw clenched. "You all have five minutes to get dressed," he announced. "We have a show to put on."

Archer slid into his *Latin* costume at record speed, then

met Mateo at the whiteboard as he was scribbling the numbers and pairings.

"This is going to be tricky." Archer frowned. "Seta will have to tango with Caleb, but we'll be missing an opening duet. Plus, the B-Boys have their paso doble showcase."

Mateo chewed the insides of his cheeks as he studied the list. "What if we made our duet twice as long to fill the gap and did the paso in their place?"

"Yes." Archer nodded without hesitation. "We can do that."

Mateo's lips curled. "Okay. That's the plan." He whirled. "Dominik, are you good to dance?"

Dominik was at the sink, washing blood off his neck. "I think so? Little lightheaded."

"Betty?"

"I'm good." She flashed a thumbs-up from the makeup table. "As long as no one else bleeds."

"And . . . Caleb?" Archer asked. Caleb hadn't moved from the chair. He had stopped sobbing, but his head was bent, rested in his palms. Archer went over and placed a gentle hand on his shoulder. "Can you dance?"

Caleb's laugh was devoid of humor. "It's all I can do."

Mateo gave a crisp nod. "I'll take that as a yes. Time to dance, people. Archer? Let's figure out what the fuck we're doing." Mateo took his hand and pulled him close. But instead of diving into the steps as Archer expected, Mateo stared into his eyes. "Are you okay?" he asked in a low murmur.

"Yeah," Archer said quickly. "I'm fine." Then he realized his knuckles were white where he gripped Mateo's hand and every muscle in his body was pulled tighter than a drum.

Mateo squeezed his waist. "Close your eyes and take a deep breath."

Archer obeyed, inhaling Mateo's scent, and letting the tension drain from his muscles as he blew it out slowly.

"That's good," Mateo rumbled. "Better?"

Archer opened his eyes and met the dark warmth of Mateo's. "Better."

"Okay. After we finish here, let's repeat the first eight bars . . ." Back to business, he began leading Archer through murmured instructions, in small, half movements, his hand always on Archer's back or waist. "And then lunge, hold for four, back up slow, three, four, and snap to center, hold my eyes, seven, eight, good."

His words rippled over Archer's skin like the heat from a fire, setting an ember inside him aglow. His world was this cocoon with Mateo, hushed, focused, firm touches, soft breaths. He never wanted it to end.

"Do you know the paso?" Mateo asked when they finished working out that part, lips inches from Archer's.

He willed himself to focus. "I've seen it enough, I feel like I do."

"Okay, let's try it."

Mateo led him through, but Archer knew most of it. He was sure they wouldn't be quite as sharp as the B-Boys, but it would do.

When they hit the final pose, Mateo's gleaming eyes met his. "Ready to dance?"

Archer nodded. *Dance? If you want, I could fly.*

* * *

When Archer woke up the next morning, the dull ache around his eye was an instant reminder of what had happened last night. For a hot minute under the dazzling stage lights, he had thought they were going to pull it off. The extended tango duet he and Mateo pieced together was flawless . . . and scorching hot. Then Dominik started bleeding again. Betty fainted. Caleb cried through the samba. Half the routines fell apart as they had to deal with those disasters on the fly. Then Archer blanked on the back half of the paso, so Mateo had to drag him through the steps. The rest of the troupe was either embarrassed or mad or worried throughout, and it did not lead to many smiles. The audience seemed baffled, tittering at first when they thought the goofs were part of the show, then descending into awkward silence, and finally, the worst insult of all, pitying applause.

After the second show, which went marginally better, Archer had looked around for Mateo but there was no sign of him. "Did Mateo leave?" he asked Betty, who was sprawled on a row of chairs with a cold cloth over her eyes.

"Yes, he said he was—and I'm quoting—'fucking done.'"

Archer's heart sank with those leaden words. *Oh.* He had imagined the heat, of course. Mateo was a pro. He had had to find a way for the show to go on, so he did. That was it.

"Fuck," Archer mumbled, now into his pillow. *Such an idiot.* Then *Fuck* again when he saw he had a text waiting from Mateo. He swiped it open, breath held.

> **Let me know when you're up. I'd like to talk.**

His stomach heaved. Was there anything worse than *We need to talk* without any context? His brain spun with possibilities, each more outlandish than the last. *He blames me for what happened with Ben and Caleb. He needs to explain why he hates me forever. He wants to kick my ass. He's going to make sure I never get another dancing job as long as I live . . .*

> **I wanted to say again how sorry I am for what happened,**

Mateo, he started typing. **So, so, so sorry. I understand if you hate me**—he stopped, staring at his words. *Jesus, Archer.* He deleted it all and tried again. **Hi, I'm up. When/where do you want to meet?**

Dining hall in thirty?

See you then.

* * *

Archer grabbed only coffee and a bagel, knowing his stomach was too worked up for him to eat much. Mateo was waiting with a mug at a small table in the back corner. He had dark circles under his eyes and looked like he'd barely slept all night. Archer imagined he looked much the same. Plus a black eye.

"I'm so sorry—" Archer started saying as he sat, right when Mateo spoke.

"Archer, I—"

They both stopped.

"You go," Archer said, swallowing down the urge to babble. His heart hammered.

Mateo took a deep breath. "I'm sorry."

Archer blinked. *"You're* sorry? For what?"

"For lumping you in with Caleb. That was really unfair of me. You're not Caleb, and it wasn't the same thing, at all."

Archer shook his head. "No, I never should have said anything to him—"

"Archer. It's okay. How could you possibly have known that he would turn around and do what he did? That's low, even for Caleb."

"Still, I fucked up. I'm so sorry that I told him anything at all, even though I was only trying to defend you."

"I know you were."

Archer willed his heartbeat to slow down, because the thudding pulse was distracting. *It's okay*, he said to himself as he took a deep breath. He met Mateo's eyes. They both smiled. His cheeks flushed as his gaze dropped to Mateo's long fingers wrapped around his coffee mug.

"Are you okay?" Archer asked. "Having that story out?"

Mateo shrugged. "I already went through it once. This is more of the same."

"Yeah, but . . . God, I can't imagine having personal shit like that in the news."

Mateo nodded then paused, looking like he was debating if he should say the next thing or not. "I reached out to Abby."

"You did?"

"Yeah." He blinked, eyes watery. "I've spent so long trying to block out that part of my life, but this made me realize I never made things right with her. And now her name is in the press again, because of me."

"Because of *me*," Archer said.

Mateo sighed. "Because of Caleb."

"Did you talk to her?"

"Briefly. I apologized—for now and for back then—and asked if she would like a public apology, too. She said no, she doesn't want to fan the flames. But . . . she's in New York filming right now and actually asked if we could meet up for coffee sometime."

Archer blew out the breath he'd been holding. "That's great, Mateo. That must have been hard."

"I should have done it sooner, but I've had my head up my ass a little bit. Guess I can thank Caleb for yanking it out."

Archer laughed. "Now that's an image."

Mateo smiled, but then it slid from his face. "Why do you think he did it?" he asked quietly, almost as if he was wondering to himself.

"I think he was trying to get back at me."

"No." Mateo leaned forward, shaking his head. "That might have been part of it, but ultimately it had to be about me."

"Either way, I'm sure he feels terrible about it now." Archer took a sip of his coffee.

Amusement flashed in Mateo's eyes. "Typical Archer, still seeing the best in people."

"Oh, well . . ." Archer ducked his head. "I mean, I dated him for a while, he can't be a total monster, right?"

Another flash. "If you say so."

They talked until their cups were drained. "Can I get you another one?" Archer asked, standing. "Cream and a half sugar?"

Mateo nodded. "Sure, thanks."

When Archer returned, he slid Mateo's coffee to him and sat down again.

"How do you know my coffee order?" Mateo asked, before he blew on it.

"Uh . . ." *Shit.* "The same way I knew you don't require much sleep."

"Which is . . . ?"

"This is embarrassing." Archer slapped a hand over his eyes. "But . . . I think it was called *Crush*?" Archer's face burned. "Some silly teen magazine. You were a 'heartthrob of the month' once. They had your answers to all kinds of little questions like that."

Mateo looked horrified. "Oh God."

"Yeah, I know. Like I said, silly." Archer busied himself

taking a gulp of the steaming coffee, ignoring how it was slightly too hot to drink.

"And you remember my coffee order?"

"Yup." No need to tell Mateo how many times he'd read it.

Mateo looked thoughtful. "What else was in there?"

"Let's see . . ." Archer shifted and their knees bumped under the table. He wiggled away. "It also said your favorite color is blue, your dream vacation is Paris, and your pet peeve is when people don't say how they really feel."

There was a pause, Mateo's eyebrow climbing. "When people don't say how they feel?"

Archer shrugged. "Apparently."

Mateo snorted. "I can guarantee you I never said anything like that. Also, my favorite color is not blue."

"What is it?"

Mateo's eyes flicked down to his own shirt, a soft, faded cherry red. "This color."

"It looks great on you."

"Thanks. This is my lucky shirt."

"I see. Trying to get lucky, are you?" Archer instantly regretted his stupid joke, cringing internally. *Why, Archer? Why?*

Mateo blushed and shifted. Their knees bumped again. Neither of them moved away this time. "Um . . ."

"Sorry. Ignore me." Archer shook his head. "That was dumb."

"It's fine." They took a sip in silence. "I would love to go to Paris, though," Mateo added, with a very kind topic change.

"Oh, same! Pain au chocolat for breakfast every day . . . er, and the museums, too, of course."

Mateo laughed. "Of course."

They chatted a while longer, finishing their second cups, and then Archer left the dining hall smiling, face and heart warm. There was only one thing still weighing him down. He headed straight back to the dorm and found the right room. He knocked.

"Hey, Steve," he said when the door opened. "Can I talk to Caleb?"

The hulking man peered down at him, frowning. Then his face relaxed into a smile. "That would be great, Archer, thanks. He's been a mess. I'll leave you to it."

Archer poked his head into the dim, silent room. "Caleb?"

"Come in," the heap under the blankets sniffled.

Archer padded in and perched on the edge of Caleb's bed. "Are you okay?"

"Don't be nice to me," Caleb muttered. "That makes it so much worse."

Archer tugged at his blanket. "Can you come out from under there?"

Caleb emerged, bleary-eyed.

"So. You and Ben, hey?"

Caleb nodded and wiped an eye. "Yeah. But I swear nothing happened until you broke up with me. I was so fucking miserable that night, and we ended up walking back to the dorm together. He helped me move my stuff and, well . . . He was just trying to console me . . ."

Archer considered the day Caleb and Ben had spent alone in the woods, and all the other times they somehow ended up next to each other. "It wasn't out of nowhere though, was it?"

Caleb stiffened. "I didn't cheat on you, if that's what you're suggesting."

"No. But Ben cheated on Beau."

Caleb traced the pattern on his blanket with a finger. "Ben said it was basically over. He was going to break up with Beau at the end of the season. He was only waiting because he didn't want to cause any more drama."

"Ha!" A sharp bark of laughter escaped from Archer's throat. "Didn't want to cause any more drama."

"Yeah." Caleb let out a dark chuckle. "Oops."

"You've liked Ben all summer, though, haven't you?" Archer asked gently.

"Yeah." Caleb met his eyes. "But I liked you too, I swear!"

"I know, Caleb." Archer sighed. "I guess they've broken up now?"

"They did. Ben texted me. They were up half the night talking. It's over. For real, for real."

"God." Archer rubbed his forehead. "What a mess. Are you and Ben still . . . ?"

Caleb shook his head. "Not for now. It's too complicated. Ben wants to be more respectful of Beau and what they had."

Archer nodded. "Probably for the best."

"I'm so sorry, Archer," Caleb blurted. "For what I did to Mateo and you."

Archer nodded. "Thank you. That was really shitty. Mostly for Mateo, though. And probably Abby. You can't mess with people's lives like that, Caleb."

"I know." A tear slipped down Caleb's cheek.

"You owe Mateo an apology, too."

Caleb nodded. "I will. I'll talk to him before the show."

A question tickled at him. "Why did you do it, Caleb?"

"Fuck, I—" He stopped, wiping at the next tear. "I'm so fucking jealous of Mateo, okay? And he had it all, then he threw it away, and . . . why would someone do that? It's not fair!"

"What? You don't even care about the show here! And you're jealous of him being on *Broadway*?"

"I do care about the show, Archer!" Caleb exploded. "Of course, I do! But my parents think it's a joke, that I'm a joke. I work in their studio, and every day it's a reminder for them that I haven't done anything with my life. So it's easier for me if I just have fun here and don't take it too seriously while I'm disappointing them."

"Caleb . . ." Archer reached out to put a hand on his knee.

"And not only did Mateo get to have it all, be a Broadway star, he got you, too. I guess I wanted to hurt both of you."

Archer's cheeks flushed. "He didn't 'get' me."

"Oh, please," Caleb said, eyes rolling so far back in his head his pupils disappeared. "You two are so fucking hot for each other it's not even funny. It's so obvious, Archer."

His eyes widened. "It is?"

"Ha! Look at you blushing."

"I am not." He definitely was. "And I really don't think Mateo is interested in me. He's here to do a job."

"A job that involves practically fucking you onstage."

"What!" Archer laughed and swung a pillow at Caleb. "It does not."

Caleb laughed too, blocking it with a forearm. "I'm saying, it's a good job."

Archer's heart warmed seeing Caleb smiling again.

"Seriously, though . . ." Caleb's eyes were earnest as his smile grew sad again. "I keep trying to tell you, Archer. There's more to life than work. Sometimes . . . sometimes hearts get in the way, don't they?"

21

So Now What Do We Do?

Archer was searching helplessly through his locker for the shoes for his hip-hop costume when Mateo leaned against the lockers next to him.

"So . . . Caleb apologized to me," Mateo said, sliding his hands into his pockets.

Archer looked up, stomach fluttering at the sight before him. God, Mateo was fucking *handsome*. First of all, his hip-hop costume was painfully sexy—dark jeans, an indecently tight bordering-on-translucent white tank top, and an unzipped black hoodie over it. At one point in the show, Mateo ripped that hoodie off and threw it to the side. That part always got Archer's heart pumping a little faster. But now, with Mateo staring at him, he also had to contend with those full lips and with those dark eyes burrowing into his . . .

Archer cleared his throat. "That's good to hear. How did it go?" Then he flushed, wondering if Caleb said the same thing to Mateo about them fucking onstage.

"Good . . . I guess." Mateo ran a hand through his hair, exposing a strip of washboard abs over his low-slung jeans that Archer did not stare at. "I kind of get what he was thinking. I'm mad at me, too."

"You're a really good person," Archer blurted. "I mean, forgiving him like that."

Mateo looked away, blinking. "I'm not sure many people would agree that I'm a good person."

"Hey." Archer placed a hand on Mateo's forearm. "I know you are."

Mateo swallowed hard, then his gaze swung back to Archer's. "So now what do we do?"

"Uh—" Archer stammered, pulse thrumming, eyes on Mateo's lips. *Kiss?*

"I feel like I need to say something after the disaster last night, rally the troops or something," Mateo continued, sighing. "I don't know . . . Despite what Eileen thinks, I'm not sure I'm the leader they need."

"Listen," Archer replied after a pause, relieved he hadn't answered Mateo's question out loud. "You know that feeling you had when you were dancing alone on the stage that time? Before I interrupted?"

"Yeah?"

"That's it. That feeling. You love dancing. Your *soul* is dancing. You need to share that with the others. They need to feel that love."

Their eyes met again. Mateo seemed to be searching for something in Archer's gaze. Then he nodded. "Thank you, Archer."

"For what?"

"For being you."

Archer floundered, unable to make any words leave his tongue, as Mateo whirled and spoke to the room. "Everyone grab a seat. Let's talk."

They were all there, even Ben and Beau, who sat on op-posite sides of the room, both of them far from Caleb.

"I just wanted to say," Mateo started, once everyone was settled, "how proud I am of all of you. Last night went to shit, let's be honest. And yet, here you all are, ready to go back out there."

The other dancers shifted in their chairs, sitting a little taller. Archer's heart swelled as Mateo continued.

"We have some things we need to sort out, for sure. Ben, Beau, it must be hard for you, but we appreciate that you're here. There's been a lot going on for all of us, so let's take a minute right now. I want you all to close your eyes and think of a time when you were dancing and you were happy. *Really* happy."

The room stilled as everyone—even Caleb—closed their eyes. Archer shut his too and thought about dancing their pas de deux in the moonlit clearing.

"Really feel it—when there was nothing but you and music and joy," Mateo continued. "*That's* the feeling I want you to remember. That feeling is why we're all here. You are *all* amazing dancers, every single one of you, and I know we can put on a good show tonight. Right?"

"Right," most of them replied in murmured agreement.

"So . . ." He looked over at Archer and smiled. "Let's fucking dance."

"Good job," Archer whispered to him after the other dancers scattered. "Look at you, leading."

Mateo shrugged, the corner of his mouth lifting. "I asked myself what you would say."

Archer's stomach flipped on his way to go find his damn shoes.

Was the show perfect? No. There was still some tension

between Beau and Ben, not to mention Caleb. At least twice, Archer had been prepared to drag those two apart based on the looks Beau was throwing. But, in the end, no one cried or fainted or bled, so it was miles better than the night before. The troupe agreed to gather at ten o'clock the next day for a meeting and rehearsal so they could talk about any adjustments that needed to be made and to polish up the choreo.

Archer was surprised and also somehow not when they arrived in the greenroom the next morning and saw Stewart talking animatedly to Mateo, Judy tucked under his arm.

"Stewart! You're back. Again." Archer hugged him and gave Judy a scritch behind the ears.

"Archer, darling." Stewart squeezed his arm. "How lovely to see you." He greeted the rest of the group as they hugged him and fussed over Judy before taking seats around the room.

"We missed you," Archer said to Stewart, adding *and that's putting it mildly* in his head. He wondered if Stewart had heard about the dumpster fire he had run out on.

"Oh, I'm so sorry, it was an emergency that required my immediate attention. We've settled the matter, but it put Judy out of sorts, didn't it, Judy?" Judy licked at his hand. He patted her head as he continued. "We needed some time to recover. I hope things didn't go too badly after"— his voice dropped to a whisper—"the breakup."

"Uh . . ." Mateo hemmed, exchanging glances with Archer. "What was it you wanted to tell us, anyway?" he asked.

"Did I not tell you before I left?" Stewart frowned. "How odd."

"Well, the . . ." Archer waved a vague hand around the room. ". . . and then you left. I hope the emergency wasn't too serious?"

"Oh, yes, that's right. Would you believe that Judy's food supplier up and moved to Canada? Ridiculous! Just when I found a suitable organic high-protein whole-meat, whole-grain food with glucosamine and probiotics, they relocated! And they canceled the rest of my orders, if you can believe it. Anyway, I spent half the night on the phone, but it's all sorted now. They're going to charge me an arm and a leg for shipping, of course, but Judy's worth every penny, aren't you, my darling?"

"Stewart. What was the news?" Mateo asked patiently.

"Oh, yes. I'm terribly sorry." He cleared his throat, and the few bits of chitchat around the circle quieted as everyone paused to listen. "I have been informed, from the most reliable of sources—you may know Cici McLannister, I directed her in *The Sound of Music* in '92, she made a lovely Maria, if not a touch platitudinous on occasion . . ." He paused for dramatic effect, relishing the rapt attention he had. "Cici's agent told her that Breckon Galloway is coming to our end-of-season show."

There was a collective gasp. "Breckon Galloway?" Caleb repeated. "You're kidding!"

Everyone knew who Breckon Galloway was, of course. Producer of last summer's smash hit, *Great Scott!*, a musical adaptation of *Back to the Future* told from Doc Brown's perspective, which was still almost impossible to get tickets for.

"He's coming here?" Dominik said, voice climbing an octave. "No fucking way!"

The room swelled with excited chatter.

"We need to do something extra special," Dominik said over the hum. "Blow his mind."

Mateo was watching Archer thoughtfully. "What about Archer's idea?"

"Which idea?" Archer asked.

"When we got that bad review for *Around the World*, you suggested adding acro."

"Oh, that was only a thought, we don't have to—"

"It was a great idea. Let's put together a whole new show for the final night. Eva Stiff will do a few numbers, and we can do our best pieces, plus a new acro routine."

"Love it!" Dominik said. "Sounds so fun." A chorus of voices joined in agreement.

"It'll be extra rehearsal," Mateo warned them.

Not one person protested, although a few cast sidelong looks at Caleb.

"Sounds good to me," Caleb said pointedly. "Let's do it."

"Brilliant!" Stewart said, with a thump of his cane on the floor. "We'll run through all of the shows today and tomorrow, then on Sunday we can start planning our finale."

They got right into a rehearsal of *Around the World*, but Archer found time to sidle up to Beau during a water break. "Hey, Beau . . . you doing okay?" he asked.

Beau offered a weak smile. "Not really. Three years, Archer. We've been together—we *were* together—for three years. To have it end like this—so abruptly, and publicly . . . with *Caleb*. I mean, God. I punched Ben!" He shook his head, blinking back a new wave of tears. "Then again . . . it wasn't that abrupt, was it? If I'm being honest with myself, he's been slipping away for a while. Maybe that's why I was holding on so hard."

"I'm sorry, Beau. That sucks." Archer slid an arm around Beau's shoulders and gave him a hug.

Beau rested his head briefly on Archer's shoulder. "Yeah."

"Is there anything I can do?"

"I don't think so. But I appreciate you asking."

"Are you going to be okay dancing with him for another month? Maybe we could rework the pairs—"

"No." Beau shook his head. "No, it's fine. I'm a grown-up. And Ben and I dance so well together." Another weak smile. "I hope that doesn't change, at least."

Archer gave him another hug. *Sometimes hearts get in the way.*

* * *

There was a hum of excitement in the air when they gathered on the stage on Sunday.

"What pieces do we want to include in our finale?" Mateo asked, uncapping a whiteboard marker. "Let's make sure we showcase everyone's strengths."

"Your pas de deux, of course," Betty piped up. "Write that down."

Mateo nodded, a smile twitching at the corner of his mouth. "Okay."

"All the tango duets!" Dominik called.

"Bollywood!"

"The hustle."

"Ben and Beau's paso."

"*Grease!*"

Mateo scribbled down the rapid-fire suggestions. Archer grinned, watching the excitement on his face. Stewart sat in his customary seat in the front row, sipping his tea and nodding wisely.

"Now what about acro, Archer?" Mateo asked when they had a list of more than enough numbers for the big show. "Where do we start?"

"Me?"

Mateo's eyes crinkled. "It was your idea, and you have more experience than most of us."

"Alright, well . . . We should probably start by figuring out who are the bases and who are the tops—Dominik, stop!" Archer cut off Dominik, whose mouth was already open for a tops joke.

Caleb snickered.

"Fine," Dominik muttered. "It was a good one, though."

Once they were paired off—Archer was with Betty—he reviewed toe pitches, where the base took the top's foot in their hands and boosted them up into the air, then braced them as they landed. It wasn't long until everyone had the hang of it, and they progressed into handstands and other more advanced skills.

He left the theater a few hours later feeling better than he had in weeks, but got a mild pang when he saw he had a text from Lynn. **Time for a call?** He realized he hadn't talked to her since right after he and Caleb broke up. She answered after only one ring.

"Archer! Hi, boo! How are you? How are things?"

"I miss you, Lynnie! And, well . . ." Archer flipped through the events of the last week and a half in his head. "How much time do you have?"

"I'm on the couch with a full glass of wine and have nowhere to be. Talk."

So he found a bench down by the water and told her the whole story—the ugly and public breakup with Caleb, *The Broadway Broad*, and the subsequent disaster show—bleeding, fainting, black eyes and all.

"Oh my God, Archer. That's insane! I'm sorry about Caleb and the whole mess. Are things better now?"

Mateo's relaxed and open face came to mind. "They're good," Archer said. "Really, really good."

"And . . . Mateo?"

Archer smiled like an idiot into the phone. "Well . . . we're definitely friends."

"Just friends?"

"Yes," he replied firmly. "Just friends. I've learned my lesson. I don't want to fuck anything up by hooking up with someone else."

"Yeah, that's fair. I'm glad you're friends, though."

"Me too." He stretched his legs out and thought about Mateo's hands on his waist last night during their pas de deux. *Friends.* "What's new with you? Did you ever figure out your trip with Sasha?"

"As a matter of fact, yes! That's one of the reasons I wanted to talk."

"So? Where are you going?"

"I found the most amazing resort in the Catskills! They had a cancellation, so we were able to get in for a weekend at the end of August."

"Which resort?"

Lynn laughed. "Shady Queens, dummy!"

Archer gasped. "You're coming here?"

"Yes!"

"That's amazing! Oh my God, I can't wait to see you!"

Lynn giggled. "I'm excited too. I finally get to propose to Sasha!"

"It's going to be so great. I'm imagining a candlelit dinner with the sunset behind you . . ."

Lynn squealed. "Right? And I'm dying to meet Mateo and Caleb and everyone."

"Hmm. You'll behave yourself, won't you?"

"Of course, Archer, darling. How dare you suggest otherwise?"

* * *

Acro rehearsals went better than expected. Every dancer could do a back walkover, and several were also able to pull off aerials or back handsprings. They had lots to work with, and a flashy routine started coming together. Dominik lobbied hard for a Taylor Swift song, and they went with "Shake It Off."

Archer laughed at Dominik twerking in celebration, cheered when Gage lifted Grace up with a toe pitch so she was standing on his hands for the first time, and took a moment to admire the way Mateo's biceps bulged while he balanced River above him in a handstand.

Archer was smiling as he and Mateo stepped into the early August sunshine on their way to grab dinner before the *Around the World* show that night.

"Archer, Mateo!" Eileen waited for them at the stage door. She was cooling herself with a paper fan, painted with delicate cherry blossoms.

"Eileen!" Archer hugged her. "How are you? We haven't seen you for a while."

"Yes, indeed." She smiled and fluttered her fan. "I met a lovely woman from Texas who was staying with her sister's family here for a couple weeks. We spent quite a lot of time together."

"That's great," Archer said, exchanging a knowing glance with Mateo. "I'm happy for you."

"How has it been for you two? I heard something about someone passing out on stage last week?"

"Oh . . ." Archer looked at Mateo and chuckled. "We had a few bumps, but it's all okay now, isn't it?"

Mateo's smile was like the sun. "It is," he agreed.

Archer savored the bass in Mateo's voice and the sparkle in his eye.

"Would you two like to come for tea again?" Eileen asked. "I'd love to hear more about how things have been, beyond the fainting."

"That sounds great," Archer said.

"An evening tea, perhaps," she said, blotting her forehead with her sleeve. "Avoid the worst of this blasted afternoon heat."

"Actually . . ." Mateo paused. "Would it be too much to ask if *all* of the dancers came for tea? Archer and I will help," he added hurriedly, "with the baking and setup and cleanup and everything. But I think it would be really nice if everyone could come."

The urge to touch Mateo's arm was overwhelming, so he did. "That's an amazing idea." The spark he felt each time their skin touched was only growing stronger.

Eileen tilted her head up and smiled at them. "*Hell* of an idea. Let's do it. Sunday?"

"Sunday."

Archer and Mateo tracked down some extra folding tables from the dining hall and set them up in front of Eileen's cabin Sunday morning. They also borrowed a carafe for hot water and some extra mugs. They spent the afternoon in her kitchen making food—cucumber sandwiches, blueberry scones, and petits fours. Eileen even made some gluten-free vegan fudge to make sure everyone had a treat, but Mateo was all over the rest of the baking.

"The trick to fluffy scones," he explained to Archer, "is using frozen butter."

"Oh, is it?" Archer replied seriously, trying not to smile at the smudge of flour Mateo had on his forehead and his overall aproned adorableness. "And you have frozen butter, do you?"

Mateo turned and rummaged into Eileen's freezer, then triumphantly pulled out a foil-wrapped brick. "You do when you plan ahead."

Archer wanted to giggle. "Wow."

Mateo's eyes narrowed. "Are you laughing at me, Archer Read?"

"Me?" Archer pressed a hand to his chest and batted his eyes. "I would never, Mr. Dixon."

"Good. Fluffy scones are no joke." Mateo unwrapped the butter and pulled a cheese grater out of a cupboard.

"And why do you have a cheese grater?" Archer fought the urge to slide his arms around Mateo's waist and rest his chin on that broad shoulder while he worked.

"For the frozen butter, of course. Keep up, Archer!"

Their laughter filled the small kitchen as they worked, hips bumping when Mateo reached into the bowl to show Archer how to mix the butter into the dry ingredients. "You want it to be coarse like this, see?" The way Mateo's hands squeezed the dough gave Archer ideas that were entirely inappropriate for the situation.

Archer studied Mateo's face instead. "Got it."

Eileen bustled around making the sandwiches, and Archer had no idea why she winked at him when Mateo took Archer's hands to help him properly knead the dough.

The tea party was a smashing success. As Archer carried another loaded tray outside, he paused on the step to look at the scene before him. Sixteen happy faces, laughing, eating, drinking, bathed in the pink and orange sky and scent of primroses. Eileen threw back her head, giggling at something Dominik said, then she leaned over to murmur a few words to Betty. Even Beau and Ben were smiling broadly while Caleb chatted with Grace and Seta.

Amid the hum, Mateo looked up at Archer and smiled.

Archer smiled back, his heart thudding.

Just friends, he told himself. *Just friends.*

Fuck.

22

All I Ask of You

"Archer!" Betty announced when he took his seat next to her again. "Eileen has a karaoke machine!"

"Okay?" Archer chuckled, helping himself to yet another scone. "And we're excited about this?"

"I love karaoke!" Betty exclaimed. "And it happens to be my birthday on Wednesday." She waggled her eyebrows. "Eileen said we could borrow it for a little party. And," she turned to Eileen and gripped her arm, "you have to come! Wednesday night, after the second show. Please?"

"Of course, if you want an old woman—"

"Yes, I do! Definitely."

"Very well." Eileen's face shone. "I'll be there."

Later, when they were back in Eileen's tiny kitchen cleaning up, Archer mentioned Betty's birthday to Mateo. "I think I'm going to head into town on Wednesday to get some stuff for a party. Do you want to come?" The invitation flowed easily from his lips, but sent his pulse fluttering.

"Sure," Mateo said casually, rinsing off a platter. "Sounds fun."

So that was how the two of them came to be hopping onto the Shady Queens shuttle together Wednesday morning. *Just friends,* Archer said to himself as he climbed on behind Mateo, taking in the curve of his butt and sculpted calves. *Not a date. But God, he's hot.*

They waved to Mrs. C, who was driving, and sat together in the first row. When a large, sunburned man clambered on after them to grab the last seat, Archer had to scoot over to the middle so he was right up against Mateo's bare arm, smelling his freshly applied aftershave. Then they were on their way, bouncing down the gravel drive.

"Do you like karaoke?" Archer asked, ignoring the jolts of electricity each time their legs bumped together. "Betty's so excited for it."

Mateo gave him a wry look. "I don't really do karaoke."

"Why not? You're an amazing singer." He felt like an idiot as soon as he said it. The man fucking headlined two Broadway shows. He didn't need some schmo from Ohio telling him that.

Mateo's eyebrow climbed even farther up his forehead. "When I get up there, people have expectations. Then they either think I suck, and I've let them down, or they're impressed, and they want me to do ten more songs. Of course, sometimes people have no idea who I am, but feel the need to approach me and tell me I should be a singer, and then it's awkward, like 'Well, actually . . .'" He shrugged. "I'd prefer to avoid all that."

"Yeah, that makes sense. Although I still hope you'll sing tonight? With just your friends around?"

Mateo avoided the question with a shrug. "What about you? Do you like karaoke?"

"Sure, it's fun. Lynn loves it too. I get up there with

her sometimes. She always wants to duet 'Paradise by the
Dashboard Light.'"

To Archer's delight, Mateo laughed at that. "Excellent
song choice. That would be fun for karaoke."

"Maybe you'll sing it with me tonight?" Archer wanted
to kick himself as soon as he said it. What the fuck was he
thinking, asking to duet with Mateo Dixon?

Mateo studied him for a moment. "Maybe."

"I mean . . . you don't have to," Archer backtracked.
"I'm not that good."

"I don't care how good you are," Mateo said. "And
you're right, it will be different with friends."

"Okay," Archer said. "If you want to." He took a deep
breath and tried to relax. Their legs touched the rest of the
trip.

Mrs. C dropped them off in the square by the general
store, and they went in there first to get a card, snacks, and
decorations. Their next stop was the vintage boutique to
pick out a gift. Archer found a kimono cardigan he knew
Betty would love—black with pink flowers—and Mateo
bought her a straw hat with a pink band that matched the
cardigan.

Finally, the Hallfield bakery. Archer hadn't been inside
the last time, but he remembered the mouthwatering smell
from when he walked by. The place was packed with sweaty
tourists, giving them plenty of time to browse the cases while
they waited for their turn. As per Hallfield's claim to fame,
there was a whole display case of pies. Archer hovered, trying not to drool.

"Does Betty like blueberry pie?" Mateo asked with a
playful nudge. "Or is this for you?"

Archer chuckled. "I'm tempted! But you're right, let's

look at the cupcakes." Archer took Mateo's arm and pulled him over to the next display case, which proved an effective distraction from the pies.

There were at least ten different types of cupcakes of all colors of the rainbow. Archer hemmed and hawed, trying to make up his mind. "Chocolate fudge, vanilla cream, strawberry cheesecake . . . Oh, man, how do we choose?" he moaned.

"Easy," Mateo said, nodding at the worker waiting to take their order. "We get some of each."

They left with two dozen cupcakes, although Archer already knew his favorite would be the chocolate fudge with rainbow frosting. Out on the sidewalk, he carefully balanced the boxes to check the time. "We still have half an hour until the next shuttle. Was there anywhere else you wanted to go?"

Mateo looked toward the park on one side of the square. Children squealed as they played in the spray from the fountain, and a stand by the entrance advertised ice-cold, freshly squeezed lemonade. "Do you want to go check out the park?"

"Yes. Love that idea."

They strolled toward the green space, Archer holding the cupcake boxes like they were made of glass.

"You got those okay?" Mateo asked.

Archer nodded, biting his lip. "Yeah, but I'm a little freaked out that I'm going to drop them."

"Here, give me your other bags," Mateo said, reaching for the handles.

"Thanks," Archer said, tingling when their fingertips touched. He knew it was ridiculous, because they were wrapped around each other on stage all the time, but this felt different, out shopping, just another couple in a happy, summer crowd. So much like a date. *Not a date*, he reminded himself again.

Mateo stopped when they got to the lemonade stand. "Can I get you one?"

Not a date. "Oh, yes, please."

After he paid, Mateo carried their drinks over to a shaded bench.

Archer set the yellow boxes tied with white string between them and frowned thoughtfully. "Would it be bad if we ate two of these before the party? Twenty-two is enough, right?"

"Well . . ." Mateo bent down and pulled a small box out of one of his shopping bags. "I thought you might say that." He opened the box to reveal two of the rainbow chocolate fudge cupcakes.

Archer's jaw dropped. "You . . . are my new favorite person. I didn't even notice you buying those!"

Mateo looked pleased with himself. "I saw the way you were looking at them. I snuck another order in when they were packing up the first one. Here." He handed Archer one of the cupcakes, then pulled the other out.

Archer peeled off the crinkly gold wrapper and licked his lips. "It's so beautiful I almost don't want to ruin it." He was also aware that there was no way to eat this without getting icing all over his face.

"Cupcakes are meant to be eaten," Mateo said, then opened wide and took a big bite. The rainbow icing left a smear over his lips. Mateo laughed and licked it off.

Archer took a bite of his too, taste buds humming at the rich fudge flavor and burst of vanilla sweetness from the frosting. "Oh my God," he mumbled through a mouthful. "This is incredible."

"Mm-hmm," Mateo agreed, licking icing off his finger.

"So good." He took another bite, then jammed the rest of it in his mouth. He laughed, wiping at his chin. "I've got icing everywhere, don't I?"

"Kind of." Archer giggled.

Mateo wiped at his face again. "Did I get it all?"

"You have a tiny bit of pink . . ." Archer reached for the corner of Mateo's mouth, but then he realized what he was doing. His fingers froze an inch from Mateo's face.

Mateo's tongue slid out and licked along his lip. "How about now?"

"Um . . ." Archer's brain tripped over the thought of what else Mateo's tongue might want to lick. "Almost . . . There you go."

Mateo grinned. "Worth the mess though."

Archer finished his too, then they sat in a comfortable silence, sipping their lemonade and watching the passersby. Two young men, maybe eighteen or nineteen, caught his eye. They were sitting on the edge of the fountain, laughing and eating soft pretzels. One of them leaned over and pecked the other on the cheek. The man looked surprised for a moment, then kissed him back. Archer's heart twinged.

"Things okay with you and Caleb now?" Mateo asked, startling Archer out of his thoughts.

"What? Oh, yes. I think so? I don't know. I mean, it's a little awkward, but . . . he knows he messed up. And he's trying."

Mateo leaned back, nodding. "That's good. I feel like he's trying more with me, too. He offered to write another email to *The Broadway Broad* asking them to retract but . . ." Mateo shrugged. "What's done is done. And I'm old news now. I don't think anyone actually cared this time."

Archer wanted to reach over the yellow boxes to pat

Mateo's hand, but instead he fiddled with his empty lemonade cup. "That's good. People have moved on, I guess."

Mateo straightened the string on the box and squinted into the bright morning light. "Yeah, maybe."

They caught the shuttle, chatting easily on the way back about fine-tuning their finale, then got to work getting ready for the party. After stashing their supplies in the cabin, their first stop was picking up the karaoke machine from Eileen's.

"Why do you have a karaoke machine here anyway?" Archer asked her as he and Mateo hefted it between them.

Eileen gave him a withering stare. "What do you mean, why? It's coming in handy right this minute, isn't it?"

Archer laughed at her wink. "You're right, you're right. I'm sorry I asked. We'll see you tonight!"

They stopped by the theater to snag a couple mic stands from the storage room, then went back to the cabin. Archer set up the karaoke in a corner while Mateo started blowing up balloons. They put up a few colorful bunches around the room and dug in the cupboard for the leftover supplies from Archer's party.

"When's your birthday?" Archer asked, as he shook out the polka-dot tablecloth.

"October," Mateo said, helping him spread it out.

"October what?" Archer asked.

"Why, are you going to show up at my apartment with some balloons?"

"I might," Archer said with a sideways glance. "Maybe even a cake, if you play your cards right."

"Hmm." Mateo pretended to consider. "The twenty-sixth."

Archer made a show of putting it into his calendar. "Okay. I'll be there."

"Great. I'll be waiting."

Archer cleared his throat, suddenly finding the room stifling. To be fair, the AC was struggling to keep up with the heat. "Deal. Now where did we put the rest of the napkins?"

* * *

Dominik, of course, was the self-appointed karaoke MC and first to grab the mic. He had paired his Hawaiian shorts and turquoise tank top with a black blazer for the occasion. "Good evening, all you shady queens." His voice boomed around the room. A bunch of the other employees turned to give him their attention, too. "I'd like to bring up a lady who I know needs no introduction. Birthday girl, get up here!"

He led the crowd in "Happy Birthday to You" as Betty, already a few drinks in, bounced to the front and took the mic from him. "Thank you, Dominik. I'll be kicking things off tonight with a song that is deeply personal to me." She nodded at Harley, who had the iPad. "Hit it."

Archer's mouth fell open as she began to sing. Betty was a rock star. She absolutely *belted* her way through "I Love Myself Today" by Bif Naked.

"Girl, you can *sing*," he told her when she was done. "That was awesome."

"Thanks, Archie. Now your turn!"

He threw his best puppy dog eyes at Mateo. "Are you in? Time for 'Paradise'?"

Mateo's gaze flitted around the room, then settled back on Archer. "Sure."

"Yes!" Archer yelped, a few drinks in himself. "Let's go." He gave instructions to Harley, then took Mateo's hand and pulled him up to the mics.

"I guess you usually do Meat Loaf's part," Mateo said. He ran a hand through his hair.

"It's okay, I'll be the woman." Archer grinned. "You always lead, after all. I've got this."

Mateo blew out a breath. "Okay."

He's nervous, Archer realized. "Hey . . . if you don't want—"

"No, I do." Mateo smiled. "It's fine."

"Okay." Archer nodded at Harley.

Archer bopped along to the opening guitar riff, gripping his mic. He'd been so concerned about Mateo he forgot to be nervous himself. Too late now.

Mateo started to sing. His voice was hesitant for the first few notes until Archer smiled at him, nodding. Mateo started tapping the beat on his thigh, and his voice got stronger.

Man, he was a good singer. Archer knew that, of course, but hearing it happen, right here in front of him . . . He was so enamored he almost missed his first line, but managed to hit it in time.

Mateo's eyebrows went up and his smile grew as Archer sang. He nodded, impressed, then jumped in with his part again. A change came over Mateo as Archer watched— suddenly, Mateo was the horny teenage boy in the song, desperate to get laid.

Archer relaxed and started to dance. It really was a glorious song, and he decided to throw himself into his love-me-or-else role. It was not a subtle one, after all.

Mateo played off Archer's energy, channeling Meat Loaf's wide eyes and hair tossing until they were wailing at each other, music crescendoing around them. They were laughing when they finished, sweaty and out of breath.

The audience cheered for them, hooting and clapping as Archer and Mateo took their seats again.

"That was fun." Mateo smiled, wiping his brow. "Thanks for getting me up there."

"That was so good, guys!" Betty whooped. "Archer, you were very convincing as a psycho girlfriend."

He poked her, grinning. "Thanks, you."

The room got louder as others took their turn. Betty sang again—"Barracuda" this time—then even Eileen took a turn with "Cecilia."

Most of them were excellent singers, but no one cared about the ones who weren't, and everyone joined in for a loud, drunken "(I've Had) The Time of My Life."

Betty bounced over as midnight ticked by and dropped onto Archer's lap. "Will you guys *please* sing another duet?" she pleaded. *"Please."*

"What did you have in mind?" Archer asked.

She drew an imaginary marquee with her hand. "A big fat Broadway number! Like, we're talking Andrew Lloyd Webber–big."

Archer looked at Mateo. "I'm game if you are."

"What song?" Mateo asked.

"Hmm, lemme see." Betty stood and reached for the iPad, then scrolled with great concentration. "Ooh! Ooh! Yes! I've got it!"

"Which one?" Archer craned his neck.

She hugged the screen to her chest. "No peeking! You'll find out in a sec." She shooed them up to the mic. "Sing your little hearts out, boys."

He shrugged at Mateo. Mateo shrugged back.

The music started. The drunken dancers whistled and hollered.

"Aw, yeah!" Dominik hooted. "Good choice, Betty!"

Archer's stomach flipped. It was "All I Ask of You" from *The Phantom of the Opera*, an achingly tender love song.

Mateo rolled his eyes, but grinned at Archer. "I'm Raoul?" he asked.

"Guess that makes me Christine." Archer sighed.

Mateo winked at him, then he began to sing. The first words poured out, liquid longing, impossibly smooth and aching. He was instantly in character, looking at Archer like he was deeply in love with him.

Archer wasn't sure if he was going to cry, melt, or explode. Or all three. Mateo's voice was nothing but heat, warming him from the inside out.

Stomach fizzing and heart thrumming, Archer started his part. Christine was a beautiful, soaring soprano, so Archer brought the melody down an octave. He had to improvise on one line that dropped too low but he didn't think anyone noticed the wobble.

Mateo stepped closer as his next turn began. His eyes didn't leave Archer's throughout the next verse.

Then Archer again. He felt a little braver now, tilting his head, letting his eyes close as the emotion swept over him.

Mateo's voice soared on the next verse. Goose bumps swept over Archer's skin, tears prickling the back of his eyes. It was impossibly beautiful. *Mateo* was impossibly beautiful. The song's intensity grew, Raoul and Christine getting closer and closer to proclaiming their love for one another.

Archer's part climbed as the song approached its climax, so he went into a mix of his chest and head voice, his melody sliding over Mateo's when their voices joined. When Raoul and Christine finally sang about love, Archer's heart was pounding so fast it was starting to affect his breathing, but he just managed to hold the last note.

As the song faded, the room erupted. Everyone went absolutely nuts.

Archer looked at Mateo, blinking back the tears that he hadn't noticed had formed, while a feeling washed over him that he'd never felt before, like his skin was too tight and too loose at the same time, barely containing him and about to disintegrate right off his body. Mateo was looking back, eyes shining. A fresh wave of goose bumps stippled Archer's skin. He took a deep breath, willing his heart to slow down. He wanted to cry. And laugh. And throw his arms around Mateo and fucking kiss him.

But Betty jumped on them first, enveloping them both in a hug. "Holy shit!" she howled. "Holy *shit*, you guys! That was . . . that was . . ." She placed a hand over her heart and shook her head. "That was the best birthday present ever. It was like our own private gay *Phantom*. Thank you so much!"

Archer swallowed, throat dry. "You're welcome."

"Seriously, wow. You two—" She looked between them. "You two are special."

Archer clutched the mic stand, room spinning around him.

"Except I think you've ruined the party. No one will want to follow that!" she exclaimed.

But Dominik came to the rescue. "I've got this," he drawled. He plucked the mic from Mateo's hand. "Excuse me, *stud*. You're in my way. Spin that shit," he told Harley.

"I'm Too Sexy" started playing. Dominik strutted around, striking ridiculous poses.

"That checks out." Archer scratched, still vibrating from adrenaline and . . . whatever else it was swirling around inside him. "Drink?" he asked Mateo.

Mateo nodded. "Yes, please." He followed Archer over to the fridge.

Archer rummaged inside, then handed him a bottle of nonalcoholic beer.

Twisting the cap off, Mateo studied him. "So . . . you can sing, too."

Archer scoffed. "Not nearly as well as you."

Mateo laughed. "I don't know about that. The way you reworked the soprano melody into your own range . . . It was flawless."

"Oh—uh—" Archer stammered.

Mateo leaned against the counter. "Thanks for asking me to sing."

"Are you kidding? Thanks for singing with me."

"Archer—" Mateo fiddled with his bottle.

"Yeah?"

He paused. "Nothing." Mateo tapped their drinks together. "Just . . . thanks."

Archer took a long pull of cold beer. There were many words spinning through his head and some emotions he couldn't name. Better keep it simple. He smiled. "You're welcome."

23

Smashed It

"Do you guys want to go for a swim? Or catch the drag show, maybe?" Archer asked Beau and Harley, his latest roommate combination. A sticky Sunday evening stretched ahead of them after a long, hot day of rehearsal, and Archer was ready to unwind a little.

"We can't today!" Harley exclaimed. "It's the volleyball game!"

"The what now?" Archer asked.

"At the end of every season, the dancers play a match. We're allowed to use the courts during the drag show."

"We're playing volleyball? For real?"

"Didn't anyone tell you? Game's at six. It's super fun," Harley insisted. "I promise."

"If you say so," Archer said, reliving his memories from middle school gym class. "Super fun" seemed super unlikely.

When Archer arrived at the court with Beau and Harley, the rest of the crew was mostly already there, milling around in swimsuits. Archer's eyes found Mateo immediately, so hot in small navy blue swim trunks it should be illegal. Dark body hair dusted his chest and made a tantalizing trail below his belly button.

"Okay, what are the teams?" Betty asked, snapping Archer out of his daze.

"I say we split up the tango duet partners," Dominik suggested, "with the height roughly equal on both sides."

"Height? What about the ability to actually play volleyball?"

"Pfft." Dominik waved a hand. "Overrated. Everyone line up with your partner, and I'll divide you into two teams."

Mateo and Archer stood facing each other.

"You any good?" Mateo said, looking Archer up and down.

Archer laughed, gaze flitting over Mateo's pecs. "Nope. You?"

"Captain of my high school team," Mateo said, with a fake polish of his knuckles.

Archer raised an eyebrow. "Really?"

"Alright, middle school," Mateo admitted.

Archer laughed again and pulled a skeptical face. "Do middle school teams even have captains?"

"Okay, fine. I wasn't the captain. But you're still going down."

"Well." Archer took a step closer, meeting Mateo's intense gaze. "We'll see about that."

At first glance, the teams looked unfair, with Mateo's strength and power on the same side as Gage and Dominik's height.

"Wow, look at the team you put together for yourself," Betty noted wryly, studying the group across the net. "Looks totally fair."

"Didn't you play in high school?" Dominik asked Betty. "I should think you can handle us."

"You just said that didn't matter!"

"Fine, you want to swap with me?"

Betty narrowed her eyes. "You know what? No. We're going to destroy you."

"Oh, yeah? Care to make it interesting?"

Archer groaned, aware that he was terrible at volleyball and there was about to be more at stake than bragging rights.

"What did you have in mind?" Betty asked, hands on hips.

An evil grin stretched across Dominik's face. "Best of three. The losing duet partner has to pamper the winner for the day tomorrow, up until the show. Breakfast in bed, massage, whatever they want."

Archer's eyes snapped over to Mateo's. He was looking back. Archer's lips quirked. *Interesting. Here's a bet I don't mind losing.*

Betty snorted. "Deal. I like poached eggs for breakfast, no salt."

Dominik snorted and started putting on a show stretching his shoulders. "Extra salt on mine, love."

Betty shook hands with Dominik, then called her team over to the center of their court. "Okay, things got interesting. I think we all know how much is riding on this game, particularly how insufferable Dominik will become, and all the crazy shit he's going to make me do. I need you to give it your all. Please. For me."

"I apologize in advance—" Archer began.

"Not accepted," Betty snapped. "You're tall and strong and can jump ten feet in the air. I expect a lot from you, Archer."

"Yeah, we can do this," Caleb said, although Archer

noticed him eyeing Ben, his duet partner, on the other side. He suspected that Caleb wouldn't mind losing, either.

"Fuck yeah, we can," Betty agreed. "Hands in for a cheer. 'Dominik sucks' on three."

Betty served first and absolutely drilled one right at Dominik's head. He all but shrieked and threw up his arms to protect his face. The ball careened off his forearm and went flying toward the water.

Betty smiled. "One–nothing," she called. "Could you get the ball for me please, love?"

Betty was . . . well, she was fucking awesome at volleyball, is what she was. She was tiny, so she couldn't help with blocking, but she picked up every goddamn ball that came within twenty feet of her. She was blindingly fast and knew where the ball was going to end up before it got there.

"You're *amazing*," Archer said, slack-jawed, after she chased down another shank out the back of the court, safely returning the ball to the other side with a windmill swing.

"Thanks," she said, panting and brushing sand off her shoulder from her dive. "I played on the state beach volleyball team in high school."

"You did?"

"Yeah." She grinned. "But then I blew out my ankle, and, once I recovered, I decided to stick with dance."

"God. We might just win this thing."

Mateo was pretty good too, which did not surprise Archer much . . . although, to be honest, he was more focused on Mateo's rippling muscles under his warm ocher skin.

When those rippling muscles smashed another ball through his block, Archer smiled and offered Mateo five under the net. "Nice spike," he said.

Mateo smiled and slapped his hand. "Thanks."

"Hey!" Betty scowled. "No fraternizing. And tighten up that block, Read. Your thumbs should be together."

"Yes, ma'am," he said, with a sidelong grin at Mateo and a mock salute for Betty.

They won the first game 25–23 after an argument about whether the ball was in or out. "The beautiful thing about beach," Betty said, stomping over to the line, "is the ball imprint doesn't lie. It was clearly out." She pointed to the mark that was a hair outside the line.

"Fine, if you're going to be technical about it," Dominik grumbled.

But Dominik's team came out swinging for the second game, now knowing what they were up against, and they won 25–21.

"Okay, huddle up," Betty said, after allowing them a brief water break. "I cannot be Dominik's bitch tomorrow, I just can't. So if you've ever cared about anything in your entire life before, I need it to be this game. Archer, listen. You can take Mateo. When you jump to block him, I want you to jump like you *know* you're going to shut him down. That ball is yours. I need some solid penetration."

"Penetration . . . ?"

"Archer. Focus, goddamnit. Get your hands on his side of the net, like right in his face. Can you do that?"

"I'll do my best."

She glared at him.

"I mean, yes," Archer amended. "Absolutely. I can do that."

"That's what I thought." She smacked his butt. "Let's go."

The next time Mateo went up for a hit, Archer jumped, and with all this might, pushed his hands over the net right into Mateo's space, thumbs together, telling himself *I am blocking this ball.*

And he did.

It rebounded off his hands with a satisfying, fleshy thud, slamming into the ground at Mateo's feet.

His team went nuts.

"That's what I'm talking about!" Betty bellowed, throwing her arms around him. "That was amazing!"

Archer had to admit it felt pretty fucking good. Particularly when he glanced over at Mateo, who looked impressed.

"Nice block, Archer," he said, nodding. "Guess I'm going to have to stop taking it easy on you."

"Oh, you were taking it easy, were you? Let's see what you've got, Dixon."

It quickly became the Mateo and Archer Show—Mateo's team set the ball to him whenever they got a chance, and Archer was right there blocking him. Archer got him at least half the time, and by the time they rotated to the back row, they were both grinning and extra sweaty. Once they were both into the front row again, it was tied at 24.

"Cap at 27?" Dominik called.

"Nah. Next point wins," Betty said, collecting the ball for her serve.

"Alright," Dominik sang. "Guess it all comes down to this. No pressure, B."

Betty hammered her serve at him. It wasn't a great pass, but he got it up in the air, and Grace set it to Mateo. Archer lined himself up with Mateo and jumped, pushing his hands forward with everything he had. Mateo swung hard, and the ball slammed into Archer's hands and flew back into Mateo's chest. He flailed at it, but it hit the ground.

"Nooooo!" Dominik cried, collapsing to his knees.

"Yessss!" Betty screamed, launching herself into the air. Her team exploded into cheers, while Dominik's team fell onto the sand, groaning.

"Archer, you beautiful man!" Betty cried, throwing her arms around Archer and kissing his cheek over and over. "You beautiful, *beautiful* man. Oh God, I'm so happy right now."

Dominik sighed, eyes raised to the sky. "Fuck."

"Poached eggs," Betty said, pointing at him. "Soft. Some multigrain toast, please."

The teams gave three cheers then shook hands along the net, Betty's team gloating and making plans for their servants' upcoming day. Mateo and Archer were at the end of their lines.

"Good job," Mateo said, holding Archer's hand longer than required for a handshake. "You really shut me down."

"Betty's a good coach," Archer said, waving off the compliment.

"So . . ." Mateo brushed some sand off his arm. "What can I get you for breakfast?"

"Oh, you don't have to—"

"No, you won the bet." Mateo gave half of an elegant bow. "Let me serve you."

"Er . . ." *Why am I blushing?* "Okay, if you're sure. A coffee and a breakfast sandwich, please . . . but only if you bring your own breakfast to eat with me."

"Deal."

The next day was Archer's best day at Shady Queens so far.

Mateo knocked at his bedroom door at ten o'clock on the nose, as agreed.

"Your breakfast, my lord," he announced, carrying the coffee tray with great ceremony.

Archer sat up, scrubbing his hand through his hair, wishing he had thought to wear a shirt to bed. "Oh, thanks."

Mateo placed Archer's coffee on his bedside table and

handed him his sandwich, then took a seat in the desk chair. He had the same breakfast for himself. The crinkling of the wrappers was loud in the otherwise silent room.

"Yum," Archer said after swallowing his first bite. "They're so good here."

"They are good," Mateo agreed, picking up his coffee. "But not as good as homemade crepes—they're my breakfast specialty."

"Yeah? I love crepes."

"Maybe I'll make them for you one day."

The *one day* hung in the air, given that there were only two weeks left in the season. *Does he mean . . . back in the city? One morning, after we—*

Mateo cleared his throat. "So, do you think we'll be ready for the finale?"

"Absolutely." Archer's answer was immediate. "We're so close already. And there's plenty of time still."

Mateo smiled softly. "You're always so optimistic."

Archer paused before his next bite. "Am I?"

"You are. All summer, you've been the one encouraging me, telling me it'll be okay, we can do it. It's . . . it's nice, having someone positive like that."

"Oh . . . that's—Thanks."

"No, thank you."

Archer smiled into his sandwich.

They ate in companionable silence, then Mateo stood to collect Archer's wrapper when he was done. "So, what else can I do for you today?"

"You really don't have to—"

"A bet's a bet. I'm all yours."

Archer's tongue twisted itself into a knot while his face's temperature cranked up a few degrees. "I can't think of anything right now . . ."

"Well, I'm at your beck and call. You let me know if you need anything."

"Okay."

"Okay."

They stared at each other.

"Want to go for a swim?" Archer asked.

"Sounds great." Mateo smiled. "Let me carry your towel."

When they got down to the dock, it looked like several of the others had had the same idea. Caleb and Ben were there, as were Harley, River, Seta, and Yuki. Ben was rubbing sunscreen onto a very pleased-looking Caleb's back.

After they spread their towels out, Mateo held out his hand to Archer. "Here, I'll do you."

"You'll what?" Archer wheezed.

Mateo chuckled. "Your sunscreen, Archer."

"Oh. Yes. Sure." He handed his bottle to Mateo, then turned his back, ignoring the smirk Caleb was giving him.

The sunscreen was cool on his skin for a second before there was nothing but the sensation of warmth and Mateo's big, strong hands on him. He was very thorough, gliding his fingers firmly over every inch of exposed skin, including Archer's neck and sides and right along the waist of his swim trunks.

It felt so fucking good that Archer bit his lip, horrified that he might actually moan with pleasure. He certainly hoped he didn't look as flustered as he felt. Mateo touched him all the time during their dances, of course, but something about the smooth, slippery rubbing on his bare back . . . "Thanks," he rasped when Mateo was done.

"I think I got everywhere," Mateo said, handing the bottle back to him. "Didn't want to miss any spots."

"Yeah." Archer's heart was pounding against his rib cage. "I don't think you did."

Mateo was right there for him, all day. Carrying his things, bringing him lunch, and reapplying sunscreen in the afternoon.

"I could get used to this." Archer grinned when Mateo held the door to the theater open for him on their way in. "I like having you around."

"I like being around," Mateo said, softly—so softly that Archer was not sure he was meant to hear it.

Archer turned to smile at him. "Well, I guess you're off duty now. It was nice while it lasted."

"Yeah." Mateo looked down at his feet, then back up at Archer. "You heading down to the cabin tonight after the show?"

Archer grinned. "Yeah. See you there?"

"See you there."

* * *

Archer showered quickly but spent a bit longer than normal choosing his late evening post-show outfit, going with a red shirt and beige shorts that looked good against his glowing tan. He stared at himself in the mirror while he fussed with his hair, which was now a little longer than he had kept it in Manhattan. There was a strange feeling brewing inside him, some energy that was building, tingling, and seeking an outlet of some sort, telling him to . . . do something.

I can't do anything though, Archer's brain argued. *I can't be the cause of another disaster breakup that destroys what we've built back up.*

But the feeling was still there.

When he got to the cabin, he spotted Mateo right away on the couch with a few of the others. He looked gorgeous, a loose, easy smile on his face, hair wet, lounging with one long, sculpted arm stretched out along the back, legs sprawled, and a buttery-soft olive green T-shirt hugging his every muscle. Archer grabbed a beer from the fridge and sat next to Mateo.

"Hey." Mateo clinked their bottles together. His dark, smoldering eyes bored into Archer's.

"Hey." Archer took a sip, not looking away.

Betty flopped onto the couch next to Archer. "Ah, what a day." She sighed happily. She patted Archer's leg. "Thanks to you."

Archer forced himself to look at Betty. "What did you get up to? I didn't see you all day."

"Well, after breakfast, Dominik did my laundry for me while I had a nap, then he drove me into town so I could peruse the used bookstore with a pack mule on hand. That guy can carry a *lot* of books."

Archer chuckled. "Amazing. Hope you found some good ones."

"Did you hear what Beau made me do?" Daniella added with a giggle. "I had to rub his feet!"

The group groaned appropriately, then there was a lot of laughter as the rest of them shared their servant-for-a-day stories. Archer half listened, his body humming with its nearness to Mateo.

Do something, his gut said.

Archer looked at Mateo. Mateo looked back.

Archer opened his mouth to say something right as the music got cranked up and Shania Twain's "Any Man of Mine" started blaring. The other lounging employees whooped as they hopped to their feet and began pushing furniture back.

"Yeehaw," Dominik cried. "Off your asses, everyone!"

Archer put his drink down, then stood and took Mateo's hand. "Come on, let's dance."

They didn't touch in line dancing, of course, but that *something* was still there, connecting them. Archer was intensely aware of where Mateo was at every second, like he was being pulled in that direction, as if his center of gravity was outside of his body and desperate to return to its home.

One song turned into several, and their eyes continued to meet, again and again.

Do something.

"Hey," Archer yelled into Mateo's ear as one song came to an end. "Do you want another drink?"

Mateo smiled, and for some reason it looked a little sad when he shook his head. "Thanks, but it's been a long day. I'd better get to bed."

"Okay," Archer said. "Well . . ." *It's better this way*, his brain reminded him. *Safer.* "Thanks again for . . . everything today."

"You're welcome."

The other voice, the one in his gut, was finally quiet while Archer watched Mateo's back disappear down the hall.

It's better this way, his brain said again.

24

Secret

As the week went on, Archer's brain started losing the argument.

It's better this way, it said.

Mateo's hand rested on Archer's back.

It's better this way.

Mateo's nose burrowed into Archer's neck during their tango.

It's better . . .

Mateo lifted Archer like he was made of air in their pas de deux, before he set him down again and they stood chest-to-chest, breath mingling.

It's . . .

Mateo's lips.

It's . . .

Mateo's eyes.

. . . What was I saying?

The connection he had with Mateo was undeniable— almost palpable and only getting stronger. Mateo had to feel it too. And yet, Mateo was also choosing not to act on it. That was the only thing Archer could hold on to, the only thing that was keeping him from throwing himself at Mateo's feet. Getting together now would be stupid, and they both knew it.

Of course, there was still dancing, at least. They spent every day together rehearsing their acro number as the final show approached, and they melted their way across the stage for their tango duet on Tuesday. Archer had to take a cold shower that night. On Saturday, their pas de deux was so intense that Archer was a little shaky as they bowed for the roaring audience.

Archer looked for Mateo in the crowd as soon as he got to Game Night. Speed Connect 4 was set up—four boards in a row along the kitchen island. They had one second to play their piece. Whoever won moved up the ladder. The loser moved down. It was chaotic and fun and distracting enough that Archer managed to mostly forget about staring at Mateo . . . until he played him.

They smiled as they faced each other across the board, fingers poised to grab their first piece.

"Ready, go!" Dominik yelled. They laughed, jammed their pieces in one at a time in a red and yellow blur, then Archer threw up his hands in celebration when he got four in a row.

"Damn it," Mateo growled, although he was smiling. "I'll get you next time."

Archer won the second time they played each other, and the third.

Mateo sighed and offered Archer a salute after his third defeat. "Guess you've got my number."

"Guess so." Archer's heart throbbed.

When the tournament ended and Dominik was declared champion—"Who's the loser now, Betty?" he gloated—

Archer went to the bathroom and to grab another beer. When he came back, Mateo was nowhere to be found. *Probably went to bed again. Smart.* He shook his head to clear it and joined in a conversation with the others, but it was futile. All he could think about was Mateo. He had barely noticed that the cabin had started to thin out as people finished their drinks and went to bed themselves, until Betty yawned and said she was turning in, too. An image of Mateo in bed flashed behind Archer's eyes, stretched out . . . naked, skin glowing against stark white sheets . . .

The cabin suddenly felt oppressively warm. Archer said good night to Betty and went out onto the porch in search of a cool breeze off the lake. But it wasn't much cooler out there, the heat of the day lingering and no breeze to be found. He leaned on the railing and blew out a breath, head spinning. The screen door slammed from around the corner and feet thumped down the stairs as another handful headed back to the dorms. Then it was still again, only a few crickets chirping to accompany his thoughts. *Maybe when we get back to Manhattan*, he consoled himself. *Maybe then.*

A creak from the shadows at the far end of the porch interrupted his thoughts. He turned and peered into the darkness. There was Mateo, sitting on the wide railing, leaning back on a thick post, one leg folded under him, one dangling.

"Oh, hi," Archer said, mouth turning to dust. "I thought you went to bed."

"I did," Mateo said in a low rumble. "Couldn't sleep."

Archer's feet traveled over toward Mateo on their own accord, then he hopped onto the railing and mirrored Mateo's pose against the other post. "Wallowing in your Connect 4 defeat?" he teased.

Mateo's laugh was like syrup, thick and slow. His gaze swung from the lake back to Archer.

"We're ready for the finale, I think," Archer said, choosing a safe topic for discussion. "Don't you?"

"Yeah." Time slowed down as Mateo slid off his seat and moved closer to Archer. He leaned against the railing, his hip touching Archer's bent knee. "I hope so."

Archer swallowed hard, giving into his impulse to reach over and squeeze Mateo's hand. "You've done an amazing job getting us there."

Their eyes met. The heat sent a charge of goose bumps over his skin, an overwhelming tingle that reached deep into every cell. The shadows slid over Mateo's face as he shuffled closer, highlighting the ridge of his eyebrows and lips. Then he shuffled closer still until he was between Archer's legs, his hip resting against Archer's dangling leg.

Archer dared to hold the gaze, even though he knew it would set him on fire. And it did, a scorching, exhilarating burn that turned his skin to ash before the embers licked at his core.

Heart thudding, blood boiling, his throat closed and his soul shrieked with need. His brain grasped to make sense of the moment, and all it could come up with was *Mateo Dixon is standing between my legs*. The smell of Mateo's sweat and deodorant and skin filled his lungs—forest and sunshine—and he wanted to drown in it all.

Their eyes were still locked, the moment stretching out until it was too thin to hold. It broke. A whimper escaped Archer's lips. And Mateo kissed him.

The kiss swallowed Archer's next whimper, then a sigh.

Their lips danced—leading, following, in perfect sync, just as the rest of their bodies were so accustomed to doing. Mateo's tongue was strong and slick as it pushed into his mouth. Archer groaned and threaded a hand into Mateo's thick hair, the other taking hold of Mateo's ass and pulling him even closer. His legs grasped Mateo's hips.

Mateo's arms slid around him, fingers gripping the back of his neck, a growl rumbling from his chest and sending sparks along every nerve ending Archer had.

Mateo's hardness pressed against his when he rocked his hips forward, the need between them molten and undeniable. It was heaven. Joy. Pure bliss.

Then Mateo ripped himself away, stumbling backward a step. "Fuck," he gasped as they stared at each other, chests heaving. "*Fuck*." He spun on his heel and bolted along the length of the deck and down the stairs.

"Mateo—" was the only word Archer could force from his lips, head swirling, blood long since drained from his brain.

But Mateo was gone, the word *sorry* echoing with the thumps on the stairs.

Archer blinked at the dark, silent porch. *Oh, hell no,* he decided and jumped off the railing, running after him. There was no sign of Mateo anywhere—the shoreline was empty, no one on the paths. But he knew where Mateo had gone.

Archer was panting when he arrived at the clearing. Mateo was sitting on the jutting rock, staring out at the lake. He must have heard Archer coming, but he didn't move.

"You had to come all the way up here?" Archer gasped.

Mateo didn't respond.

"Mateo," Archer said softly.

He shook his head, jaw clenched. "I'm sorry."

"What do you mean, sorry? That kiss was—"

"I shouldn't have done it."

"What are you talking about?"

His voice was flat. "Nothing can happen between us, Archer."

"Mateo, I don't—" Words flitted through Archer's head but refused to come together in any rational way. "Why not?" he asked. From the moment Mateo's lips touched his, he officially no longer cared that they had to work together, that a breakup might spell disaster. There were only eight days left in the season, and fuck it. He needed more.

"You're young, you've got your whole future ahead of you in New York. You don't want some washed-up has-been dragging you down."

Archer shook his head, reeling. "What are you even talking about? First of all, 'a washed-up has-been'? That's crazy! You're *made* for Broadway! Nothing has changed about that since the first time I laid eyes on you. And as for me, a future in New York—Mateo, I don't belong there. I'm nothing. I'm going nowhere. I'm an accountant from Ohio!"

Mateo turned to face him, eyes aflame. "Don't you get it, Archer? You can do anything. Anything. I don't even know why you're here."

A bitter laugh bubbled out. "No one wanted me, Mateo. No one. But you? You're a fucking star."

"No one wants me either."

"But you haven't even tried!"

Mateo turned back toward the water, shaking his head. "Archer . . . I've seen you dance. I've felt you dance. You have what it takes."

"Then why did I end up here?"

"I don't know. Maybe you were nervous at your auditions, or it was bad luck, or maybe it's just a random, shitty business where talent doesn't always matter."

"Maybe I dance better with you."

Mateo half smiled. "You've come alive this summer, Archer, and it's not only with me. You've only gotten better. You're outdancing me. You will get a job. A big one. It's inevitable."

"So could you. You've got everything, Mateo. I know it."

Mateo's head dropped. Then his shoulders started to shake. He was crying.

Archer climbed onto the rock and slid an arm around Mateo's shoulders. "What is it?"

It took him a minute to get the words out. Archer waited patiently.

"I'm afraid, Archer," he finally said. "I'm terrified of trying. What if everyone hates me? What if I . . . what if I blow it all again?"

"I get it, it's going to be hard, but . . . what if I were with you?"

Mateo looked up at him, wet eyes sparkling in the dim light. "You don't want to do that."

"Oh, Mateo. I very much do," Archer insisted, a soft laugh punctuating his words. "You're Mateo Dixon, don't you know? I had your face on my wall."

Mateo laughed, but it was still half sob.

"Even if you don't want to . . . *be* with me, we can just be friends. I will go with you to every audition until you get a part, before I have to go back to Ohio. And let's be honest, it will probably only be one audition."

"If I don't want to be with you?" Mateo repeated.

"Um, we just kissed—a really fucking amazing kiss, by the way—then you said *fuck* and ran away."

Mateo shook his head, lips quirking. "Of course I want to be with you. I— Are you sure that you—"

Archer leaned in. "I'm sure." He pressed his lips to Mateo's.

They kissed on their rock in the moonlight while the lake glittered below.

* * *

"Oh God," Archer breathed a while later, dizzy from the lack of oxygen, lips tingling. "You're a good kisser."

"So are you." Mateo tilted Archer's chin toward him for yet another.

"This isn't a bad idea, is it?" Archer asked him when he could breathe again, over the sound of his pounding heart. "We're so close to the big show. Are we going to mess anything up?"

Mateo nuzzled Archer's neck. "I've been thinking the same thing. Maybe we should wait until we get back to the city?"

Archer breathed in Mateo's scent as he brushed his lips along Mateo's cheek. "That's probably smart. What's a few more days?"

Mateo's hand crept up Archer's thigh. "We can do it."

"Okay, that's the plan." Archer sighed before they started kissing again.

It was a while until they dragged themselves back down the mountain, holding hands and being careful not to lose their footing in the dark each time they got distracted. Where the path split at the bottom, they paused.

"One last kiss at Shady Queens?" Archer asked. "And then we're not together." Overhead, the maple leaves whispered their secret in air thick with the smell of late summer flowers.

"Right," Mateo agreed. "No one can know."

"Good night," Archer murmured, lips ghosting over Mateo's.

"Good night," Mateo replied. "Sweet dreams."

Archer's dreams, indeed, had never been sweeter.

* * *

Mateo was the first thought Archer had the next morning. His eyes flew open at the memory, a smile stretching across his face. *Holy fuck. HOLY FUCK. I kissed Mateo Dixon. Like, a lot.*

He reached for his phone to send Mateo a text and saw that Mateo had already had the same thought. **Good morning. How did you sleep?**

Archer wanted to squeal like a teenager. **Good. So, so good. You?**

Also very good.

Good.

Did you want to meet for breakfast?

"What are you smiling at?" Beau asked from the doorway.

Archer jumped, stammering. "Uh, nothing. Just, er—a funny meme."

Yes, that would be great. I can meet you there in 15?

"Can I see it?" Beau asked.

"Can't, gotta shower," Archer called, already halfway out the door, running for the bathroom.

Mateo was waiting for him outside the dining hall. Archer's heart sang as soon as he saw Mateo's tall frame against the pink of the primrose bush.

"Hi." Archer smiled at him, hands in his pockets.

"Hi." Mateo smiled back.

They smiled some more.

Archer studied Mateo's lips before casting a glance around them. He nodded at Gage as he went by.

Mateo read his mind. "We can do this," he muttered.

Archer nodded. "Right. Breakfast."

They joined a few of the other dancers and sat across from each other, legs threaded together under the table. Archer tried to occasionally look at places that were not Mateo's gorgeous face or statuesque shoulders or strong, capable hands. He failed miserably.

"Oh my God," Betty hissed when Mateo got up to return his and Archer's trays. "Did you two—?"

"No!" Archer squeaked, his face burning.

Betty inhaled a deep breath like she was about to start shrieking, but Archer frantically shook his head. "No! Nope. No."

Betty blew the breath back out. "Okay," she said quietly, squeezing Archer's knee. "Got it."

Betty's eyes were still on them when he stood and joined Mateo strolling back out into the sunshine.

It was torture being around Mateo all day and not being able to kiss him. He started wondering if maybe they could break the rules and sneak a kiss here and there, but as long as they were at rehearsal, there was always someone around. When the group paused for lunch, Archer and Mateo lingered in the greenroom. Mateo decided it was a good time to untangle the jumble of extra metal hangers in the closet, while Archer scrubbed the makeup mirror. When Caleb, the straggler, finally left, their eyes locked across the room. They each took three long strides, reached for the other . . . and Stewart came in, Judy trotting at his heels.

"Mateo, there you are!" he cried.

Archer and Mateo screeched to a halt, hands awkwardly falling to other tasks. Archer scratched his nose.

"I was thinking, do you suppose we ought to make a fuss for Breckon Galloway?" Stewart wondered. "Or do we pretend we don't even know he's there?"

"Ah . . ." Mateo cleared his throat, gaze drifting down Archer's body. "Pretend we don't know he's there, I think. Don't want to look like we're trying too hard."

Archer didn't think he was imagining the emphasis Mateo put on the last word. He smirked back and thought about Mateo's plump bottom lip between his, their bodies pressed together.

"That was my initial thought as well," Stewart said, linking arms with Mateo and pulling him along to the exit. "But some of these theater types, you know, they love to be fussed over, don't they? Not me or you, of course, but did I ever tell you about the time Dame Judi Dench came to watch my production of *Don't Stop Believin'*, the Journey tribute? She sent me the most scathing letter afterward, complaining that I hadn't put a reserved sign on her seat . . ."

Archer trailed after the two of them on the way to the dining hall, winking at Mateo when he cast a helpless look over his shoulder.

After the show that night, they walked back to the dorms together. When the coast was clear, Mateo took Archer's hand and yanked him into a patch of hazelnut bushes.

"Fuck," Mateo muttered before their lips met in a frantic, exhilarating kiss.

"Yes," Archer whispered back when they came up for air. *More,* was all Archer could think. He wanted more.

"But we're not doing this," Mateo reminded him when they paused after the next kiss, resting their foreheads together. "We're waiting."

"It's going to be so hard . . ." They laughed. "But you're right," Archer breathed. "No more."

"Right." Mateo sighed.

Archer's stomach swirled at the thought of what they were waiting for. For now, the best he could hope for was a week of longing glances and accidental finger brushes.

And the dancing.

There was always the dancing.

25

Two as One

They were cooling down after rehearsal early Thursday afternoon when the backstage door clanked shut and light feet trod up the stairs. Archer looked up at River's gasp, then almost let loose a screech himself when he saw the figure entering the stage.

"Abby Hodge," he said in disbelief, and in unison with at least four others. The last time he had seen her was on Lynn's television screen at the Oscars in her midnight-blue Valentino gown. She was in blue again, loose linen shorts and tank top, graceful brown leather sandals, hair in a perfect, sleek bob, and lips bright red. She looked every bit the movie star. Archer snapped his mouth closed and tried to stop staring.

Abby's eyes had already found Mateo.

Mateo stared back. "Abby," he stammered. "You're— What are you doing here?"

She smiled. "It's nice to see you too." Her tone was teasing, but her smile was uncertain.

"Right. Sorry, I—" He noticed the fifteen other people

staring at them. "Uh, this is Abby Hodge. Abby, this is . . . everyone."

"Hi." She beamed at them, her eyes sweeping the room. "Nice to meet you all." Her gaze went back to Mateo. "Eva is actually a good friend of mine and she invited me to see the finale." She shrugged. "I thought I'd surprise you."

"I'm surprised." They watched each other another few seconds, the silence deafening. "Well, I'm done here. Would you like to go grab that coffee?"

She nodded once, movie star smile back in place. "I'd love to."

Mateo quickly gathered his things and led Abby back toward the steps. His eyes met Archer's on the way by.

Good luck, Archer mouthed at him.

Mateo nodded, shoulders tense. *Thanks*, he mouthed back.

Archer sent them all the good vibes he could muster as they disappeared down the steps.

* * *

When Archer came back early for the six o'clock show, Mateo and Abby were sitting together at the piano in the greenroom. Abby was slowly teasing out the right hand of a piece Archer didn't recognize.

"There he is," Mateo said when he saw Archer come in. He stood. "Abby, this is Archer. Archer, Abby."

"It's an honor to meet you," Archer said, shaking her hand. "You're so talented."

"Thank you, Archer. You are too, from what I hear. Mateo hasn't shut up about you the whole day."

Mateo gave an indignant gasp while Archer grinned. "Is that so?"

Mateo poked Abby. "You said we were cool!"

Abby laughed. "We are. But I had to get one shot in."

"Fair enough." They shared another smile.

"Well." Abby stood, too. "I'll leave you two to get ready for your show. I can't wait to see it."

"I hope you aren't expecting too much—"

"Oh hush, Mateo. If you're involved, I know it's amazing." She hugged him. "Maybe you two can stop by my cabin for a drink tomorrow?"

Mateo nodded. "We'd love to."

"It was nice to meet you, Archer." She swapped cheek kisses with Archer and slipped from the room.

"So? It went well?" Archer asked the second the back door closed.

Mateo slumped onto the piano bench like his legs were about to give out. "Really well," he breathed. "Really, really well. We talked for hours. I'd forgotten what a great friend she is."

"I'm so happy for you," Archer said, sitting next to him and pulling him in for a hug.

Hugging Mateo was so easy, even easier than dancing with him, the way their bodies melded together so perfectly. Archer never wanted to let go.

When the hug ended, Mateo pulled away, opening his mouth to say something, but then the back door wrenched open and they heard Dominik screeching.

"NOBODY MOVE! ABBY HODGE SHOOK MY HAND!" He appeared in the greenroom, grinning from ear to ear. "Mateo, why do you get to have such cool friends? I can't believe she's here! Oh my God, is Abby Hodge going to be *watching* us tonight? I am *literally* dying."

But Mateo barely seemed to notice Dominik's theatrics. He bumped shoulders with Archer. "Thanks. I'm happy too."

* * *

"ARCHER!" Archer was walking across the center green Saturday afternoon when the shriek reached him.

He turned. It was Lynn, barreling toward him, holding her hat with one hand. Sasha followed behind, towing their suitcases. Archer's smile was so broad it hurt his face. "Lynnie!"

She threw herself into Archer's arms. "Hiiiii! I missed you so much!"

"I missed you too!" He hugged her hard. "I can't believe you're actually here!"

"Me neither, especially after hearing about it all summer!"

Sasha puffed up to them, sweat already sliding down her temple in the heat. "Hey, Archer," she said, with a hug of her own.

"Hi, Sasha. Wow, you two look gorgeous!"

They were both wearing long, flowing pastel summer dresses and wide-brimmed hats.

"Oh, these old things?" Lynn declared with a wink.

Archer knew Lynn had done a special shopping trip to pick out some memorable outfits for their sure-to-be-memorable weekend.

"Where's your cabin?" Archer asked.

"One-oh-five, I think?" Lynn said, digging in her bag for the keys.

"Ooh, a nice one! Right down by the water!"

Sasha frowned at Lynn. "I hope you didn't spend too much, love."

Lynn booped her on the nose. "Don't you worry about that."

Archer pointed them down the right path. "I'm on my way to grab some food before the show, but your cabin is that way."

"Yes, we should go get settled in, but we'll see you at the theater! Which show is tonight again?"

"*From the Heart*, the contemporary one. Then tomorrow is the big finale."

"And when do we get to meet Mateo?" she asked with a grin. "Not to mention Caleb! And I really need to meet Dominik. And Betty."

Archer laughed. "Maybe if you're good, I can give you a backstage tour between shows."

"Yes!" Lynn whooped. "Perfect. We'll be on our best behavior."

"I mean it, Lynn! No one knows about me and Mateo."

"It's still a secret?" she said, sharing a look with Sasha.

"It's better this way," Archer explained. "We're waiting until we get back to the city. No drama if no one knows. It all has to go perfectly tomorrow."

Lynn mimed zipping her lips closed. "Promise."

* * *

After the first show, Lynn and Sasha waited in their seats as instructed while the rest of the crowd shuffled out.

"Hey!" Archer popped out onto the stage and waved them up the stairs. "Come on up!"

Lynn squealed and rushed up to him. "Oh my God, Archer! You were so fucking amazing! You made me fucking *cry*. And I do not cry."

"So gorgeous!" Sasha agreed, kissing his cheek.

"And, fucking hell, I think I got pregnant watching you and Mateo." Lynn fanned herself. "You two are scorching hot."

"Shhh!" Archer hissed, craning his neck to peek around the masking draperies to make sure no one had heard.

"Sorry," she whispered. "But *damn*."

Despite himself, Archer grinned. "Thanks. Let me introduce you."

He led Lynn and Sasha into the greenroom and over to where Mateo was pulling on a T-shirt. "This is Mateo. Mateo, this is my roommate—er, former roommate Lynn and her girlfriend, Sasha."

Lynn beamed. "Mateo! It's so nice to meet you. I've heard so much about you."

Mateo leaned in to kiss their cheeks. "Likewise."

"You are an amazing dancer," Lynn said. "I can see why Archer likes you so much."

Archer cleared his throat, cheeks heating. "Thanks, Lynnie."

Mateo laughed. "It's okay. I like him too. A lot." He threw a smoldering look at Archer, causing his cheeks to flush further.

"If you look at each other like that very often," Lynn said with a chuckle, "trust me, everyone knows."

Archer dragged his eyes away from Mateo's. "Come on, then, let's meet the rest of them."

Lynn, Sasha, and Betty hit it off right away, and Archer could barely pry them apart. "Okay, you guys can talk about the best art galleries in Brooklyn another time. We have another show to get ready for."

"Yes, heaven knows Archer Read is never late for anything," Lynn said with an eye roll.

"Right?" Betty agreed. "He's late more than anyone!"

Archer's jaw flapped. "You—I—"

"Yes, yes," Lynn soothed. "We're going." She kissed Archer on the cheek. "See you tomorrow."

"Lynn and Sasha are great," Mateo said, watching the two of them leave.

"Yeah," Archer said fondly. "I'm really going to miss living with Lynn."

"Have you had a chance to look for an apartment yet?"

"I took a quick look at some roommate-wanted ads yesterday." Archer pulled a face. "It was scary."

"You know . . ." Mateo said slowly. "I have an extra room in my apartment. You could stay with me. While you look for something."

"Really? Even though we're . . ."

"Yeah, I know the timing is a little weird but . . . you need a room and I have a room. It doesn't have to be anything more significant."

A thousand-pound weight lifted off Archer's shoulders. "If you're sure . . ."

"If I'm sure?" Mateo said, eyes crinkling. "This is basically me begging."

Archer wanted to throw his arms around Mateo, but he remembered just in time they were in the greenroom with fourteen other people. "Yes. Thank you. That would be . . . perfect."

"Good."

"Good."

* * *

Archer stepped onto the darkened stage. Mateo's shadow waited for him. The audience hushed as the first strains of music filled the theater. Archer took his position, in third, arms extended. He exhaled. The spotlight turned on and illuminated them both.

Their eyes met.

Mateo's beauty took his breath away.

Archer's heart crashed into his rib cage, a bird that refused to be contained, that needed to fly.

So, he flew.

He pirouetted and reached for Mateo. Their hands met, firm and yet gentle. Mateo grasped his waist, then his thigh as Archer dove toward the worn boards. Then his waist again, his shoulders, as the music took them. Their arms and legs threaded together, weaving a story, a spell that captured them both. Mateo lifted Archer to the swell of the music, held him. They breathed at the same time, their sweat mingling on flushed skin. The thump of Mateo's pounding heart vibrated through Archer's hand when he rested it on Mateo's chest. His fingers brushed Mateo's face, and then they turned and came back together once again. Archer fell, Mateo caught him, safe and secure in those arms.

The audience vanished; it was only the two of them as one. As Archer stretched and turned and leaped, he knew Mateo was there, right where he was supposed to be, perfectly in sync, never a hand misplaced, never a missed beat. Archer lost himself in the dance, let the emotions take over, put every grain of every feeling into his legs and toes and arms and fingers, neck, torso—his body as fluid as the flame that burned inside him.

When the music faded and the roar from the audience rushed back, they held hands and bowed, then exited the stage while the others went on.

They stood in silence in the shadows, watching each other, chests heaving. Every hair on Archer's body stood on end. His every cell, alive and wanting.

"Mateo," he breathed.

Their lips met, bodies wound together again, slotting together perfectly. Archer dissolved into an ocean of bliss.

It wasn't until they heard their next cue that they broke apart, panting.

Mateo nodded, took Archer's hand, and squeezed.

He didn't need to say anything.

After the show, Archer tingled, as if he and Mateo were tied together by an electric wire, humming and singing with an undeniable current.

He stole glance after glance at Mateo as they changed and stored their gear. Mateo was always looking back.

When there was nothing else left to put away and the room had thinned out, Mateo approached him. "Archer."

"Yes?" He waited, pulse humming.

Mateo leaned in, his lips nearly brushing Archer's cheek as he whispered. "Tonight . . . would you like to—I think we should . . . that is, do you—"

"Are you asking me out on a date?" Archer winked, eyes sliding over Mateo's face, taking in every inch of skin, every hair, wanting to remember this moment.

Mateo closed his eyes briefly, embarrassed. "Yes, and doing a terrible job at it."

Archer tilted closer, lips grazing Mateo's cheek in turn. "Yes, I would love to, thank you."

Their eyes met. Mateo smiled. "I'll pick you up at your room in thirty minutes."

Archer shivered. "Make it twenty."

Nineteen minutes later, Mateo was rapping on Archer's doorframe. "Ready to go?"

Archer smoothed his hair with one last look in the mirror. "Where are we going? Night out on the town?"

Mateo took his hips and pulled him in for a kiss. "Would it be ungentlemanly if I took you straight back to my room?"

"Do you care if—?"

"I don't care who sees. I don't care who hears. I don't care what anyone thinks. I just want you."

Archer's heart tried to squeeze its way through his rib cage. "Then yes, please, and hurry up about it."

Archer barely remembered the walk down to the cabin, aside from the feeling of his fingers laced through Mateo's. He barely remembered climbing the stairs and rushing down the hall, only Mateo's warm hand in his, tugging him along.

But he remembered Mateo's bedroom door slamming closed as Mateo kissed him against the back of it. He remembered Mateo's hands on his body, pulling his shirt up, pushing his shorts down. He remembered every kiss.

He remembered the way they moved.

Archer reached for Mateo. Their hands met, firm yet gentle. Mateo grasped his waist, then his thigh, his shoulders. Their arms and legs threaded together, weaving a story, a spell that captured them both. Mateo lifted Archer, held him. They breathed at the same time, their sweat mingling on flushed skin. The thump of Mateo's pounding heart vibrated through Archer's hand when he rested it on Mateo's chest. His fingers brushed Mateo's face, and Mateo held him, so safe, so secure in those arms.

The only thing that existed was the two of them as one.

* * *

"So . . ." Archer traced Mateo's strong jaw with his finger. "We're doing this? We're telling people?"

"I can't wait any longer," Mateo murmured, eyelids fluttering. He kissed the fingertip that drifted over his lips. "What's the worst that could happen?"

"Oh, God. Don't say that. I don't want to find out."

Mateo chuckled. "Fair point. It's been quite the summer."

Archer kissed Mateo's pec. "When did you first know . . . you wanted this?"

"This?" Mateo took Archer's hand and laced their fingers together and kissed the back of it. "From the first moment I saw you."

Butterflies danced around Archer's stomach. "Really? All summer?"

"Remember when we were blocking out our pas de deux in the clearing?"

"Yeah?"

"And I did the full-on fucking pirouette-into-tour like an asshole?"

"What?" Archer laughed. "That was fucking hot."

"Such a show-off."

"Trust me, it was appreciated. You're hot when you show off. But why didn't you say anything, ever? I thought you hated me!"

Mateo barked a short laugh. "You ended up with Caleb so fast. But I took my shot, Archer. Remember your birthday? I got like two hours of sleep that night so I could get up at four in the morning and ice your fucking cake."

"You did?"

Mateo groaned and covered his face with his other hand. "Was it not completely obvious? I thought you were rejecting me. For Caleb!"

"No! I . . . Fuck! I thought it was just a cake."

Mateo arched an eyebrow. "Do I seem like the type to stay up half the night baking cakes for my coworkers?"

Archer groaned too. "When you put it that way, I'm an idiot."

"Yeah." Mateo pushed a piece of hair back off Archer's forehead. "A sweet idiot, though. A beautiful idiot."

Archer propped himself up on an elbow, sliding his fingers around Mateo's neck. "An idiot who would like to kiss you now."

"Please."

A while later, they flopped back onto the mattress, panting. Archer rolled onto his side and studied Mateo's perfect profile as he got his breath back. His eyelids drooped and the idea of time briefly flitted through his head. "We should probably get some sleep," he murmured. "Big day tomorrow. Er, today."

"But you'll sleep here with me?" Mateo snaked his arms around Archer's waist and pulled him closer. "You'll stay?"

Archer smiled in the darkness. "I'll stay."

26

The Finale

Archer woke up with Mateo's chest pressed to his back, arm around his waist, nose on the nape of his neck, tickling him with each breath. He smiled, chest rising and falling in a deep, contented sigh.

"Can we stay here forever?" Mateo whispered in the silence.

Archer wiggled around, smile growing, sliding his arms around Mateo's neck. "Yes." He kissed Mateo's cheek, then his lips, morning breath be damned.

"Archer," Mateo murmured, pressing their bodies even tighter together. "Archer," he breathed again, sliding his hand down Archer's stomach.

The heights Archer reached with Mateo were like none he had ever known before. His body responded in ways he never thought possible. When he danced with Mateo, it was like he entered another plane that was all electricity and tension and fire. But being with him like this . . . it was a whole other universe. Stars, planets, comets—they all whizzed by him, through him, compressed space and time down to one singular point of bliss.

"Oh, God," Archer panted when he sagged onto the mattress again, goose bumps shivering over his skin, pleasure still radiating from his center. "*Fuck.* You are . . . you are really good at that."

Mateo smiled and planted a kiss on Archer's shoulder. "So are you."

"Better than I am at dancing?"

Mateo laughed and gave him a half-hearted shove. "Yes. Even better than you are at dancing."

Archer let out a low whistle. "Damn. I *am* good at this."

Mateo's laugh vibrated through Archer's chest, perfectly in time with his heart.

This.

This right here.

"So . . . we go home tomorrow," Archer said, tiptoeing up to the conversation after some more cuddling.

"Yeah. Hard to believe the summer's over already." Mateo's fingers drifted up and down his arm.

"Am I really going to move in with you?" Archer asked in a rush. "Are you sure you want me invading your world?"

Mateo's eyes were serious when they met his. "Archer . . . I haven't had anyone in my life in a very long time. And I am absolutely sure. I feel like . . ." He blushed and looked away to fiddle with the sheet. "I feel like I've been waiting for you."

Tears flooded Archer's eyes. "I've been waiting for you too."

They kissed again, a slow, gentle kiss that was a promise of many more to come.

"If I don't get any jobs in a few months though . . ." Archer had to warn him. "I'm almost out of money. I'll have to move back to Ohio."

"Fuck Ohio," Mateo said with a growl. "Breckon Galloway is going to see you and fall in love. I know it."

"Hah. If anything, he's going to fall in love with you."

"Well, I'm taken."

Even though he was already rubber, Archer managed to soften further. Joy swelled up his throat as he snuggled under Mateo's jaw, ear pressed to the steady rhythm of Mateo's heart.

* * *

Mateo paused outside the stage door and squeezed Archer's hand. "You ready?"

They were meeting early for a dress rehearsal before the night's finale, and they had officially agreed: no more hiding. A handful of maintenance people had seen Archer coming downstairs with Mateo this morning anyway, all disheveled, and who knows who had seen them sprinting to Mateo's room the night before. Better to get it all out in the open now so there were no surprises later.

Archer nodded. "Ready."

They walked into the greenroom, fingers laced.

Betty's face lit up when she saw them. "Hiii!" she squealed and ran over, hugging them both. "Oh my God, yes! So happy for you two."

Dominik stood and shouted, "You owe me ten bucks!," although it wasn't clear who it was directed at.

"'Bout time," Caleb said, shaking his head.

"Well, we didn't want to cause any drama or anything, you know," Archer said, rubbing the back of his neck.

"It is possible to date without causing drama, you know," Betty said dryly.

"I don't really blame them," Caleb said. "Every other couple ended in disaster."

"Uh, no they didn't!" a voice piped up.

It was River. Every head swiveled over to them.

"Gage and I are still together," they said, alarmed at having so many people staring at them. "No drama."

An awkward silence ensued.

"Er, right. Well, clearly you two are an example of how to do it," Archer said. "Well done."

Once Eva arrived, they did a full rehearsal, and it all went perfectly. When it was over, the dancers gathered in a tight huddle in the middle of the stage.

Mateo spoke, his head slowly turning to meet each person's eye. "This is it, team. We made it. I'm incredibly proud of each and every one of you. It wasn't without its bumps"—Caleb studied his feet—"but I truly believe we have put together an incredible show, one that will absolutely blow away Breckon Galloway."

"Hell yeah, it will!" Dominik cried, backed by cheers and enthusiastic agreement.

"Go get some food and be back here at six. Last one, team."

They put their hands in and cheered.

Mateo exhaled as the group dispersed.

Archer slid his arms around Mateo and hugged him tight. "Speaking of being proud," Archer said. "You should be incredibly proud of this show."

Mateo hummed and tried to deflect the compliment. "Stewart—"

"Nope." Archer cut off his deflection with a kiss. "This

is as much your show as it is Stewart's, the entire thing.
You led us the whole way through. And I'm really proud
of you."

Mateo blinked rapidly. "Thank you, Archer."

Archer took his hand. "Now let's go eat."

* * *

Archer was just finishing his last bite of dinner in the dining
hall when his phone buzzed. It was a text from Lynn that
was only a picture—Sasha's hand, with a pink teardrop diamond shining from her finger. Behind was a table set for a
candlelit dinner and the lake sparkling in the background.

> **Oh my Goddddd! Congratulations! You did
> it! I'm so happy for you two!**

> **Thanks, boo! Do you have time to
> join us for a super quick glass of
> champagne before the show? We're
> on the deck of our cabin.**

Archer checked the time—five forty-five. The finale—
only one show this time—was at seven, and even though
he was technically supposed to be there at six, if he was a
touch late arriving, Eva Stiff went on first, so he had a bit of
a time cushion. **Sure, if I hurry! I'll be right there!**

He kissed Mateo on the forehead. "I've gotta go see
Lynn and Sasha real quick—they just got engaged! I'll be at
the theater by six though . . . ish."

"Okay, hurry back." Mateo squeezed his waist. "And
congratulate them for me too, please."

Archer pocketed his phone and hurried out the door
into the heavy afternoon heat, settling into a jog toward
Lynn's cabin, sweat beading on his forehead. When he

came around the bend by the lake, there was a small, lone figure crumpled in the middle of the path.

Archer's heart wrenched in two when he recognized the purple floral dress.

"Eileen!" he cried, racing to her side. He fell to his knees and reached for her hand. Her eyes were closed, face stark white. "Eileen," he said again. "Eileen, are you okay?" He pressed his fingertips to her neck trying to find a pulse, but all he could feel was his own hammering heart.

Then her eyelids fluttered.

"Thank God," he muttered, scrambling to pull his phone out of his pocket and dial 911.

He did his best to answer their questions and listen to instructions. When the dispatcher put him on hold, he sent a text to Mateo with shaking fingers.

> **Something's happened with Eileen. I found her unconscious. I'm on the phone with 911.**

> **Where are you? I'll be right there.**

> **We're on the path by 101.**

"Someone's coming, Eileen," Archer murmured to her. "It's going to be okay. Please, hang in there." There was no response, but her chest rose in the odd shallow breath.

The dispatcher's calm voice returned. "An ambulance is on its way. I'm going to give you some more instructions to help Eileen. Are you ready, Archer?"

"Yes. Yes, I think so." He followed the steps to put Eileen in the recovery position, and he sent a bystander to the front desk to alert them to the situation.

Mateo came running up. A wave of relief flooded Archer's chest at seeing his face.

"Archer! What happened? Is she okay?" he panted.

"I don't know." Archer dragged a hand through his hair and reached for Mateo.

Mateo fell to his knees next to them and followed the same motions Archer had—checking her pulse, listening for her breath, searching for any encouraging signs. "Has she moved at all?" he asked.

"Just an eyelid." Archer picked up Eileen's fallen sun hat and clutched it with white knuckles.

A few more curious onlookers gathered, then Mrs. C arrived, carrying a first aid kit.

"She's breathing," Archer told her. "Barely."

Mrs. C checked her over, as well. "Poor thing," she murmured, brushing Eileen's hair off her forehead. "She mentioned before that she has poor circulation. I wonder if that has something to do with it."

"I don't know," Archer said, his voice rough. "Is there anything else we can do?"

"They'll be here soon, Archer. Eileen knows you're here with her."

They finally heard the ambulance approaching, and then the siren cut out once the ambulance pulled into the long drive. A minute later, two EMTs came into sight walking down the main path with a stretcher. They waved the crowd back and set their cases down.

"Archer?" one of them asked.

"Yes," he nodded, mouth dry.

"I'm Caroline and this is James. We are emergency medical technicians and we're here to help Eileen."

"Yes, please," he said, letting go of Eileen's hand and gripping Mateo's instead as they moved back.

Caroline and James knelt next to Eileen's small figure.

"Eileen, can you hear us?" Caroline called.

Eileen's eyes fluttered again.

"Eileen?" Caroline gave her shoulder a shake.

Her lips moved, as if she were mumbling something, but Archer couldn't hear any words.

Once their assessment was complete, they lifted Eileen onto the stretcher. Archer, Mateo, and Mrs. C followed the medics up the path.

Eileen's eyes drifted open as they approached the ambulance. "Archer," she croaked when she saw him.

"Eileen!" Archer took her hand again. "Are you okay?"

"I don't know," she breathed. "I was walking up the path and . . ." Her voice faded and her eyes closed again.

"It's going to be alright," Archer said, doing his very best to keep his voice calm. "The paramedics are here, and they're going to take you to the hospital."

She looked so small and frail in the back of the ambulance, surrounded by medical equipment and sterile white walls. Her eyes opened again. "Will you stay with me, Archer?"

"Of course I will." He turned to Mateo. "I'm going to go with her. I'm sorry, I know—"

Mateo cut him off. "I'm coming too."

"What? No! Mateo, it's the final show."

"I don't care. I need to be with Eileen. And you."

"Okay." Archer nodded, relenting. Of course Mateo would want to go. "Thank you."

"Do you have a car?" Caroline asked.

"You can take mine," Mrs. C offered.

"We're going to St. Luke's," James told them. "If you go to registration in Emergency, they can tell you where Eileen is."

"Okay, thank you so much. Eileen"—Archer turned back to call to her—"we'll be at the hospital, okay?"

She didn't reply, her eyes closed again.

It was a blur as Mrs. C handed them her keys and told them where to find her car. They ran to the staff parking lot and, breathless, Archer texted Betty from the passenger seat. **Something happened to Eileen. Mateo and I are going with her to the hospital. We're so sorry to miss the show. We know you guys can fill in the gaps.**

Of course, Betty replied right away. **Send Eileen our love if you can. Let us know how she's doing, please.**

I will. Love you.

Love you too.

He texted Lynn too, then didn't remember much of the drive, only staring blankly out the window, watching the trees go by in a green smudge. At the hospital, they were directed to a waiting room and were told someone would come find them with an update once Eileen was stabilized.

Archer paced the dingy linoleum until Mateo handed him a bag of Reese's Pieces from the vending machine. He sat and ate them in three handfuls, leg jittering.

"Are you Eileen Lamb's friends?" A woman in a white coat with kind, tired eyes approached them.

Archer shot to his feet again. "Yes, that's us."

"I'm Dr. Farag. Ms. Lamb is resting comfortably, and you may see her now."

"We can?" Tears filled Archer's eyes. "She's okay?"

"It was likely heatstroke. Our tests show she was dehydrated, and her blood sugar and blood pressure were low. She might have been overdoing it in this heat for someone her age. She's doing much better now and will be just fine."

Archer sighed and pressed a hand to his heart, willing it to slow down. "Thank you, Doctor."

They followed the instructions to find Eileen's room. Archer pushed open the door and they crept in.

"Archer. Mateo," Eileen said when she saw them, her voice thin. "Oh, what you must think of me. How embarrassing."

"Shhh." Archer leaned over to leave a gentle kiss on her forehead. "Don't be silly. We're glad you're okay."

Mateo bent to kiss her too. "It's nothing to be embarrassed about. We're just relieved."

Eileen sighed. "That's getting old for you. No fun at all."

"Did they say how long you'll have to stay in the hospital?" Archer asked, rubbing her shoulder.

"Overnight for monitoring. What time is it?" she asked, squinting at the clock on the wall. "I've lost all sense."

"It's eight thirty," Archer said.

She gasped. "Wait—the finale! You didn't miss it, did you?"

"It's fine," Archer said. "It's only a show."

"You're more important," Mateo said, squeezing her hand.

"Well, that's utter nonsense," she grumbled.

Archer laughed. "Glad to see you're back to your old self."

* * *

Archer texted Betty on the drive back to let her know Eileen was okay, and Betty assured him that the show had gone well. **Not as good as if you two had been here. But good!**

Did Breckon Galloway like it? Archer asked.

I think so. He was talking with Stewart after.

That's great!

**Drive safe. Come by the cabin when
you get back!**

By the time they parked and found Mrs. C to return her keys, it was almost ten. But instead of the cabin, their feet took them toward the theater, sitting dark and silent in the still night.

"I can't believe we missed it," Archer sighed. After everything that had happened on that stage over the summer, the realization that he would never dance there again left a hollow ache in his chest.

"Yeah." Mateo studied the old building, then turned to look at Archer. "You want to do it now?"

"What?"

"Come on." He pulled Archer down the hill.

They giggled as they tiptoed in, grasping for a light switch.

"Should we change?" Archer whispered, for some reason reluctant to disturb the silence.

"Nah." Mateo led him up the stairs to the stage and kicked his flip-flops off, then tossed his shirt. "Gimme a second to get the music ready."

Archer similarly stripped down to his shorts.

Mateo turned on a single stage light, then the music began, quieter than normal, just loud enough for them to hear. It was not the same pas de deux they had performed thirty times before this summer. It was a little looser, more dreamlike, their smiles and lines gentle in the white light. When it was over, they hugged, breathing in the stage together one last time.

"That was beautiful." The voice came out of the shadows.

Archer whirled. A man with a vaguely familiar face was making his way down the aisle of the theater.

That's not—

"Breckon Galloway," the man said, stopping below them. "Nice to meet you, Archer, Mateo. My niece has been telling me all about you two all summer."

Archer's jaw dropped. "W—Your *niece?*"

Breckon turned to wave at somebody who was lurking at the back in the shadows. The shadow began moving toward them. A blond shadow.

"Betty?"

Betty waved sheepishly. "Hi."

Archer and Mateo shared a confounded look, then Archer turned back to Betty. "This is your *uncle?*"

"Yep."

"Why—why didn't you tell us?"

"Oh, you know, the old cliché. Wanted to make it on my own, et cetera."

Archer's jaw hung open for a second before a question occurred to him. "How did you know we'd be here?"

"I had a feeling. Plus, Breckon saw you go in and texted me."

Archer turned his attention to Breckon. "We're sorry we missed the finale, our friend—"

"Yes, Betty told me. I'm sorry to hear that. She's doing well now?"

"Thankfully. She'll be okay."

"What a relief. You know, I actually caught the performance last night, too."

"You did?"

"Mm-hmm. You're both stunning, and your chemistry? Insane." He paused, studying them for a moment, then gave a small nod. "It just so happens, I'm casting my next show in September, and you two would be perfect for it."

Archer choked on his tongue while Breckon pulled two business cards out of his wallet, reaching up to hand one to each of them. "Send my assistant an email with your contact information. I want to make sure you're at the auditions."

"We will," Archer rasped. "Thank you, Mr. Galloway."

"Call me Breckon." He paused and examined Mateo for a moment. "I saw *Robin's Egg* twice. You have a gift. Broadway has missed you."

Mateo gulped. "Thank you, sir."

Breckon nodded. "We'll talk soon."

Betty winked at them as she followed Breckon back up the aisle. The sound of the door swinging closed echoed back at them.

They stared at each other.

"Did that just happen?" Archer asked.

"That just happened," Mateo replied, a laugh bubbling up.

Archer jumped into Mateo's arms.

Mateo caught him, as usual.

Epilogue

"Would you hurry up?" Mateo called.

"One second!" Archer replied.

"That's what you said five minutes ago!"

"But for real this time." Archer gave himself one last look in the mirror, then stepped out of the bathroom, arms wide in a *ta-da!* pose. "How do I look?" His navy suit fit him perfectly, a recent bespoke purchase.

Mateo's mouth fell open. "You look . . . wow. Amazing."

"Naw." Archer swatted at Mateo, then reached to straighten his bow tie. His suit was dark gray, highlighting his wide shoulders and slim waist. "*You* look amazing."

Mateo took hold of Archer's hips and kissed him soundly.

"Okay, we both look amazing," Archer allowed, once his lips were free again.

"Yes, and we will both be late. Get your sexy ass in the elevator."

"Pshhh." Archer waved a dismissive hand on his way

out the door. "Lynn knows I'm always late. In fact, I bet she gave me a fake time."

Mateo rolled his eyes as he locked their apartment behind him. "She did not. I checked. The reception is actually at six. She trusted me to get you there on time."

"Oh. Well then, shit, we'd better hurry up."

Mateo grabbed his hand and squeezed it as they hurried to the elevator. "You're lucky you're cute."

Archer squeezed his hand back. "You love me."

The doors slid shut behind them. Mateo took his chin, eyes dark, and kissed him again. "Yes, I do."

Archer's heart fluttered. He never got tired of hearing that.

The first time was twelve months ago, the morning of their audition for Breckon Galloway.

"I'm so nervous," Archer remembered saying over breakfast, picking at his toast, leg jittering under the table. "My stomach is in knots. I think I might actually vomit."

Mateo had nodded and put his spoon down. He had oatmeal for breakfast every single morning. "Do you want to move in?" Mateo asked, words loud and sure. "For good?"

Archer's leg stopped jittering. "What?"

Mateo took Archer's hand. "Move in with me. Stay. Please." His eyes crinkled. "This is me begging again, to be clear."

Archer tried to swallow, throat dry. "I—What if we don't get this job? I'm almost broke—"

"I don't care if we get it or not." Mateo took his other hand. "You will get a job. I know it. You belong here, Archer. You belong in New York. You belong with me. Please stay."

Archer nodded, struggling to put together a sentence. A tear slipped out as he smiled. "I'll stay."

A little bit later, after they celebrated, Mateo whispered the words into his skin. "I love you, Archer."

Archer took them and folded them into his heart. "I love you too."

He had never had a more satisfying conversation with his parents. "I belong here," he told them, knowing it was true, deep down inside, the same way he knew he was meant to dance.

They crushed their audition for Breckon's show, and the next day he got the rest of his stuff from Sasha and Lynn's place. He found the sunniest windowsill in Mateo's apartment—their apartment—for his plants.

"Did you miss me?" he had whispered to Danny and Belle and Spot as he arranged them next to Eileen, the new plant Mateo gave him, a little cactus with purple flowers.

Now, a year later, Lynn and Sasha had had their wedding ceremony earlier that day at city hall, with their parents present. And Archer and Mateo were about to be late for the reception at a charming French restaurant in the West Village.

"We're here, we're here!" Archer cried, rushing from the cab to the wrought iron front door where Lynn waited with Sasha, tapping her foot. "Congratulations! You look beautiful!" he cried, pausing for a quick cheek kiss for each of them before he and Mateo scurried inside. Both women wore simple white dresses—Lynn's was a strapless sheath, and Sasha's was soft and flowy, with lace cap sleeves and an empire waist.

The restaurant was draped with fairy lights, eucalyptus leaves, and Queen Anne's lace, candles flickering on every table. Archer and Mateo hurried in and sank into the two empty seats next to Betty and . . . Caleb?

"Caleb! Hi! What are you doing here?" Archer leaned over to give him a hug.

Betty grinned. "He's my plus-one. We wanted to surprise you." Betty, Lynn, and Sasha had become fast friends in the year since they'd met at Shady Queens, and they all had kept in touch with Caleb, too.

"How are you?" Archer asked him. "What's new? It's been a few months, things have been so crazy . . ."

"I'm good," Caleb said. "I opened my own dance studio."

"You did? Good for you!"

"Thanks, Archer." A smile stretched across his face. "It's going really well."

"And . . . Ben?"

The smile turned a little bashful. "He's coming to visit again next month."

Archer reached over to squeeze his arm. "That's great, Caleb. Seriously, congratulations."

"But enough about me," Caleb said, swatting Archer away. "Look at you!"

"Excuse me, everyone!" Lynn's uncle called from the door. "Could you please stand to welcome . . . Lynn and Sasha Molina-Grimes!"

Archer stood with the rest of his table and cheered and cheered.

Later, after dinner and the speeches, but before the cake and dancing, Archer leaned over to mumble at Mateo. "People are staring . . . specifically that entire table over there." He tilted his head, a smile frozen on his face.

"Get used to it," Mateo said, casting them a glance. He stretched an arm across the back of Archer's chair with a smirk. "That's the life of a Broadway star."

"I don't think I'll ever get used to it," Archer said,

throwing an awkward half wave to the table. They tittered and waved back.

"They'll want autographs after a few more drinks, I expect." Mateo laughed while Archer groaned. "It's your fault for being so talented, I guess." He smiled and rubbed Archer's shoulder.

Their show with Breckon had debuted a month ago to rave reviews and instant sellouts. They had been on the front page of the *New York Times* Arts section with Breckon, smiling below their marquee. Archer's mom had even called squawking, ordering him to go buy up all the copies he could get his hands on so she could give one to everyone they knew in Dayton. Funny how it turned out that not even twenty-nine was too old. It was just a beginning.

Archer leaned over to kiss Mateo. "At least I get to be famous with you," he said, catching a whiff of forest and sunshine. "I can do anything with you."

Mateo touched their foreheads together. "I love you."

"I love you too."

As the night went on, he watched Lynn and Sasha dancing in the soft glow of candles and fairy lights. Lynn twirled Sasha out and back, laughing.

Archer sighed, his heart full. *Life is sweet.*

Mateo slid his hand onto Archer's thigh and then laced their fingers together, leaning in close to murmur in his ear. "Care to dance?"

Archer smiled at him. "Always."

Acknowledgments

First, I would like to thank my mom and dad, who were the best parents anyone could ever hope for, and my husband and children for their love and support, and for letting me have the best corner of the couch.

Over the last few years, I have learned that writers need writing besties who believe in them, cheer them on, and offer insightful, thoughtful, and kind suggestions on their writing. I am lucky to have so many of these people in my life. Thank you to Hanna Kubicka, who loves my work, makes it stronger, and has cheered me on since I wrote my first word—and, in fact, encouraged me to write that word in the first place. To John, whose endless kindness, positivity, and tech support have gotten me through many rough patches. I am so grateful for his time and talent. To Andrew Padgett, my fellow nerd, who helped with Archer and Mateo's singing duet, and who reads every word of mine carefully so he can offer brilliant ideas. Thank you to Rebekah Rodriguez-Lynn, who had a huge hand in emotionally fine-tuning this book and made it so much better with her thoughtful suggestions. To K. C. Carmine, who somehow finds the time to read my work and support me, despite constantly working incredibly hard herself.

The idea for *Flirty Dancing* was sparked by the talented and beautiful dance troupe at the Hyatt Ziva Los Cabos in July 2022. About three minutes into *Retro Night*, I knew I had to write a book about a dance show. Thank you to everyone involved! I would also like to thank the artists and creative forces behind *Dirty Dancing, So You Think You Can Dance,* and *Noises Off.* . . . Their DNA winds throughout *Flirty Dancing*.

So many people helped bring this book to life and I can only hope I have remembered all of them: Jane, who told me about the dancers on the cruise ship she worked on; Alexander James, who helped with New York geography and gave me "ass end of Brooklyn," a phrase that continues to delight me to this day; Jenny Sandvold, who helped with dance lingo; James Larose and Andre, who gave me feedback on the paramedic language; Gwen, who can spot a typo a mile away; and Tyrell Johnson, who has been a constant source of calm, reassuring, and wise text support (and who writes beautiful books you should check out).

When my first book was published last year, I was not expecting the wave of love, support, and excitement that came from my family and friends. I was so touched by their enthusiasm, and want to thank each and every person who read *A Hard Sell,* especially those who took the time to share their enjoyment with me. Publishing can be a long, hard road, and you all keep me going.

Thank you to my agent, Jordy Albert, for her work behind the scenes and endless positive vibes, and to early readers of *Flirty Dancing* Amanda Sellet and Jayne Denker, as well as Sidney Karger and Lindz McLeod.

A massive thank you to Leni Kauffman for the breathtakingly beautiful cover that I will always treasure. Really, I still get goose bumps when I look at it.

It has been a joy working with the team at St. Martin's Griffin. My heartfelt thanks to Morgan Garces, Ginny Perrin, Natalie Montanez, Zoë Miller, Austin Adams, Olga Grlic, Chrisinda Lynch, Brant Janeway, Janna Dokos, Omar Chapa, and Meryl Sussman Levavi. Thanks as well to the audiobook team at Macmillan. My deepest apologies if I missed anyone—please know that I am incredibly grateful for your contributions.

Heaps of love and thanks to Grace Gay, my editor, who has made all my dreams come true. Grace has been the kindest, most supportive and thoughtful editor I could ever imagine working with. Grace, thank you for loving this book and making it even better with me.

And finally, thank you to you for reading *Flirty Dancing*. I hope it made you smile.

About the Author

Jennifer Moffatt believes that there are so many more romantic stories to tell than the ones that have traditionally been lined up on bookstore shelves, and she plans to write as many of them as she can. Her short stories have appeared in multiple anthologies and literary magazines. *Flirty Dancing* is her third novel. Jennifer loves hot summers and potato chips and lives with her family in British Columbia, Canada.